The Family Jewels

and Other Stories

The Family Jewels

and Other Stories

Dorothy Cannell

Five Star • Waterville, Maine

Additonal copyright information on page 237.

This collection is a work of fiction. Names, characters, places, and incidents are either the product of the author's imagination or, if real, used fictitiously.

Five Star First Edition Mystery Series.

Published in 2001 in conjunction with Tekno-Books and Ed Gorman.

Set in 11 pt. Plantin by Elena Picard.

Printed in the United States on permanent paper.

Library of Congress Cataloging-in-Publication Data

Cannell, Dorothy.
The family jewels and other stories / Dorothy Cannell.
p. cm.—(Five Star first edition mystery series)
ISBN 0-7862-3144-0 (hc : alk. paper)
1. Detective and mystery stories, American. I. Title.
II. Series.
PS3553.A499 F3 2001
813′.54—dc21 2001033055

To my friends
Sandra and John Lyons
with love

Table of Contents

Introduction

I first encountered Dorothy while riding in an airport shuttle to my first Bouchercon, which was in Minneapolis in the late 1980s. When I heard a mellifluous British accent, I immediately turned around to make sure the speaker was neither P. D. James nor Ruth Rendell. Relieved that I had not yet encountered anyone who was Alarmingly Famous, I relaxed until the woman and I arrived at the hotel desk and she told the clerk her name. "Author of 'The Thin Woman'? " I gasped, then ducked behind the nearest plastic plant to reconsider my definition of Alarmingly Famous.

Dorothy may sound as though she just got off the boat, but she most certainly did not just get off the turnip truck. She retains her accent because of her finely tuned ear for the nuances of both spoken and inner language. Her characters come off the pages to walk across my living room when I snuggle up with Ben, Ellie, the vicar, the ne'er-do-well cousin, and the dauntless Mrs. Malloy (there's something oddly familiar about that name, but I can't quite put my finger on it). Her prose is so elegant and tinged with satiric undertones that I find myself rereading sentences simply to marvel over them. Well, okay, even to analyze them in hopes of deciphering how she manages to add a dollop of arsenic to the teacup and a slathering of venom atop the scones, all without succumbing to the contemporary trend to substitute gratuitous violence to mask weakness in plot and character definition. Comedic fiction is, in my humble opinion, much more challenging to write; drug dealers and their unsavory ilk are easier targets than eccentric yet believable residents of a quiet little village where nothing much happens—except murder most foul. To find a way to approach this with wit requires a deft hand, and Dorothy is the virtuoso. Were Jane Austin to toss a bloodied body in the drawing room, I suspect she would first study Dorothy's mystery novels. I know I do.

Joan Hess

The Purloined Purple Pearl

The news that Sir Robert Pomeroy was to marry Mrs. Dovedale was greeted in our village of Chitterton Fells with great excitement. Neither party was young, nor uncommonly handsome as would seem required for heady romance. They were both widowed; the late Mr. Dovedale having passed to his reward in the fullness of a substantial Sunday lunch some years previously, Lady Kitty as behooved her exalted position in the community, going out with a good deal more fanfare.

She had not been generally liked. "Interfering and uppity" being among the gentler epithets bestowed upon her. The vicar in extolling her ladyship's virtues at the funeral looked hollow-eyed and worn to the bone as if having spent several sleepless nights before coming up with "thrifty and industrious." It was, however, possible to legitimately address her death as a tragedy, in that Lady Kitty had been murdered. Many in the community voiced surprise that she had not been bumped off years before. But there were those who felt that in death her lady ship had finally added some lustre to her husband's ancestral home, which heretofore had been sadly lacking in ghoulish tales of murder and subsequent hauntings.

Prior to Lady Kitty's demise, visitors paying two pounds a head for the privilege of touring the house and grounds often voiced disappointment at not once glimpsing a spectral figure disporting itself on the ramparts. Pomeroy Hall, having been built in the reign of George III, possessed no battlements, dungeons or other gothic embellishments suited to the sensibilities of ghosts, a species known to be somewhat set in their ways. But the paying visitors failed to accept these architectural limitations as an excuse for the lack of headless spooks and the morose clanking of chains.

According to Mrs. Goodbody, the housekeeper at Pomeroy Hall, some thirty years previously one of the kitchen maids had taken it upon herself to invent a melodrama aimed at sending shivers down the spines of the susceptible. A shilling would pass hands and the fabrication told of a daughter of the house left to perish in a secret room behind the wainscoting in the library, for refusing to wed a dreadful old earl who ate nothing but hard boiled eggs and wore his nightshirt in public. Several people reported having heard the Undutiful Daughter's piteous moans and to have seen books leaping off the library shelves. But all too soon the maid, whom Mrs. Goodbody charitably refused to name, was seen waylaying a group of visitors entering the gates, and was dismissed on the spot.

After that no stories of dark doings were told at Pomeroy Hall until the occasion of Sir Robert's marriage to Lady Kitty. And that tale only involved a theft. Mr. Alberts who conducted the tours (being at other times the head gardener) did his best with the material at his disposal—stressing the fact that the purloined object had never been recovered. Still the visitors continued to hanker for a ghost. And when Lady Pomeroy's body was discovered floating in the ornamental pond behind the west wing, the village waited with bated breath until the official word came that she had indeed been the victim of foul play. Naturally Sir Robert was suspected, but his name was quickly cleared when the murderer was caught and cheerfully helped the police in their inquiries by making a full confession.

The baronet looked suitably bereft at the funeral. His tie was crooked and his coat misbuttoned, as was to be expected after nearly thirty years of marriage to a woman who had sucked away his self-confidence to the point where he was barely capable of dressing himself let alone having a thought to call his own. He was known to have spent a great deal of time playing with the model train set when he wasn't patrolling the estate looking for poachers at his wife's behest. Lady Pomeroy apparently had lived in hourly dread that old Tom Harvester would be overcome by a salivating desire for rabbit stew. Poor Sir Robert! A sad excuse for a man was how the village long viewed him. But within weeks of becoming a widower he began to blossom. His face fleshed out and took on a ruddy hue. His tentative walk became a stride—one might even say a strut. He took to wearing sportier jackets and mustard cravats. It was said that he had not only taken up pipe smoking, but now had his moustache professionally styled. Certainly, the village began to see a good deal more of him. On and off the hunting field.

I got to know Sir Robert when he joined the Chitterton Fells Library League. Another of our members was Mrs. Dovedale who owned a grocer's shop on the corner of Market Street and Spittle Lane. At first I thought I might be reading too much into the sideways glances that I often saw exchanged between her and the baronet during weighty discussions such as whether we should serve sandwiches in addition to cake at the annual meeting. But I soon got the scoop from Miss Whiston, the niece of Mr. Alberts who was still head gardener cum guide at Pomeroy Hall. And Evangeline Whiston was not someone to be readily doubted. Hers was a pious disposition which found outlet not only in endeavoring to get books "of a certain kind" banned from the library, but also in doing the flowers and polishing the candlesticks at St. Anselm's Church with enthusiastic regularity.

Miss Whiston was, despite her prim manner, a woman who enjoyed telling a story. And she was quick to point out she was not such an antique at fifty that she had forgotten what romance was all about. Her account was that Sir Robert and Maureen Dovedale had shared a youthful passion. It had begun when he was a boy, home from boarding school for the holidays and would go into the grocery shop to buy sweets and bottles of fizzy drinks. His over-the-counter chats with Maureen about comic books and football matches had developed into something more when they reached their late teens. The two young people had begun to meet for Sunday walks along honeysuckle-scented lanes. Secretly. An alliance between a Pomeroy and a grocer's daughter being unthinkable, however much they might both want it.

"Life is full of heartbreak," said Miss Whiston. "A friend of mine that worked up at the hall told me how things were. When the time came Sir Robert did his duty and wed the woman his parents chose for him and a couple of years afterwards Maureen married Ed Dovedale. All very sensible. But who's to say what will happen now that he and Lady Pomeroy are both underground?"

It was a question voiced with increasing frequency in Chitterton Fells, making Mrs. Goodbody the center of attention at many a Hearthside Guild meeting. As Sir Robert's longtime housekeeper it was assumed she had to be in the know, and her insistence that her lips were sealed only fanned the flames of curiosity. But at last the word was out. Evangeline Whiston said she had it from the vicar that the wedding was to be on the first Saturday in March. And Tom

Harvester boasted he'd had it straight from the horse's mouth that Sir Robert didn't give a damn what anyone thought. He'd already wasted half a lifetime and counted himself the most fortunate of men to have won the hand and heart of the woman he considered a pearl beyond price.

"I expect he be wishing he could give her the one what was stolen all them years ago," Evangeline's uncle, now approaching his eightieth birthday, looked soulful. He was one of a group of us who had gathered at the church hall for a special meeting of the Hearthside Guild to discuss what we could do as St. Anselm parishioners to prepare the church for the wedding. Naturally, those most closely involved with Pomeroy Hall were the ones who set aside other obligations to show up at short notice on a blustery winter evening. Other than myself, that is. I lived within a stone's throw of the church, liked Maureen Dovedale a lot, and I'll admit had been glad of the opportunity to leave my husband to put our three-year-old twins, Abbey and Tam, to bed.

Mrs. Goodbody, Tom Harvester, Evangeline Whiston, and Mr. Chistlehurst—a wooden faced man who had been the estate manager until Sir Robert's marriage to Kitty—all nodded knowingly when the old gardener mentioned the theft. But as a relative newcomer to Chitterton Fells I was eager for details. I knew of course that a pearl of a glorious purple had vanished some thirty years ago. This was the story recounted to visitors to Pomeroy Hall in an attempt to make up for the lack of a ghost on the premises. Until her ladyship was murdered and Tom Harvester—in return for being allowed to poach at will—had started the rumor which had soon become local lore. On moonless nights Lady Kitty's spirit was now said to rise up from the pond in which she had drowned, thence to drift up to the house where she would check all the rooms to make sure the servants weren't slacking off. Writing her initials in any dust on the furniture. But the theft of the purple pearl wasn't myth. And it haunted me that I knew only the barest outline.

Mrs. Goodbody had always made it clear that she did not like to have it talked about and as she was a person held in considerable deference, her wishes on the subject were respected even when she was not present. Until now, that is. The excitement of Sir Robert's impending marriage had loosened Mr. Alberts' tongue, and Mrs. Goodbody did not silence me with a shake of the head when I pressed for more information.

"I reckon there's no way round it, Mrs. Haskell, the story's bound to be dredged up now that Sir Robert is to remarry. And better you hear it from me than some of the tattle tongues that make up what they don't know as they go along." Mrs. Goodbody was a stout elderly woman, with hair as white as the collar and cuffs of the navy blue dresses she invariably wore. Drawing her chair closer into the table around which we were seated, she dropped her voice to a whisper and glanced around before continuing. "If Myrtle Bunting should walk in we'll have to start talking about something else on the quick. Poor soul! She's never got over it, and there's not a day goes by that I don't pity her from the bottom of my heart."

The story so far . . . As members of Chitterton Fells' Hearthside Guild are discussing how best to prepare St. Anselm's Church for the eagerly anticipated wedding of local lord of the manor Sir Robert Pomeroy and village grocer Maureen Dovedale, Mrs. Goodbody and company are regaling Ellie Haskell with the scandalous tale of The Purloined Purple Pearl . . .

"It was the Pomeroy's butler, Myrtle's husband Horace, that was blamed when the pearl went missing," Mrs. Goodbody raised her voice a notch to be heard above the wind rattling the windows, as if some embodiment of darkness demanded re-entry to the world of the living.

"Bear in mind this wasn't just any pearl, Mrs. Haskell," Mr. Chistlehurst informed me in his dry-as-toast voice, "it was famous. Immensely valuable. Incomparable. I have heard it said that Keats wrote 'An Ode To A Purple Pearl,' before his publisher advised him that one to a Grecian urn had more classical appeal. And would thus be more marketable."

"I've never seen a purple pearl," I said, hugging my cardigan around me.

"Well, that be old Mother Nature for you," responded Mr. Alberts, looking more shriveled by the minute. "Always a one for her little surprises she is. I mind many's the time I gone planted red roses and got white or yellow ones instead. And Lady Kitty didn't half give me what for! A terrible temper that woman had," eyeing Mrs. Goodbody through lizard lids. "If you speak true, my old friend, you'll tell Mrs. Haskell here that it was her ladyship's spitefulness that killed Horace Bunting."

"Killed?" I forgot the cold.

"Her ladyship can't be blamed for his death," Mrs. Goodbody reproved the old gardener, then sighed deeply. "Still, there's no getting round the fact that it was her hysterical carrying-on that got a good man dismissed on the spot. After him and his wife working at Pomeroy Hall for more years than most people can count. Of course Myrtle couldn't stay on, not after what happened. Had one of those bad nervous breakdowns she did. And afterwards went to live with her daughter in Canada."

"Mrs. Bunting only returned to Chitterton Fells last month," contributed Mr. Chistlehurst. "Still not over the tragedy by the looks of her. I'm sure she never accepted the possibility that her husband was the thief. The only thing keeping her going is the hope that one day he will be exonerated and a public apology offered by the Pomeroy family. There is none so blind as a doting wife, but one cannot but feel for the woman."

"Needs something to occupy her time does Myrtle Bunting," Tom Harvester, who had made a career out of idleness, was always eager to put other people to work. "Let the past lie buried is what I say."

"I still don't know exactly what happened." I tried not to sound plaintive.

"It was the Saturday before the wedding." Mrs. Goodbody's mouth was set in a grim line. "Lady Kitty—well, she was Kitty Cranshaw then—she'd come down for the weekend and it was one of those lovely summer days you mostly only get to read about in books. The sun was shining like it had just thought up the idea and the flowers, thanks to Mr. Alberts here, made the garden a real picture. So after luncheon I had the stable lad set up deck chairs on the lawn and everyone went and sat under the trees."

"Everyone?"

"Well, let me see." Mrs. Goodbody twined her blue-tinged hands together. "There was the engaged couple, and Mr. Robert's parents—he hadn't come into the title then, of course—and then there was you, Mr. Chislehurst . . ."

"Quite so, I was always treated like one of the family, which is in fact the case." His lips twisted into a smile but the eyes behind the rimless glasses gave nothing away. "I am in fact a third cousin to Sir Robert, the requisite poor relation; given a job on the estate and expected to be suitably grateful."

"Now let me think," Mrs. Goodbody's furrowed brow cleared. "Ruby Estelbee was also there. She who's now the church organist. At that time she was one of those sporty young women; leastways she was good enough to hit a ball over the net if the wind wasn't blowing the wrong way. She often used to get invited up to the Hall to partner Mr. Robert who was keen on a game of tennis. But I think it wasn't really meant for Ruby to come that day. I remember hearing Mr. Robert say he was sure he'd rung to put her off. Him and his intended had a real set-to about it, voices raised, doors slamming. I thought to myself well, the engagement's off. Maybe it's for the best. But of course bridegrooms the like of the Hon. Robert Pomeroy didn't grow on trees."

"And it weren't like Lady Kitty was a bonny lass even with youth on her side," supplied Mr. Alberts. "What's more, she didn't have what we called in my day the come-hither look. Not like Evangeline here. Led all the lads a dance in those days she did. The fellow Ruby Estlebee was courting broke things off, he was so mad for Evie."

"Well, the row blew over between Mr. Robert and his bride-to-be," Mrs. Goodbody got the story back on track, "or so it seemed when they went out in the garden. I was back and forth with mugs of lemonade and sunshades for his mother. I heard her say, 'Son, why don't you give Kitty the pearl now, after all you won't be seeing her on the wedding morning. You know it's tradition that it's always presented before the marriage. I took it out of the wall safe in my bedroom before lunch; it's in its box on my dressing table.' "

"You have it down pat, Mrs. Goodbody." Mr. Chistlehurst nodded over his steepled fingers. "Robert got up and went into the house, only to come back within minutes to say he had encountered Bunting in the hall and sent him up to fetch the box. I vividly recall, Mrs. Haskell, that the very air seemed charged with excitement as we waited for Bunting to parade in his dignified way, across the lawn. But I cannot claim to have sensed any portent of alarm. I had never seen the pearl. I know only that it was shaped like a bird's egg and hung from a gold chain. But my eagerness to see it was nothing to that of Kitty."

"Then the unthinkable happened," Mrs. Goodbody shivered. "Mr. Bunting came across the lawn at a run—something total out of character for a man always so controlled in his deportment. He practically stumbled over to Mr. Robert and flung back the lid of the box. It was empty. Nothing inside but the red velvet lining."

"All hell broke loose," Mr. Alberts' rheumy old eyes stared back into the past.

"You were there?" I asked.

"Clipping a hedge," he said. "Not in view, you understand, but close enough to hear what was said, just as you was, Tom Harvester, hanging round the side door of the west wing."

"Aye, so I was. It wasn't rabbits I was after that day, but a mug of tea and perhaps a slice or two of bread and dripping from Mrs. Goodbody here, or Myrtle Bunting. Always a soft touch was Myrtle. Wouldn't have minded marrying her myself, but from the time she was sixteen she never looked at any man but her Horace."

"You get the picture, Mrs. Haskell," Mr. Chistlehurst's face became so wooden it could have sat on a mantelpiece. "There were several people who could have entered Robert's mother's bedroom that day. She was known to forget to replace pieces of jewelry in the wall safe. Her husband often chided her for leaving rings and necklaces on her dressing table tray, saying it was unfair to the servants—putting temptation in their way. But as she rightly said, the staff had been with them for years and there had never been any trouble."

"I can vouch for that," Mrs. Goodbody nodded her white head. "Not a hat pin lifted in all the years I'd been housekeeper. And I'd have noticed. It's been a matter of pride with me to know if so much as an ornament was moved half an inch. Very strict I was—same as Mr. Bunting; but kind with it, I hope. That's always the way to get the best out of your staff. But I'm not saying they shouldn't all of them—myself included—have been put through the wringer when that pearl went missing."

"The police were summoned immediately," intoned Mr. Chistlehurst as if addressing us from the bench, "everyone who had access to the house that day was questioned. I imagine I placed high on the list of suspects, the resentful poor relation. Then there was Ruby Estelbee who may have harbored hopes that Robert would marry her. And might have decided that at least Kitty would not get the pearl. As for you, Tom Harvester . . ."

"I know," the other man looked none abashed, "a layabout like me! Truth is I've made me mark in life as the local suspicious character, and it was humbling in its way not to be singled out from the rest. But I heard one of the coppers say, 'It won't be Tom, the old goat's happy with a sack for a blanket and a shed roof over his head.' "

"I wasn't what you could call put through the wringer," Mr. Alberts shifted in his chair. "I'd helped my father in the gardens at Pomeroy from the time I was big enough to push a toy wheelbarrow. And the family had been good to me, letting me live in the old lodge at the gates when I married the Missus. But what the police didn't ask and I didn't bring up was that I'd felt some hard feelings toward the family for a couple of years."

"Uncle!" Miss Whiston who had appeared lost in thought, pressed a hand to her lips.

"I know, Evie, but with everyone here talking so straight forward. Let's bring it out in the open. Mrs. Goodbody's always been good about making sure none of the staff let on it was you that . . ."

"Well, I felt I owed that in part to you, Mr. Alberts," said that lady. "And I do try to be a Christian."

Mr. Alberts reached out a trembly hand and laid it on his niece's shoulder. "It had nowt to do with theft, but many's the day I've blamed myself for not letting on that I hadn't felt quite the same towards the Pomeroys since. After what they done to you, Evie. Just a young lass larking about. And as I told at the time, it wasn't like you kept those shillings the visitors gave you telling them ghost stories. Always put them in the church collection, didn't you, lass? Never doubted your word on that, I didn't."

"Miss Whiston," I stared at her in awe—trying and failing to picture her as a mischievous imp, still in her teens. "You were the maid who was dismissed for making up the tale of the Undutiful Daughter? I've always thought that was so enchanting, apart from the part where you were caught and dismissed on the spot."

"Sir Robert's father was a hard man. He prided himself that was why his staff toed the line as they did." Something sparkled in Evangeline Whiston's eyes. Anger? Or something as strong as hatred. Then her face softened and I caught a glimpse of how she might have looked years ago. "Mr. Bunting was kindness. He said he'd speak up for me, explain that I was a good worker—one of the best. I was crying and he put his arm around me and stroked my hair. Someone must have seen and said something because that was one of the things Lady Kitty brought up against Mr. Bunting. That he was a faithless husband. And a man who would deceive his saint of a wife was likely to be a thief as well."

"That wasn't a day I thought ever to see at Pomeroy Hall," Mrs. Goodbody reached into her handbag for a handkerchief to dab her eyes, but resisted the weakness. "All the staff, along with Tom here, huddled in one room and the family and visitors in another. It wasn't just the shame of being searched," her voice cracked, "the worst part was knowing that if that pearl wasn't found, a cloud of suspicion would hang over every one of us for the rest of our days. And of course that's what happened. The house was ransacked from top to bottom and every inch of the grounds gone over, but from then to now there has been no sign of the purple pearl."

"How did Mr. Bunting come to be accused of the crime?" I asked.

"He wasn't by the police," Mr. Chistlehurst replied. "I was present when the detective inspector informed the family that there was no reason to assume the butler did it. Bunting could have entered Lady Pomeroy's bedroom, just as he said, and upon seeing several jewelry boxes on the dressing table opened each of them to make sure he had the right one. None contained the pearl and—ominously one was empty. It was agreed that he was in and out of the house in minutes. And of course, his person was searched. But there was no reasoning with Kitty. She was vicious in her attack of the man, insisting she had heard he had been carrying on with one of the maids. That he was a sneaking hypocrite attending church every Sunday morning—when he should have been attending to the preparation of luncheon—just to throw everyone, especially his long-suffering wife, off the scent as to the villain he really was. Mr. Robert spoke up for him—he was still able to face off against Kitty in those days. But his father sided with her. The upshot being that Bunting was escorted from the house as soon as the police left."

"It was a terrible thing," Mr. Alberts sat head hunched into his shoulders, "and I suppose I took it particular hard after what was done to Evie—her being the daughter and the wife I never had. All these years I've tried to be grateful that at least her name wasn't dragged through the mud. We was able to put it about that she gave up working at the hall so she could take care of our own patch of garden. And it was her taking flowers up to the church regular that got the old vicar to feel a soft spot for her. She went to work at the vicarage typing his sermons and letters and such a couple of days a week. After a while she was able to get a good paying job as a proper secretary." Pride gleamed in Mr. Alberts' eyes, but quickly faded into sorrow. "Poor Mr. Bunting, he didn't get no second chances. He was killed the very evening he was give the sack, hit by a bus crossing the road to his house."

"Don't suppose he was looking where he was going, poor devil, all wrapped up in his sorrow." Tom Harvester produced a grubby handkerchief and blew his red nose. "Small wonder if Myrtle Bunting thinks her man was murdered by the Pomeroys."

"What I find amazing," I said, "is that with people so eager for a haunting at Pomeroy Hail, word didn't spread of the shadowy figure of a butler being glimpsed gliding down the corridors with a silver tea tray."

"My dear Mrs. Haskell," Mr. Chistlehurst's wooden demeanor became even more pronounced. "The family would quickly have nipped talk like that in the bud. It would hardly have reflected well upon them, especially Kitty. There were certainly those who believed she had leaped at the excuse to be rid of Bunting because she resented Robert's dependency on him, in such matters as delivering messages not so long before to Maureen at her father's shop. Kitty had to know Robert was in love with someone else, and given her temperament she was not averse to venting her venom on any one who had played even a small role in helping that romance along."

"The staff was ordered not to discuss it on or off the premises," Mrs. Goodbody leaned in to say. "And Myrtle Bunting going to pieces like she did—well, she wasn't in a state to do any talking. She went into one of those psychiatric hospitals the night her Horace died. When she came out she went straight to their daughter in Canada. But now she's back and Mr. Robert's going to marry Maureen Dovedale. So it's a new beginning of sorts, which is why I finally felt free to talk about what happened."

"Put the past where it belongs," Mr. Alberts nodded. "I'll admit I've relished talking to paying visitors about the missing pearl—not mentioning Mr. Bunting of course, because that would have cost me my job. But knowing all the while I was a thorn in Sir Robert's as well as his lady wife's side. But time comes to move on. And I'd like to see Maureen Dovedale happy and the Hall back to its old self."

"Lady Kitty was all into Danish modern and stainless steel," Mrs. Goodbody came as close to turning up her nose as was possible for a woman of her restraint. "All the wonderful antiques went up into the attics and the silver and brass got put away in drawers—except for that candelabra, the one that was given to the church in celebration of Reverend Marshwind's twenty-five years at St. Anselm's. It always does my heart good to see how beautifully you keep it polished, Evangeline." The kindly housekeeper reached out to squeeze Miss Whiston's hand. "And Mr. Bunting would be more pleased than anyone; most particular he was about the silver. Did most of the cleaning himself, and always supervised the rest."

"Speaking of cleaning," I looked up at the wall clock and saw that a couple of hours had passed, "does anyone have any suggestions as to how we can spruce up the church for the wedding?"

"I do my very best to keep our house of worship looking its

best," Miss Whiston sounded just a little resentful. "In addition to doing the flowers, I make any necessary repairs to the altar cloths and, as Mrs. Goodbody just said, I polish the candlesticks . . ."

"Your contribution is invaluable," Mr. Chistlehurst continued briskly, "we are all most appreciative of the time you devote to St. Anselm's. But what we are talking about here is in the nature of a spring cleaning. Something every church needs every three or four hundred years. And it seems to me that there is something symbolically important in such an undertaking, given the fact that in essence Mr. Robert is cleaning house—emotionally speaking—by marrying Maureen Dovedale."

"What I think would be best of all," said Mrs. Goodbody, "would be if we could get the new covers for the kneelers finished. If we all plied our needles a bit faster they could be ready for the wedding."

This was a project that had been occupying the Hearthside Guild for the past five years. A St. Anselm's parishioner had visited another small country church where the kneelers had been recovered in needlepoint, each incorporating in its design words taken from a Biblical verse. As our red plush covers were getting threadbare it had been agreed that the Hearthside Guild would supply canvas and thread to anyone who knew a needle from a haystack. My canvas, which I had decided would say 'Behold the Lilies' and include a graceful flower or two, had not progressed well. Fortunately my mother-in-law had paid a recent visit and, after brightening visibly at my ineptitude, had offered to take the lop-sided bunchily stitched rectangle home with her. I was sure she would unpick every stitch and return the finished piece so perfectly sewn that it would be impossible to tell the back from the front.

Thus, I was able to say, with just enough hesitation to ensure I wouldn't be asked to take on another one, that I believed my cover could be finished in time for the wedding. Mr. Chistlehurst was more frank. He admitted to having paid another parishioner to do his for him in addition to her own. Miss Whiston said that she had already completed three covers and would be happy to take on another couple if necessary. Mr. Alberts reminded us that he had made a financial contribution to the enterprise. And Tom Harvester proudly announced he was coming along nicely doing an inch a night.

As we were all buttoning our coats, Mrs. Goodbody asked, "Who shall we have do the upholstering? This is just a suggestion, but how would it be if I were to ask Myrtle Bunting? She did a beautiful job recovering the dining room chairs when she worked at Pomeroy Hall. I think it might give her an emotional lift as well as putting some money in her pocket."

It was agreed, without dissent, that Mrs. Goodbody should immediately get in touch with Myrtle Bunting. Mr. Chistlehurst was leading the way toward the church hall door, when it flew open, and a figure in a flapping coat charged into our midst. A woman recognizable to all of us, even though her face was distorted with fury. She was the church organist, Ruby Estelbee, who had been one of those on the scene when the purple pearl was stolen. Her fury was directed at Evangeline Whiston. Who as young Evie had caught the eye of the man who had been previously courting Miss Estelbee.

"It was you!" she cried, stabbing a finger in Evangeline's direction. "It's always you that leaves the church door unlocked, so that when I go in to practice I never know if some deranged maniac is lurking in the vestry or up in the choir loft ready to slit my throat. You have a key! I have a key!" The words came spitting out of Ruby Estelbee as she strode toward Evangeline Whiston. "But only one of us ever remembers to use it upon shutting the door."

"Isn't it rather late for you to begin practicing?" Mrs. Goodbody stepped between the raging inferno and Evangeline. "And on such a nasty night, too. We're all," eyeing the rest of us, "eager to be off home."

As the angry color drained from Ruby Estelbee's face, it was possible to see that she was still a handsome woman and might have appeared to even better advantage if she had known how to look pleasant. Was it possible, I wondered, that she still harbored feelings for Sir Robert and her display of temper sprang partly from a raging disappointment that he was to marry Maureen Dovedale? Evangeline said primly that if she occasionally forgot to lock the door it was because she was sometimes overly fatigued after working at her secretarial job all day—before fulfilling her church obligations. Her uncle took her arm and they both marched out into the night and the rest of us trailed after her, Ruby Estelbee taking up the rear, then watching to make sure Mr. Chistlehurst locked the door.

In the weeks that followed, I often thought about the purple pearl and the tragedy it had brought to Myrtle Bunting. Mrs. Goodbody did speak to her about doing the upholstery work on the church kneelers, and she agreed to do it free of charge. A couple of weeks before Sir Robert and Maureen's wedding, she came to a Hearthside Guild meeting to collect the new needlepoint covers. She was a thin woman with a sad, gentle face and clear, sweet voice. It was only because she was standing at my elbow that I was able to hear her telling Mr. Chistlehurst she had never blamed Sir Robert for what had happened to her husband. Was she a saint? Or did she secretly rejoice that Lady Kitty was to be replaced with such a public display of enthusiasm on the part of the inhabitants of Chitterton Fells? I was inclined, feeling suddenly humble on meeting her quiet gaze, to believe that Myrtle Bunting was indeed one of those rare people whose hearts may break but whose souls remain intact.

After coffee and cake, we presented her with our completed covers. Mine was quite beautiful, thanks to my mother-in-law. Bordered with lilies, the wording was exquisitely stitched in lavender and rose. The others were also spectacular—except for the one proudly handed in by Tom Harvester. His needlepoint wasn't bad, but it was almost entirely composed of big letters stating "Esau Was a Hairy Man." Before the close of the evening it was agreed that we would meet at the church a couple of evenings before the wedding to return the kneelers to the pews.

Mrs. Goodbody phoned me the afternoon of that meeting to ask if I would bring a thermos of coffee, as a couple of the others were doing. It would be chilly in the church even with our coats on. And she mentioned during the conversation that Myrtle Bunting might still be working on the last of the kneelers, because she'd had a bad cold earlier in the week and was a little behind schedule.

Even with my coat buttoned to the chin and a woolly hat pulled down over my cars, I shivered as I made my way down the path that divided the churchyard with its sagging gravestones from the vicarage garden. It was only seven o'clock, but it might have been midnight. The moon peered out from the clouds like a frightened face and an owl hooted. At least I hoped it was an owl, and not Lady Kitty risen from her grave, trying to attract my attention. It was all too easy to imagine Sir Robert's first wife with lumps of earth in her hair and a face whitened to bone, slinking after me to enter the church and lurk in the shadows waiting with the patience known only to the dead until the wedding morning arrived and the vicar spoke the words, "Does anyone here know of any impediment why these two should not be joined together?" At which point her ladyship would rise up in all her foul splendour and bride and groom would drop dead on the spot.

I was so completely trapped in the nightmare of imagination that I was halfway down the aisle before I realized I was the last of the group to arrive. They were gathered by the vestry door: Mrs. Goodbody, Mr. Chistlehurst, Tom Harvester, Mr. Alberts and Evangeline Whiston. The odd thing was they didn't look real. They all wore the same expression. And it didn't match any of their usual faces. Their heads jerked and their eyes blinked as if pulled by invisible strings. Then as a unit they looked down. It took me a minute, but somehow I found the strength to do likewise.

Myrtle Bunting lay dead on the floor. No possibility that she was pretending, even had she been the sort of person to pull such a nasty stunt. Her hair was matted with blood and her eyes gazed full square into eternity. Beside her lay an overturned kneeler, the old plush-covered cushion pried half out of the wooden frame. Next to it—just inches away—was the silver candelabra that usually stood on a table beneath a plaque dedicated to the memory of one of the Pomeroy forebears. Like the kneeler, the candelabra wasn't all of a piece. The upper part that formed the two branches had separated from the stem.

"Someone clobbered her with it." Tom Harvester's voice seemed to come at me from the rafters instead of his mouth.

"I was the first one here." Mrs. Goodbody aged ten years with every word. "The lights went out for a few moments and I almost stepped on the poor soul in coming down the aisle. Thank God, Mr. Chistlehurst arrived just minutes after or I think I would have fainted, something I've never done in my entire life."

"Someone must have crept up behind her when she was working on the kneeler." Mr. Alberts' knees buckled and he groped his way to a pew to stand clutching the post. "But why her? A woman that never did no harm to nobody?"

"Perhaps it was the other way round," Mr. Chistlehurst suggested in an expressionless voice. "It could be that Myrtle walked in on someone attempting to steal the candlestick, who struck her down before fleeing the scene. You may have been lucky, Mrs. Goodbody. It occurs to me that the lights may not have gone out because the electricity failed. The killer could still have been in the church when you arrived and flipped off the nearest switch in order to slip away unnoticed."

"But they came on again! Why would anybody making their escape bother with that?" Miss Whiston was almost as glassy-eyed as the corpse.

"To make us think that whoever did this wasn't one of us?" I heard myself talking, but it was as though I were somewhere else, safely back at home with my husband and children. And I knew it was the same for the others. Their physical beings were here, but their minds had run for cover.

A voice crashed through our collective daze, a voice attached to a face we struggled to bring into focus.

"It was you!" A finger came stabbing into view. And I saw that it belonged to Ruby Estelbee. For a moment I was back at that other Hearthside Guild meeting when she had come charging into the hall to accuse Evangeline Whiston of failing to lock the church door. Even when my brain cleared a little, I thought she was making the same complaint, rage making her oblivious to Myrtle Bunting's body at her feet, but then I saw the emotion that drove her wasn't rage. It was triumph. Again she was pointing the finger at Evangeline Whiston, who was now cowering against the vestry door.

"I saw you," Ruby Estelbee lowered her voice and it was clear she was savoring every word. "I was up in the choir loft getting ready to practice the wedding hymns. Do you think I'd let it be said I wasn't up to playing when Robert takes another wife? I leaned over the balcony when you came in, you sanctimonious hypocrite. I saw you talking to Myrtle Bunting. She was bent down working on her upholstering and just as you turned away she pried out the old pad and pulled out a piece of paper. I heard her say clear as a bell that there was a gap down the side of the kneeler. Then she unfolded that piece of paper and read out what was written on it. Would you like me to refresh your memory, Miss Whiston?"

"No, oh please, don't," whimpered Evangeline, "not in front of Uncle."

"Evie." Mr. Albert's voice was every bit as anguished.

"Yes, Evie," Ruby Estelbee smiled. "That's how the note began: 'My darling Evie, it's in a safe place but the witch got me blamed and I've been turned out. Don't worry. As soon as things quiet down, I'll get back into the house one night, collect the you-know-what and get another message to you as to where we will meet to begin our new lives.' There wasn't a signature, but of course Myrtle didn't need one. She recognized the writing and the context spoke for itself." Miss Estelbee allowed her gaze to drift around the entire group. "No wonder you were always so eager to do the church flowers, Evangeline," she continued, "it gave you the opportunity to retrieve the notes your Mr. Bunting hid in the kneeler during the Sunday morning service. Had you picked up this last one, your life might have gone along in the rut you'd settled into so sensibly."

"He was killed," Evangeline licked her lips, no longer looking at her uncle, "on a Saturday. He'd always left the notes on Sundays. He said it was important to stick strictly to a routine so no one would suspect we were seeing each other until we could run off together. Anyway, I didn't care once he was dead. Not about the pearl. Not about anything. He was years older than me, but I loved him desperately. It started when he was kind when I was dismissed for telling ghost stories. He kissed me and told me he couldn't help himself, not after being married for years to a saint who didn't understand anything of a real man's nature."

"You didn't have to kill her," whispered Mr. Alberts.

"I didn't mean to," Miss Whiston (I could no longer bring myself to think of her as Evangeline) clasped her hands and bent her head as if in prayer. "If Ruby Estelbee wasn't so full of hate she could back me up on what happened. It was Myrtle that grabbed up the candlestick and came at me with it. Something snapped inside her head, I suppose. Just like it did when Horace died and she went into that hospital. And I doubt any of you will blame her for lashing out at me. What I did all those years ago was wrong. I've tried to make my peace with God and myself ever since. But I see now that the past doesn't die, it just lies low, waiting for the right time to pounce. In struggling to get the candelabra from Myrtle, I struck her and it separated into two parts. And what should fly out into my hand but the purple pearl." There were tears now in Miss Whiston's hand and I couldn't help but feel pity for her. It was the age-old story—flighty young girl taken in by smooth-talking older man.

"I remember now," she continued, "that the candelabra was in Mr. Robert's mother's bedroom, so it would only have taken Horace a matter of seconds to push the pearl way down into the hollow stem of the base where it would fit snugly enough that it could only be unwedged by a forceful shake. To think of all the years I've polished that candelabra without ever guessing what it contained."

Miss Whiston slipped her hand into her coat pocket, then held it out palm open. It was truly a thing of beauty, that purple pearl. But I doubted the new Lady Pomeroy would choose to wear it. I hoped that its discovery would allow some of the ghosts to go to their rest, and one love story to have a happy ending that would become a beginning. It doesn't hurt to dream, does it? In the thick of winter, even in Chitterton Fells, spring is always just around the corner.

Cupid's Arrow

"You know what happens to wicked people, don't you, Giselle?" said Great Aunt Honoria.

"They go to hell," my ten-year-old self addressed the implacable hands on the wheel as the elderly Daimler proceeded decorously down the country road. "But surely you have to do something really bad, like murder one of your relations." I savored the prospect as a blackbird fluttered in front of the windscreen and was instantly sent into backward flight by a blast of the horn. "It was only a very small lie."

"You told me that you had been chosen to play Little Red Riding Hood in the school play." Aunt Honoria's voice deepened to a rumble that echoed the thunder that was trying to scare the car into a ditch. "It was a complete fabrication. There isn't a play. And you aren't in it."

"No, Aunt." I withdrew my gaze from her granite profile and studied my shoes.

"I always know what's inside a person, Giselle." She made this sound as though it were a special talent, like playing the piano or being able to climb a rope. While the Daimler purred on down the road, flattening out any bumps that had the impertinence to be in its path, I thought with satisfaction that she had not caught me out in my really big lie.

Aunt Honoria had asked me when we stopped for lunch in

Mobley Cross if I were enjoying myself and I had told her I was having a super time. Now that was a complete fabrication! My mother had warned me that the day might not be loads of fun.

"She's a bit of an old dragon, darling! And she doesn't have a clue about children. But try to remember she is a lonely old lady with not as much money as she once had. In fact, I'm sure she's down to her last fur coat, so don't stand looking at toys in shop windows and please think small when it comes to meals."

As it turned out I didn't have to fend off the urge to gaze adoringly at teddy bears. Aunt Honoria did not take me walking past any shops. In the morning we visited the hospital where she had worked as a volunteer when she was a young woman and no one now remembered her. When we sat down to lunch at the Thatcher and Aunt Honoria ordered us each a bowl of clear brown soup, it was hard for me to adhere to Mother's instructions and keep my lips zipped. God would not have put fish-and-chips in this world if he had not meant them to be eaten. And when the people at the next table started tucking into treacle pudding, I was tempted to inform Aunt Honoria that Mr. Rochester's mad wife may have ended up that way because someone had starved her in the presence of other people licking their sticky lips and sucking on their forks. But I had smiled bravely and told my noble lie which, if there was any justice in this world, should have canceled out any number of bad lies, including the Red Riding Hood story.

"I don't think I'm going to hell," I told Aunt Honoria as a woolly gray mist wrapped itself around the car windows and the thunder crept closer and growled more menacingly. "At the worst I will go to purgatory for a few hundred years."

"Nonsense. We're Church of England, so you can't go to purgatory because we don't believe in it." She put her foot down on the brake, brooking no argument from the Daimler or me as we came to a barely visible red traffic light. I was hoping we were on our way back to my parents and the London flat. But after crawling along for another few minutes down a lane, we passed a building that might, or might not, have been a church and turned onto a drive lined with evergreens. These appeared to have been sketched with charcoal and the house that presently rose up from the mist to greet us, also looked the product of a fevered imagination.

"Is this your house, Aunt Honoria?"

"Good gracious, no! Do I look as if I am made of money?" She pulled down the cuffs of her fur coat and turned off the engine with a snap. "This is Thornton Hall, an Elizabethan house now open to the public. I thought we might take a look at it if you will promise not to climb over the ropes and bounce on the bed that was slept in by Charles the Second."

"Oh, Aunt Honoria! What a treat!" I bundled out of the car and skipped around to where she stood tapping her cane impatiently on the ground. "It looks just like the house in *Jane Eyre*. And the name is almost the same."

"You're much too young, Giselle, to be reading such books."

"I did have trouble with some of the big words," I conceded, "but I looked them up in the dictionary and—"

"That's not the point." Aunt Honoria cut me off in a way that would have been considered rude in a child of my age. "You should be reading about nice people doing nice things. It's far too soon for you to know anything about illicit passion."

Rubbish, I thought. I had felt very passionate about that treacle pudding.

"Mr. Rochester had no business falling in love with Jane Eyre when he had a wife upstairs in the attic." Aunt Honoria thrust aside the mist with an imperious wag of the cane and marched without a sideways glance at topiary or sundials toward the lighted windows of the house.

"Yes, I suppose it was a bit naughty of him," I agreed dutifully, "but he paid for his sin, didn't he? I don't suppose it was much fun going blind and losing his hand in the fire."

To my relief Aunt Honoria did not seize upon this statement to continue her lecture on the well-stoked furnaces of hell. After admonishing me not to trip over my tongue, she followed the arrow signs posted along the edge of the flower beds and stalked up a short flight of steps to a door marked ENTER.

"Wipe your feet, Giselle." She gave me a poke with the cane as we stepped into the heavily beamed combination tearoom and gift shop. Oh, how lovely! China dolls dressed in a range of period costumes from stiff Elizabethan frocks and lace ruffs to frothy Victorian crinolines were displayed among the toasting forks and horse brasses on the wall shelves. My nose twitched in appreciation of the smell of toasted teacakes that warmed the air. But a glance at Aunt Honoria put to rest any hope that she was about to ruin my character by indulging me with butter-dripping treats.

"Is it still raining?" A dark-haired woman wearing a wool frock and a pleasant smile came around from the counter that stretched across, a corner of the room.

"No, but the mist is turning to fog." Aunt Honoria spoke as if leveling a criticism of how things were run at Thornton Hall. "We could hardly see anything of the grounds so I hope"—she looked sternly down at her black leather handbag—"that we will get our money's worth here in the house."

"We only charge adults a pound for looking around the place and children are half price." The nice lady smiled at me. "Having a day out with Grandma, are you, honey?"

Before I could open my mouth Aunt Honoria set the woman straight on her mistake, then added accusingly, "You sound like an American."

"From Chicago. My husband and I have always loved England, and two years ago we decided to pull up stakes, move over here, and buy this place. It's been exciting if"—an expressive shrug—"a little daunting. The people round here are taking their time accepting us."

"Give them three hundred years," said Aunt Honoria, "and that may change."

"Sometimes," the woman responded with an attempt at a laugh, "I'm not sure we'll last three years. It's a lot more work running a place of this size than either my husband or I realized, and we're beginning to think we're not cut out for being cooped up with the past. Now this part of the business I do enjoy." She looked around at the tables with their yellow-and-white-checked cloths and the shelves lined with gifts. "It's cheerful in here. And my husband enjoys the gardens; he's out in the greenhouse now. But mostly we leave the guided tours to old Ned. He came with the house," she explained as Aunt Honoria raised an interrogatory eyebrow. "The man has to be a hundred if he's a day and knows the history of Thornton Hall backward and forward."

"Then I suggest we meet this treasure before I reach my centenary." Aunt Honoria's lips stretched into an attempt at a smile.

"You wouldn't like a cup of tea first?" The woman stepped toward a cast-iron cooker in the corner and held up the kettle invitingly. "And the little girl looks as though she would enjoy a toasted tea cake."

"Giselle has enjoyed lots of toasted tea cakes in her short sojourn upon this earth." Aunt Honoria looked pointedly down at my portly form. “But I have brought her here to feed her mind, thank you all the same, Mrs. . . . ?”

“Perkins.” She led us through a round-topped oak door into a wainscoted hall that was bigger than the one where I suffered through ballet class, and into a room with narrow leaded windows and a great many portraits in heavy frames on the walls. A while-haired old man wearing an apron and pair of grimy leather gloves stood at a refectory table polishing away at a brass candlestick. This he set down next to its still-tarnished fellow when Mrs. Perkins ushered Aunt Honoria and me toward him.

“Ned, honey,” she said brightly, “these folks would like the guided tour, and I need to stay in the shop in case we should get lucky and have a busload of people arrive all wanting tea and crumpets.”

“Very good, Mrs. Perkins.” The old man put down his polishing cloth, straightened his stooped shoulders, and turned to Aunt Honoria and me. “If you will kindly follow me, madam and little miss, we will get started.”

“Don’t let us rush you,” my relation responded austerely. “By all means take the time to remove your apron.”

“It doesn’t make much sense to do that. I’d only have to put it back on again when I’m done with you.” Ned waved a glove at the army of candlesticks, kettles, and warming pans. “The copper and brass won’t decide to clean themselves.”

Aunt Honoria muttered the word “Uppity!” and, while I was hoping I was the only one who had heard her, Mrs. Perkins retreated from the room. Fixing me with a piercing blue gaze, Ned said, “Little miss, this isn’t one of the really grand houses such as Chatsworth or the like, and for the admission price of a pound, you don’t get a tour guide with military posture wearing gold braid and silver buttons.”

“I’d much rather have you,” I said truthfully, because

something in me warmed to his gloomy voice and wrinkled visage—*visage* was one of the words I had looked up in the dictionary while reading *Jane Eyre*. Stepping up to him I reached for his hand, but he tapped me ever so lightly on the shoulder and led us toward the fireplace with its beaten-copper surround and ornately carved mantelpiece displaying a row of silver hunt cups.

"I gather we are about to be shown the priest hole," Aunt Honoria said, as if announcing we were to have cucumber sandwiches for tea, but I noticed a sparkle in her eyes and realized she had not brought me here for the improvement of my mind alone. Old houses, I decided, were her passion. Without making any comment, let alone saying abracadabra, Ned touched a carved rose and a section of wainscoting slid sideways to reveal a dark aperture.

"Gosh!" I whispered, feeling the stirrings of an enthusiasm that might one day transcend treacle pudding.

"It was never used to hide priests or other followers of the popish faith," Ned told us in a voice that creaked with age, as did the floorboards. Drawing a torch from his apron pocket, he shone its yellow beam into the narrow rectangle that was no bigger than my toy cupboard. "The Thornton family turned Protestant without need of the thumbscrews at the Reformation. From that time forward they were rabid opponents of the Roman church. This hideaway was used for the concealment of royalist sympathizers during the rule of the Lord Protector."

"Oliver Cromwell," Aunt Honoria informed me as if I were four years old. "I imagine we are looking at a box of tricks with a secret staircase that offered the fugitive some hope of escape should the Roundheads show any intelligence."

Ned smiled and showed us a cunningly concealed

trapdoor in the flagstone floor. Our tour of Thornton Hall began in earnest with a visit to the wine cellars, which continued the merry little game of hide-and-seek by providing hidden access to a lichen-covered tunnel which exited, so our guide told us, at the far edge of the apple orchard.

"It's all so romantic!" I gave an ecstatic sigh as we trooped back up the stone steps.

"I don't suppose the royalists thought so when they were captured and sent to the Tower of London. Having one's head chopped off, Giselle, has never been my idea of a good time." Aunt Honoria tapped out an impatient tattoo with her stick, but I could tell she was enjoying herself behind her grim lips.

Ned closed off the panel to what I still thought of as the priest hole and preceded us at a stooped-shouldered but vigorous pace back to the main hall with its massive stone fireplace. The blackened oak staircase rose up forever until it was lost in a ceiling painted with an azure blue sky, banks of clouds, and golden-winged cherubs whose rosy plumpness suggested that they shared my fondness for treacle pudding and other earthly delights.

"This ceiling was painted in the eighteenth century by Wynward Holstein, who is thought in some quarters to have influenced the work of Sir Joshua Reynolds." Ned paused for me to say. "Gosh!" in what I hoped was a suitably reverential voice. He then led us through a series of doors into rooms whose Tudor and Jacobean furniture won grudging approval from Aunt Honoria. Her stick quivered with enthusiasm when she pointed at a tapestry that depicted in finely stitched detail the Great Fire of London. It seemed to me, however, that Ned's responses to her questions concerning court cupboards and pewter platters became more perfunctory as we poked our way about those rooms on the ground floor. When

I watched him open the only door we had not yet entered, I fell suddenly terribly sad.

The feeling was almost as bad as when my cat had died. And that was ridiculous because I'd had Tabitha for as long as I could remember and Ned was only a man in an apron with a face as old as time. Perhaps I only felt down in the boots because I hadn't had a proper lunch or because the rain had begun weeping against the windows to the accompaniment of wistful sighs from the wind. Perhaps Ned was tired to the bone and fed up to the teeth with trotting bossy old ladies and little girls in and out of doors and up and down stairs.

The room we now entered should have brightened my mood. It was unlike any we had yet been shown. The walls weren't paneled in carved oak. They were papered in a striped ivory-and-pale-green silk that matched the scroll-armed sofas, which like the curtains were edged with rose-colored cord. The fireplace mantel was done in what Aunt Honoria whispered to me was gold leaf, and several of the delicate tables were inlaid with the same veneer of sunlight. The paintings that hung from gold cords were all of flowers—so fresh and real I was sure that if I reached up I could pluck them from their frames and gather them into a bouquet that would still be wet with dew and heady with the scent of a summer from long ago.

"Charming," said Aunt Honoria, but when Ned stood aside she did not step more than a few feet into the room. "I suppose the Perkinses did all this!" She poked at the velvety rose carpet with her cane while her lips tightened in a look of disapproval edged with something softer, and I found myself moving up close to her and wishing she would take hold of my hand. Did she feel it too, the terrible empty waiting for something or someone who had once filled this room with a happiness brighter than gold leaf or sunlight?

"Mr. and Mrs. Perkins did redecorate this room upon taking up residence," Ned said, "but they did it from an old watercolor sketch, so it now looks very much as it did at the turn of the eighteenth century when Sir Giles and Lady Thornton occupied the house."

"It's very pretty." I smiled up at him but he had already turned back toward the hall as if eager to be done with us so he could get back to cleaning his brass. Aunt Honoria did not rap him on the shoulder and demand that he give us the history of the secretary desk or the harp-backed chairs. Perhaps she had realized that Ned was also an antique of sorts and should be treated with a measure of respect. Or could it be she was growing a little tired herself? After all she was getting on in years and might now prefer a cup of tea to climbing that extremely tall staircase. I wasn't particularly eager myself, and my voice came out in a whisper that was almost lost in the wind that was beginning to sound like the big bad wolf.

"Ned, is there a ghost at Thornton Hall?"

"I never saw one, little miss," he replied, and went ahead of us up the uncarpeted stairs.

"The house must have its stories." Aunt Honoria came tapping fast upon my heels.

"It's said three of the Thornton children died in the plague of 1665," Ned spoke over his shoulder. "And the eldest son of the sixth baronet was killed in a duel fought on the grounds."

"How awful," I said, feeling much more cheerful. The house had seen a lot in its day. Good times and sad. So some rooms, like the one now used for the teashop, were likely to be cheerful as copper kettles, while others, like the pretty ivory-and-green room, would have their moments of melancholy. But it wasn't as though Thornton Hall was a person. Houses don't cry until they're all wet on the outside and dry on th side. They don't love till it hurts and wish they could die, as I had done when Tabitha had to be put to sleep.

Ned took us into several upstairs rooms with enormous four-poster beds and I asked him if Charles II had really slept in any of them.

"I don't believe so, little miss, but maybe one of his lady friends did. The Merry Monarch had enough of them to fill all the beds in his kingdom." Ned smiled so that his mouth became the biggest wrinkle on his wrinkled face. And I found myself wishing I could tuck him into an easy chair and stroke his white hair until he fell asleep.

I was not a particularly affectionate child, except where animals were concerned, but I wasn't as coldhearted as Aunt Honoria, and even she seemed to be mellowing as we continued our tour. She only pointed her stick at one piece of furniture and denounced it as a blatant reproduction, and once or twice I discovered a gentle light in her eye as she looked at Ned. Goodness! I thought. Was it possible that she had fallen madly in love with him on the way upstairs and was plotting how she could lure him into having a cup of tea and perhaps a crumpet with her before we left Thornton Hall?

My head filled with romantic possibilities and calculations as to how many years Aunt Honoria and Ned might reasonably have left in which to gaze rapturously into each other's eyes. As a result I almost tripped over her cane when they stopped in front of a portrait displayed in an alcove whose gallery railing overlooked the hall.

"What a lovely girl!" Aunt Honoria's voice descended to a rumble. Following her gaze I could see why she was impressed. The painted face was so alive I was sure that if we looked long enough her lips would move and she would speak to us, or that the young lady would lift the hands that held a pink rosebud and brush back the soft brown ringlet that brushed against the shoulder of her muslin gown. She was not exactly beautiful, but she seemed lit from within by a golden glow and there was a look in her eyes of such joy and—

"Love!" said Aunt Honoria. "It's in her face!" The rain slipping and slithering down the windowpane to our left was the only answering sound until Ned finally spoke.

"Wynward Holstein, who painted the ceiling in the main hall, also did this portrait. She's Anne Thornton. The only daughter, the youngest after five sons, of Sir Giles and his lady. They had that salon downstairs"—he looked down at me from under his shaggy white eyebrows—"the one you thought so pretty, little miss, decorated for her because she loved the way the sun came in at its windows. And they hung the walls with paintings of flowers because her father called Anne the sweetest blossom in his gardens."

"How old was she when this portrait was painted?" Aunt Honoria shifted her handbag up her arm and stood with both hands on her cane.

"Seventeen, Madam."

"What happened to her?" I asked Ned. "Did she get married and go away to another house?"

"She never left Thornton Hall, little miss."

"Oh!" I said, picturing a sad decline of the girl's radiant youth into years of knitting mittens for the poor and tending her parents in their old age.

"She died, Anne did, shortly after the completion of the portrait." Ned stepped away and indicated with an inclination of his white head for us to follow him down the hallway.

"Her eyes! Look how they watch you!" Aunt Honoria went tapping after him, but I lingered behind, stepping to the right and left trying to see if she was correct about the magical properties of the portrait. We had a copy of *The Laughing Cavalier* on the stairs at home, and when my cousin Freddy had come to visit I had pridefully shown him how the roguish eyes followed us whichever way we went.

"Don't dawdle, Giselle!" Aunt Honoria's voice rapped me smartly on the head and sent me scurrying after her ramrod-straight back and Ned's stooped shoulders. "How did the girl die?" she asked him. "Did she succumb in proper eighteenth-century fashion to a fever or take an ill-prompted tumble from her horse?"

"I will show you where she died." Ned opened a door set beside a tall window overlooking the rose garden and led us up a narrow stone staircase that coiled around itself in ever-narrowing circles that threatened to squeeze the breath out of me. "Here we are, madam and little miss." Ned stepped into a round tower room that was empty of so much as a table or chair under which to huddle from the wind. It came gusting in through the gaping slits of paneless windows with such force that even Aunt Honoria had to struggle not to capsize like a sailing vessel cast upon stormy seas.

"Here?" Her shadow caricatured the waggle of her cane as she stood with feet apart on the flagstone deck. "Anne Thornton met her untimely end here?"

I shivered as a spatter of rain hit me squarely in the eye. "Did she get locked in by mistake and freeze to death?"

"No, little miss," Ned said, "she was shot by Cupid's arrow."

"Rubbish!" Aunt Honoria snapped. "If you have brought us here to tell us a fairy tale, my good man, you have another thing coming! I have already had quite enough of such folderol for one day!" Her baleful glance at me informed me she was referring to my Red Riding Hood story.

"Oh, please! Do tell us about Cupid's arrow!" I reached for Ned's hand, but he had already mounted the stone lookout perch that surrounded the rim of the room, very much in the way that our vicar, also an old man with white hair, might have ascended the pulpit.

"Very well, my good man! Indulge the child." Aunt Honoria grimaced up at him. "There is no peace for the wicked and I am sure if I think long and hard I will realize what I have done to deserve catching pneumonia while Giselle listens openmouthed to the Legend of Thornton Hall."

"No peace," Ned murmured. Gloved hands folded on his apron front, he shook his hoary head and began to tell us what befell the sweet-faced girl of the portrait. "Anne's parents held a masquerade ball to celebrate her betrothal to a young gentleman by the name of Roger Belmonde. The two families had been closely connected for many years and the engagement had long been hoped for by Sir Giles and Lady Thornton. Everyone of any social standing in the county was invited to the ball except"—Ned paused as if the wind had forced the words back down his throat—"except the Haverfield family, which was comprised of Squire John, his lady wife, and their son Edward, a young gentleman who was still some months from attaining his majority."

"That means he had not yet turned twenty-one," Aunt Honoria told me with a poke of her stick, which missed me by several inches, suggesting that despite her earlier protests she was becoming caught up in the story.

"Why weren't Edward and his parents invited?" I asked.

"The Haverfields were of the Roman faith." Ned said as if reading off words printed behind his eyes. "And as such the Thorntons shunned any association with them even though Haverfield House lies only a few miles from here. Sir Giles had instructed Anne when she first began to ride beyond the grounds that Edward and his parents would in less lax times have been put to the chopping block for their popish ways. He forbade her to acknowledge the lad should they chance to meet upon one of the bridal paths."

"And in those days," Aunt Honoria said for my benefit, "a young girl never set foot outdoors unaccompanied by her groom or governess. But that didn't always put a stop to misbehavior. I suspect from what we saw of her face that Anne was the darling of the household and such being the case her chaperons would not betray her to Sir Giles and Lady Thornton when she inevitably met young Edward and embarked on a budding friendship with him under the greenwood trees. One wonders"—she looked at Ned—"how he reacted to her engagement to Roger Belmonde."

"Edward came to the ball." Ned stepped down from the stone ridge and looked at us with a pensive smile further creasing his face. "It was easily done with all the invited guests masked and in costume. He slipped into the thronged hall at a little before midnight when the revelry was at its zenith. He came in the guise of Cupid with a quiver of golden arrows. He merged with the press of faceless youth in their wide silk skirts or satin knee breeches. Among the dancers, bowing and curtsying as they traced out the steps of the minuet, while the old ladies in powder and patch drank sack and the old men propped their gouty legs on footstools and talked hunting days of yore, Edward found Anne Thornton."

"A planned meeting, I presume," said Aunt Honoria.

"Most certainly, madam. Anne escaped the watchful eyes of her betrothed by telling Roger Belmonde she had left her fan in her green-and-rose sitting room. She went with Edward gladly to the tower room even though she knew she was going to her death."

"I don't understand." I wrapped my arms around myself to ward off the cold.

"Edward Haverfield and Anne Thornton loved each

other," said Ned. "They had done so from their first meeting, through stolen rendezvous and the fear of discovery. He was the lamp who lit the flame of joy we saw in her face. Marriage to the man chosen for her by Sir Giles and Lady Thornton would have been for Anne a living death. And her loss unending anguish for Edward. So the lovers decided upon a means that would ensure none would ever part them. They agreed he would come to the ball in the guise of Cupid with a golden arrow in his quiver and she would go with him to this tower room. It seemed so right to Anne that after one last kiss Edward would draw his bow, piercing her heart with love's arrow, and her soul would be set free to wait for him to join her within moments on a far rainbow-lit horizon."

"Why didn't they just run away together?" I asked.

"Where could they have gone, little miss?" Ned responded softly. "Their families would have cut them off without a shilling and seen them starve in the gutter sooner than recognize their union."

"But death is so horribly final!"

"Don't babble, Giselle!" said Aunt Honoria as our shadows loomed monstrously upon the walls. "I'm sure Ned would like to get back to cleaning the brass today, if not sooner." She speared him with an eye as sharp as Cupid's arrow. "How did young Mr. Haverfield intend to achieve his own demise? Step into one of those windy apertures and throw himself off the tower?"

"That was the plan, madam, but when the moment came and he stood poised to jump, his courage failed him and his limbs locked. He closed his eyes against the dizzying drop to the courtyard below; he tried to picture Anne waiting for him with outstretched hands, but his mind was blinded by panic. He stumbled down from the aperture and crawled to where her lifeless body lay upon the floor. Cradling her in his arms, he wept over her, begging her forgiveness and praying that his fortitude would revive."

"What a rotten egg!" I pressed my hand to my mouth and my cruel shadow mocked the motion. "I don't feel the least bit sorry for him."

"Neither, little miss, did Roger Belmonde," said Ned. "That young gentleman had grown uneasy upon finding his betrothed missing when he returned to the ballroom with her fan. He was truly devoted to Anne, and a lover's instinct brought him up the stairs to this tower room. He found it locked against him and, fighting down a dreadful sense or foreboding, he summoned up the strength of angels and battered his way through the door. Picture, if you will, madam and little miss, the anguish of Roger Belmonde when he beheld Edward Haverfield crooning in demented fashion over the dead girl."

"Oh, I wish Anne had loved him," I said. "He sounds ever so much nicer than the beastly Edward and I expect was heaps more handsome."

"Incensed with grief and rage Roger set upon the other man," Ned continued, "but the murderer fled the tower to lose himself in the throng of dancers still stepping daintily to the minuet. He escaped the house by way of the secret passage, the location of which Anne of the trusting heart had described to him. But do not fear, madam and little miss"—Ned smiled wryly down at my cross face—"Edward Haverfield did not elude retribution. Anne Thornton's brothers, I told you she had five, rode out in a thundercloud of black cloaks to hunt down her murderer, and when they found him skulking in the hollow of a giant oak they . . ."

"Yes?" Aunt Honoria's shadow stiffened upon the wall.

"They . . ." Ned glanced from her to me and back again. "In the manner of their times they made sure Edward

Haverfield would never shoot another arrow. And afterward they bound him with cords, tossed him facedown across the eldest brother's saddle, and rode back with him to Thornton Hall. There Edward was handed over to the justice of the peace who, still flushed with an evening's worth of ale, promised a swift trial and a slow hanging."

"I think it would have been better if he had languished in prison for a long time first," I said nastily.

"As it happened he did, because his father, being a man of prominence, managed for some years to stay the execution. And so, having made a short story long"—Ned shepherded us out the door and onto the stone staircase—"so ends the story of Anne Thornton and Cupid's arrow."

"Very interesting." Aunt Honoria tested the drop between one step and the next with her cane. "You are a fine teller of grim tales, Ned. No doubt Giselle here will be afraid to close her eyes when she goes to bed tonight."

"No, I won't!" I said as the walls spun me around in ever-tightening circles. "It was awfully sad about Anne, but not creepy the way it would be if Thornton Hall was haunted because of what happened. I'd be scared to meet a ghost"—I hesitated over where best to place my foot on the narrow stair wedge—"but at the same time it would be rather exciting. And as Mother and Father say—every child should be exposed to new experiences."

"I suspect they meant that you should start helping with the washing up," Aunt Honoria breathed fiercely down my neck. "Ah, almost at the bottom! Step smartly, Giselle," she said, following me into the light blazing off the hallway walls in contrast to the gloom of the stairwell. "This is the conclusion of the guided tour, is it, Ned?"

"I'll walk you back to Mrs. Perkins in the tea shop." He looked for the flicker of a second toward the portrait of Anne

Thornton before making his stooped way to the main staircase.

"Not so fast," Aunt Honoria caught up with him at the banister rail. "Here"—she tucked her cane under her arm, opened her handbag, and pulled out a black coin purse—"I must give you a little something for your trouble."

"There's no need of that." He waved a hand at her, but she pressed a two-shilling piece into the grimy palm of his brass cleaning glove. And I saw a look pass between them. I didn't think it was one of mad passionate love because I had decided when he was telling the story that his crusty old heart belonged in true romantic fashion to the memory of Anne Thornton. I sensed that the look was about tired feet and reaching a place in time where the present, not the past, becomes dim with age. Aunt Honoria pocketed the coin with surprising meekness when Ned returned it to her with the grunted suggestion that she take me to the old church at the corner of the lane and light a candle at St. Bartholomew's altar.

"Is that where she is buried?" I asked, but before he could answer Mrs. Perkins came panting up the stairs to announce that several carloads of people had arrived, half of them wanting tea and the rest wishing to be shown around the house before closing hour.

"No rest for you, Ned honey!" She gave him a harried smile, rippled a distracted hand through her dark hair, and bustled down ahead of us into the main hall and along to the tea shop, which was crammed with people jostling for seats at the yellow-and-white-checked tables or crowding around the gift items on the shelves. When the place thinned out by a dozen or more, Ned disappeared also. Mrs. Perkins gave us a frazzled smile as Aunt Honoria caught up with her at the cash register to pay for our tour.

"Did you enjoy yourselves?" Her eyes stopped roving the room and came back to us when the till drawer smacked open and caught her in the midriff. But immediately her attention was demanded by a woman's voice exclaiming that if she didn't have a cup of tea and a cream cake this minute she would drop dead on the floor.

"Come along, Giselle." Aunt Honoria prodded me with her stick and headed for the door.

"But aren't we . . . ?" My longing look at the Victoria sponge sitting next to the till finished the sentence for me.

"I'm not hungry." Her lips came together in a click of false teeth. "And I can't imagine how you could eat a bite after the lunch you ate."

"I suppose I did make a bit of a pig of myself." My sarcasm was wasted on Aunt Honoria, who marched me through the drizzling rain, down the drive where the trees lined up like leaky umbrellas, to where the Daimler sat like an obedient dog who had been ordered to stay or face a lifetime without the occasional table scrap. I was about to open the passenger-side front door and climb sullenly aboard when my relative asked me how I could suppose she would waste running the engine for such a short distance.

"But we are miles from home," I said.

"And only a stone's throw from the church."

"Oh!" I stopped being cross and skipped to keep up with her. "Then we are going to light a candle for Anne Thornton! I'm glad because anyone with a bit of imagination could see Ned is in love with her portrait."

"Not just the picture, child!" The *rap-tap* of Aunt Honoria's voice kept pace with her stick as we turned left into the black ribbon of lane toward the church.

"And her story, of course! Telling it over and over again to people like us he couldn't help falling under its tragic spell."

"Really, Giselle! It should be obvious to anyone with sense that Ned is in love with the girl herself."

"You mean"—I stumbled on a loose stone and had to grab her arm to save myself from going smack down on the ground—"you mean her ghost? But Ned told me the house isn't haunted."

"That is not what he said."

"Yes, he did!"

"He said he had never seen a ghost at Thornton Hall, but you and I saw one, Giselle."

"We did?" I stopped walking and addressed the back of Aunt Honoria's fur coat as she marched onward. "Do you mean one of the shadows on the wall in the tower room shouldn't have been there?"

"I mean," the voice came floating back to me, "that Ned is the ghost. Surely you know that Edward is commonly abbreviated in that way."

"Mr. Rochester was an Edward." I scurried to catch up with the back that had disappeared into the mist. "And Jane Eyre never shortened his name to anything except Sir. I hate to say it, Aunt Honoria," I said kindly, "but I think you are letting your imagination run away with you. The name business is just a coincidence. Ned couldn't possibly be the ghost of Edward Haverfield. He was much too real."

"As opposed"—disparaging sniff—"to other ghosts of your acquaintance?"

"And he's far too old," I persisted.

"Do you want to argue, Giselle, or would you like me to tell you why I am sure whereof I speak? Very well, I will assume you are nodding your head in agreement, not because it is loose on your shoulders." We had entered the churchyard and stood under a weeping willow that lived up to its name by dripping all over us. But I hardly noticed that I was growing damper by the minute. "If you remember, Giselle, I remarked to Ned that the eyes of the girl in the portrait followed his every movement."

"I thought you meant she was watching all of us."

"Then you need to bone up on your grammar, my girl! Did I not use the pronoun *you* when addressing him? Never mind. I pondered upon the fact that those eyes possessed a glow only to be seen on the face of a woman in love. You're too young, Giselle—"

"I'm not! I saw it too!"

"And I thought the only passion you understood was for treacle pudding! Indeed, yes!" Aunt Honoria shook her fur coat the way my cat Tabitha used to do after coming in from the rain. "I read your face at lunch with the same skill with which I read Anne Thornton's. And even you noticed Ned's feeling for her."

"He's a nice, dear man," I said, "and I don't want to believe he was ever a murderer, and a sniveling one at that!"

"He paid the price for his act of betrayal, Giselle, in the moldering cell that I imagine quickly changed him from a handsome youth to a white-haired old man. And from that time forward he has existed in purgatory."

"But you told me there's no such place," I objected.

"I said no such thing." Aunt Honoria gave the weeping willow a whack with her stick in hopes perhaps of discouraging it from dripping all over us. "I said that you and I as members of the Church of England do not believe in purgatory. Therefore we don't end up in a place between heaven and hell, but Edward being a Roman Catholic was bound by the tenets of his faith to serve out his time of penitential suffering in the manner prescribed by his faith."

"You mean polishing brass at Thornton Hall?"

"No, Giselle." Aunt Honoria began walking down the

broad path toward the church. "His penance is in having to tell with agonizing truthfulness the account of Anne Thornton's death and his subsequent cowardice, day in and day out, to people wishing to tour the house and wallow in a lurid tale."

"Yes, Aunt Honoria," I said as we stood on the steps of the church, which I now saw from the posted sign was Roman Catholic. But I was still a long way from being convinced.

"You think I'm a dotty old woman." To my amazement she actually smiled, but the creaking sound came from the doorknob turning under her hand. "But Ned himself provided me with the proof that I was correct in my summations. When I put the two-shilling piece into the palm of his glove I remembered what he had said about Anne's brother's making sure that Edward would never shoot another arrow. You see, Giselle"—Aunt Honoria pushed open the church door and stepped into the light—"there was no hand inside that glove, just some soft substance like cotton wool. And"—she frowned at me—"don't go thinking you put the idea in my head by your talk of Mr. Rochester and how he lost his hand for his sins. My imagination did not get the better of me."

"No, Aunt." I smiled at her.

"And when you get home don't start babbling to your parents about any of this. Not that I wish you to lie."

"That would be wicked," I agreed.

"But there is no harm in being discreet, as Ned was when you asked him if there were ghosts. And we don't want your mother and father to get the wrong idea and not allow you to come out with me again, if you should wish to do so."

"Yes, please!" I said. "I've had a super time."

"Changed your tune since lunchtime, haven't you, child?" Aunt Honoria cleared her throat. "Well, don't stand gawking. We must find St. Bartholomew's altar and light a candle for the repose of Ned's soul. I would like to think we could speed up his reunion with Anne Thornton who, if I know anything, is still waiting for him at the pearly gates." Aunt Honoria poked me toward the nave with her stick. "He was never wicked—just once young and less than heroic, and in my eyes he found honor as a man of truth. Such men are rare indeed, as you will discover when you have the misfortune to fall in love, Giselle. I don't suppose there's much hope you will develop some sense and take a leaf out of your Great Aunt Honoria's book. Thank God I never had a romantic bone in my body."

"Rubbish!" I said as her hand closed over mine and together we lit the candle.

One Night at a Time

It was an evening in late October of the kind of which I am particularly fond. An east wind whipped around the corners of the London street, chasing off any chance wayfarers with their coattails between their legs. The moon gloomed behind a ragged curtain of cloud, and rain spat cheekily upon the windows as if in hopes I would relax my clasp of the curtains and charge off to seize up the poker, in order to challenge the peeking shadows to a duel.

I was restless to be out and about, if to do no more than explore the dark alleys and courtyards with which that part of town abounded. My rooms were at the top of a repressively humdrum building, and it is my belief that they were as tired of me as I of them. The wall lamps did their best in lending a feverish blush to the wallpaper, but the sofa and chairs sat stolidly where they always sat, like dogs told to "stay" and subsequently forgotten by an absentminded master. The books and papers on my desk had all been squared away by my secretary, before she escaped to whatever life she knew beyond these walls. Not a pencil required sharpening, not an inkwell filling. Assuming a seat by the fire, I reminded myself that this confinement to quarters was of my own making. A scant week before, I had invited an old acquaintance to take up residence with me until he could establish himself elsewhere. This offer was not made purely out of the goodness of my heart. Ours was a relationship of doctor and patient, for although I do not hang my shingle in vulgar display upon the door, I may lay claim to certain credentials as a medical practitioner.

The clock on the mantelpiece struck nine, and I arose with more alacrity than was merited by the occasion to set out a pair of decanters and some glasses. Ah, yes! My guest had awakened. A creaking sound, coupled with a nose-nipping draft, indicated the opening of the bathroom door. Upon his arrival I had strongly urged him to a more conventional medium of repose, but he had insisted he would rest more soundly in the mahogany-enclosed bathtub.

When he now entered the sitting room I perceived the chill of porcelain still upon him, heightening the somber effect of raven locks winging back from a pallid brow. The shadows beneath the sunken eyes appeared more pronounced tonight, and I made haste to play the genial host.

"Ah, Batinsky!" I spread my hands with a flourish. "I trust you slept well?"

"Tolerably, my dear Warloch." The smile he bestowed on me was as frayed about the edges as the aged smoking jacket he wore, causing me to suspect that his rest had been assaulted by dreams in which all the old, forbidden cravings reimposed themselves.

When Batinsky had first approached me seeking "a cure" I had thought him foolish indeed. I have never experienced a burning (so charming a word) desire to join the human race. But he had brought me by degrees to the realization that he had come to find his present existence intolerable. Recalling, albeit grudgingly, a service he had once performed to me at some risk to himself, I fetched down my alchemist's vials from the cupboard and set about mixing up a potion that would provide, when taken daily, the nutrients his particular chemistry required and were no longer to be ingested through his favorite libation.

I had previously had occasion for experimentation with a case similar to his. The subject had been my secretary, the inestimable Miss Flittermouse. Finding her shorthand tiptop, but her tendency to bare her fangs at me—upon being asked to work late—disconcerting, I had been moved to try to assist her in rejoining the common herd. (The particular inducement for her was a gentleman: a curate of all unsuitables, in attachment that happily withered on the vine once Miss Flittermouse took "the cure.") I may say, without fear of correction, that hers was a success story. True, there were days when she was a little flighty but I put this down to the time of the month, when the moon was full, and in the main was well satisfied with her.

Front the outset I had known Batinsky's would be the more challenging case. Traditionally, the male sex tends to be harder to reclaim, and, unlike Miss Flittermouse, he was no recent acolyte. His addiction had been created over centuries, and no potion, however exactly compounded, could entirely rid him of a dependence both emotional and physical. His only real hope lay in total abstinence. There must be, I told him with all attempt at lightness, no social imbibing or talk of "one last nip for the road." Having explained the situation as plainly as I might, I urged him to seek out some other form of diversion for his energies, but he made no response to the suggestion, and, to my increasing irritation, seemed bent upon boring himself into oblivion.

"A drink, Batinsky?" I said now, holding up a decanter.

"Yes, but not port, I think," he smiled wryly. "I would prefer, if I may, a glass of tomato juice. If not the flavor, at least the look and consistency, my dear Warloch."

Relieved to find him up to even this meager jest, I made haste to procure him the requested beverage. "And what is your pleasure tonight, sir?" After filling my own glass, I waved him to a chair. "After we have dined, we may, if you wish, visit some friends of mine in Kensington."

"To play parlor games with a crystal ball?" Batinsky seated himself and stared broodingly into the fire. "Your efforts to entertain me are unceasing, old friend, and do you the more credit for being all infernal nuisance." At my murmured denials he paused to sip his drink. Setting it aside he said, "You cannot deny you must have been wishing me off"—a derisive chuckle—"in some belfry all week. But let me tell you now that your advice to bestir myself did not go in one ear and out the other. I have thought long and hard, through the dark reaches of the night, as to how best to redirect my life and now am come to a decision."

"Splendid!" I sat down across from him, leaned back comfortably and rested my glass of port on my waistcoat front. "Relieve my curiosity, sir! Or must I pry the whole out of you?"

"Yesterday I placed an advertisement in *The Spectre*."

"My! We *have* been industrious!"

"In it I announced my availability in matters requiring the services of a private detective."

"Indeed?" I was somewhat at a loss.

"For people of our sort."

"Of course."

Batinsky leaned forward, his bone-white hands resting upon the knees of his old-world breeches; the shadow cast by the bureau behind him lent an eagle swoop to his shoulders. "You may recall that I have upon occasion engaged in the solving of certain riddles that perplexed and troubled members of our acquaintance."

"Certainly. I am unlikely to forget your timely assistance in recovering the journals that recorded my family's history, after they were appropriated by that impudent puritan. A woman skulking under the name of Mercy, if I remember rightly!" Rising, I trod over to the window and stared fixedly out into the night. "Doubtless I would have withstood the rigors of interrogation; but I will admit to you an unmanly fear of the ducking stool."

My sharp ears picked up the sound of Batinsky's shrug. "An abominable indignity," he said. "And I do not forget that to the hunter you and I look the same in the dark. But let us return to the present. Do you then wish me success in my labors?"

In truth I was of two minds about the matter. My friend did well to contemplate an emergence from his lethargy; however, the uneasy thought occurred that he might have fallen prey to the desire to atone for his past life by embarking upon a course of good works—a most unhealthy attitude—but before I could urge him to consider the possibility of card-sharking as an alternative diversion, my attention was caught by the movement of a figure in the street below.

"A veiled woman." I followed the words with a sour chuckle. "If ours were the world of detective fiction, Batinsky, she would undoubtedly be making for our door to consult you upon a matter of gravest urgency."

"Do not despair!" Before I could turn towards him, Batinsky was at my shoulder. "Life is no less predictable than the printed page. Smooth down your shirtfront, Warloch, and prepare for a visitor."

"So you make your deduction," I responded with heavy sarcasm, "because the fish-and-chip shop next door is closed, the boxing club across the way does not cater to females, and because you know the other inhabitants of this building, all in all a sterling lot, are not given to receiving callers at unreasonable hours."

"Very true." Batinsky turned to face the door.

"And next you will be telling me you can ascertain by the weary turn of the lady's head and the languid drift of her skirts that she has traveled a vast distance by means of a milk cart with a broken axle and a horse lame in the near foreleg . . ."

"She has certainly come from far-off places," he conceded in voice of one humoring a child, holding up a hand to solicit my silence. Before I could raise an eyebrow the doorknocker sounded with a thud, causing the mantel clock to execute a series of jumps. Batinsky and I moved as one, but we were not halfway across the room when the woman walked through the door. Please understand, she did not turn the knob and enter in the prescribed manner. Rather, she passed through that door while it stood closed and barring the way, as was its earthly function.

Her voice was soft and anxious as a child's. "Which of you gentlemen is the Baron Batinsky?"

"I have that misfortune, Madam." My friend executed a low bow, and our visitor advanced upon him, her outstretched hands as transparent as her draperies, her countenance of less substance than her veil. But what she lacked in flesh and blood she more than made up for with the force of her presence. It was not only that she brought with her the dew-washed fragrance of woodland flowers; there was an urgency to her movements that charged the room with the energy of an electrical storm.

"Sir, I am come to you for help." In the heightened glare of the wall lamps, she stood with head bent. "Do not, I beg of you, send me away."

"Allow me instead," Batinsky spoke gently, "to present my colleague, Dr. Warloch."

"I am honored." The lady turned her veils in my direction, and I made the necessary responses even as I began to feel quite grumpy. Splendid! Here I am, cast in the role of the old duffer who feeds the great detective's intellectual vanity by asking the wrong question at the right time, while he, with all due nobility, basks in the attentions of a woman whose soul is her only attraction. Trying to restrain my irritation, I asked our visitor if she would care for something to drink.

"A glass of brandy, Madam?"

"Thank you"—her voice held a hint of innocent mirth—"but I did not partake of spirits, even before I became one. I will, however, take a seat, and you gentlemen may join me." Whereupon she glided over to the settee, and Batinsky and I availed ourselves of the fireside chairs. "And now you would like me to explain my intrusion on your evening." As she spread her shadow skirts, I became convinced that she had been hardly more than a girl when events brought her to her present pass.

"You have not told us your name." Batinsky—perhaps in contrast to her vaporous form, or possibly because his boredom was deserting him—looked more alive than I had yet seen him.

"Elspeth Sinclair."

"You are"—I could not resist a smug glance at the great detective—"Lady Sinclair?"

"The same."

"Then I remember something of your story," I proclaimed triumphantly. "A dozen serving wenches may come to grief without any fuss being made; but when a lady of your quality meets an untimely end, it is a different matter. Also, the date on which calamity struck your ladyship happens to be of cultural significance to me."

Silencing me with a slight stiffening of his shoulders,

Batinsky turned squarely towards our guest. "The suspicion occurred to me when you first appeared, Madam, that death had not come to you in one of its more acceptable forms."

"It was assumed I took my own life, but the cruel truth is that I was murdered." Her voice came in a whisper, even as the rest of her seemed to gain strength, so that the contours of her face were now discernable and her eyes burned through the veil. "Last year on the night of All Hallows' Eve I was thrown from a fourth-story balcony."

"An accidental fall was not considered a possibility, by those involved in the investigation?" I asked.

"The height of the railing ruled out misadventure."

"And you come to me seeking revenge upon your murderer?" Batinsky reached out a hand towards her and as quickly drew it.

"No!" Her cry was one of such abject despair that even my tough old heart was touched. "I want you to discover the name of the one who hated me so much that he . . . or she would want me banished from the earth, because not knowing who or why keeps me from my rest . . . were there not an even more compelling reason for the truth to be known."

"You had no enemies?" Batinsky asked.

"None."

"And what of lovers?"

"I had a husband." The mere words breathed life into her, and I saw, or thought I saw, her eyes turn the color of bluebells on a spring morning and her hair blossom into wheaten gold. Hers was the kind of beauty to which I am not usually partial, one enhanced by sweetness of temper and winsome laughter. But I had forcibly to remind myself that I could be her great-great grandfather. And that she was dead.

"Ours was one of those great loves." She was leaning towards Batinsky, her hands fleshing out as she twisted them in bitter hopelessness. "There were many who said our marriage would not work because Justin was twenty years my senior and had not lived a monk's existence before we met. But I never doubted his devotion. He told me again and again, in the most tender and impassioned way, that I had renewed his soul and that without me he was nothing."

What *you* must tell us, Lady Sinclair, I thought, with all my accustomed cynicism, is of those events leading to your unscheduled departure for the other side.

"So you must see I cannot leave Justin in the torment of believing I took my own life," she declared, spectral tears pooling.

"I will help you if I can," promised my friend, offering her his handkerchief.

"And in order that you may do so"—a stilled sob—"you will need as much information as I can provide."

"I would like to know where you were and with whom," came Batinsky's almost dreamy reply, "on the night in question."

"At a masked ball in Chiswick, given by Mrs. Edward Browne."

"Where no doubt a great many of your friends and acquaintances were present."

"I am sure of it, but you must understand we were not only masked but in costume and thus unrecognizable one to the other. And I, for one, had upheld the stricture of the invitation that we keep our disguises secret."

Batinsky did not make the obvious point that Sir Justin must surely have been privy to his wife's costume. Instead he asked, "What did you wear, Lady Sinclair, to this All Hallows' ball?"

Her answer was a moment in coming, and I saw her mouth

for the first time, sweetened by the rosiest of smiles. "My husband insisted that I go as Marie Antoinette. He had a yearning to see me in a powdered wig and silk gown of sea green trimmed with forget-me-nots and French lace. What merry times we had that last month! Every fitting was an occasion because Justin made a point of being always present with suggestions—for an alteration, perhaps, to the bodice or more ruching for the skirt. Yet you must not think him a tyrant, for he lavished praise upon the little dressmaker, who entered into the spirit of the thing with her pretty, teasing ways."

"Lady Sinclair," I said, determined not to be backward in coming forward, "did this seamstress have a name?"

"Millie Tanner."

"What Dr. Warloch would intimate"—Batinsky's expression was hidden beneath his hooded eyes—"is that this young woman may, with no malice intended, have discussed your costume with one or another of her clients."

"She was a chatterbox," Lady Sinclair affirmed, yet she sounded doubtful. "Millie had sewn for me once before, and it was as much for the liveliness of her personality as her exceptional talent with the needle that we hired her back. But even if I concede the possibility that she forgot her vow of silence and let her tongue run away with her, it makes no difference, because when I was thrown over that balcony I was not in costume as Marie Antoinette."

"The peasouper thickens," I quipped, the truth being that for once a woman had me under her spell. However, I suspect it was the brooding intensity of Batinsky's silence that encouraged Lady Sinclair to approach the climax of her story.

"It was a night of one vexation after another. While my husband and I were dressing—he was to go as a Versailles dandy—his valet brought him up a letter that had been delivered to the house. Justin would have slipped the envelope into his pocket without opening it, but I insisted it must bear tidings of some urgency to have been sent round at such an hour. And so it proved. After scanning the note, Justin began to pace the floor in great agitation before gathering me up in his arms and begging my understanding. A dear friend, a member of his club, had suffered some misfortune—I do not know of what nature and am not sure that Justin was clear on that himself—and was summoning him. What could I do but tell him in as cheerful a voice as I could muster that he should go to this friend at once?"

"Did he suggest joining you later at the ball?" Batinsky's eyes appeared to look right through her (which was, of course, entirely possible).

"Yes, but I would not allow myself to hope, for there was no knowing how long he would be detained. And no sooner had I arrived at Mrs. Browne's house than calamity struck again. A villainous-looking pirate, who was about to take his departure, reached for my hand and was bestowing a very hairy kiss upon it when I felt the seam of my gown rip all the way from my underarm to the waist. I made my excuses to my hostess, and would have gone immediately home, but she insisted that I accompany her to the attic where she was certain we could find a costume for me among the trunks. Before her marriage Mrs. Browne was for some years an actress, in musical comedies, I believe, and would seem to have held on to every flower-seller's hat and feather boa she had worn upon the boards."

"Did the good lady remain with you while you picked out a change of costume?" I asked before Batinsky could do it.

"No. She was in haste to return to her other guests. And Mrs. Browne was not an intimate friend of mine. We had met on but two prior occasions. It was Justin who knew her from his bachelor days. Indeed I think it likely there may have been more to their relationship than mere friendship, because at first he had been hesitant to accept the invitation to the ball and then, when I persuaded him, was so lovingly determined that I look my very best.

"Always I assured Justin that what had gone before meant nothing; only the present counted with me. And had I experienced any foreboding when standing in Mrs. Browne's attic that I would within minutes be consigned to the past, I would never have donned the Nell Gwyn costume I found in the first trunk I opened. But, I tell you, my skin did not prickle nor my hair stand on end. Indeed, when lacing up the bodice and abandoning my powdered wig for a mobcap with ringlets attached, I began to see the humor in the situation and think myself peevish for being so put out by one failed evening, when my life was in the main so richly blessed."

"Did you encounter anyone upon leaving the attic?" I inquired. A sound question, but one posed, I must confess, because I was strangely unwilling to take that final walk with Lady Sinclair.

"No one was about when I went down the short flight of stairs to the fourth floor where the ballroom was located. But when I was passing down the corridor something did occur to startle me. I heard a cry—a woman's voice—emanating from one of the bedrooms."

"And you investigated?" Batinsky sat like a wax exhibit in a museum.

"Yes, to my undying . . ."—a sound between a moan and a laugh—"mortification. The room would have been in darkness but for there being a full moon that night, making it possible for me to see the shapes of a pair of lovers upon the bed. I could really tell nothing about the woman, whose hair was loosened upon the pillow, because he was on top of her, his hands upon her neck or shoulders. He did look up when I was backing out the door, and I can scarcely doubt he was as embarrassed as I."

"But he, like you, was masked?" Batinsky asked.

"Yes, along with the added camouflage of some head-covering of dark cloth and a beard to hide his blushes. Once back in the corridor I made every effort to put the incident behind me. I was, after all, a married woman, not a schoolgirl. But, after entering the overheated ballroom and wending my way through the crush of gentlemen in togas and ladies clanging Gypsy tambourines, I felt flushed to the point of faintness and soon escaped through one of the many doors to an anteroom, whose French doors stood invitingly open. I . . . heard footsteps approaching as I went through to the small balcony, but before I could turn, let alone experience the least flutter of panic . . ."—her voice faltered—"I was grabbed from behind and lifted up, like in offering to the gods, and hurled over the iron railing."

The wind stilled, as if it, along with Batinsky and myself, had ceased breathing, and, when I forced myself to meet Lady Sinclair's gaze, the blue had ebbed from her eyes and the gold from her hair. She was, as she had been upon entering my sitting room, but a shadow of her former self.

Gliding up from the sofa in a cobwebby drift of veils, she whispered, "My time is up, Baron Batinsky."

"Dear lady," I intervened, "you must not rush off. Our friend here does not charge by the hour."

Her sigh came as a dying breath. "My strength is all but exhausted. And I fear that this intrusion upon your time has been in vain, for I cannot think I have told you anything to assist you in discovering the identity of my murderer."

Batinsky chose not to exert his fabled power with the fair sex to reassure her; instead, he asked, "Have you been able to make contact with your husband?"

"I see him." Lady Sinclair was fading as we watched. "I see him in all his anguish. I watch him pace the house in the dead of night and I hear him crying out my name. But he does not feel me reach out to comfort him or know that I am there. Imagine, if you can, how he must feel in believing I took my own life. He must doubt his own sanity, for I know he can never doubt my love for him. I beg you, Baron"—she was now reduced to a pair of outstretched shadow hands—"discover who did this to me, so that I and my beloved may know some peace."

"It will be done, Madam."

"I have not spoken to you of payment."

"In giving my thoughts a new direction, my lady, you place me in your debt."

"Tomorrow . . ." Her voice came soft as a raindrop, from over by the door. "I will come again at this time tomorrow night. Pray God you will have an answer for me; and may He bless your endeavors, dear Baron."

Before either of us could murmur our adieux, the great detective and I were alone, with only the blank-faced furniture for company. Had it not been for the lingering fragrance of wildflowers, there would have been nothing to suggest we had not conjured up the Lady Sinclair out of our imaginations.

"Tomorrow," I said, pouring myself a liberal glass of port. "You know what day that is, Batinsky!"

"All Hallows' Eve."

"My feast day," I could not forbear reminding him, "and the anniversary of our . . . your client's murder."

"Timeliness is of the essence, my dear Warloch." He roamed the room in so somber a mood that even his shadow would seem to grow nervous.

"You need a drink," I told him.

"Indeed, I do"—his eyes burned into mine—"and something stronger than tomato juice."

"Your wish is my command," I said, deliberately misconstruing. "I will mix it with a splash of vodka and we'll entitle the brew a Bloody Betty . . . or Mary, given your penchant for virgins."

Taking the glass I handed him and downing the contents in a single swallow, Batinsky said, "Her perfume was both delightful and distinctive, was it not?"

"The very essence of the woman."

"It occurs to me"—he resumed his prowling—"that a husband might fail to recognize it on grounds of familiarity, whereas someone else might well . . . pick up the scent in tracking down his . . . or her prey."

"Irrefutably." I retrieved his glass as it went past me for the fourth time. "But I do not think you should readily dismiss Sir Justin as a suspect. Church bells, Batinsky! There is no denying that when it comes to the human tragedy, the husband is always the most likely culprit."

"I hear you, my dear Warloch." He ceased his perambulations in front of the fireplace, and the clock gave a nervous ping as if asking permission to proceed with chiming the hour.

"But do not think me blind to other possibilities," I said when silence reigned once more, "blessed as I am with an evil mind. I see all the advantages to the hostess of the ball, Mrs. Browne, in removing the wife of her lover."

"Former lover, if we are to believe the lovely Lady Sinclair," countered Batinsky. "And men of Sir Justin's walk of life are not prone to marry their mistresses, who are in the main chosen from the lower orders to dispel those very aspirations."

"You forget." I sat down and planted my hands in the

manner of a righteous cleric upon my waistcoat. "You forget that Mrs. Browne had already married up in the world. Her late husband, a Yorkshire mill owner, was no blueblood, it is true, but he was rich to the point of respectability, making it not implausible that his widow might set her sights even higher the second time around."

"What an invaluable source of gossip you are." Batinsky's eyes were darker than the night, and even more adept at concealment.

"One does one's best to live in the real world," I responded mildly. "And I admit the facts speak strongly against Mrs. Browne in that the Nell Gwyn costume came from her store of theatrical finery."

"There is no discounting, for all the emphasis upon the masquerade, that she may have mentioned Lady Sinclair's change of attire to one or other of the guests."

"Most probably to Sir Justin, were he to come looking for his wife," I replied with some complacency. "But in focusing upon him as our villain, do not think I fail to note the implications of Lady Sinclair's entering that bedroom to interrupt a passionate encounter, whose revelation might prove exceedingly awkward for the parties involved. Indeed, it appears to me probable that our unknown gentleman, using the term loosely, may have had sufficient glimpse of her ladyship, alias Nell Gwyn, to track her down."

"But surely murder would seem excessive under the circumstances described."

"Sometimes, Batinsky," I said, "one gets the impression that you have no inkling of how life is lived beyond the confines of your personal twilight zone. If one or both lovebirds were married and liable to be cut off without a shilling, or the male speared in a duel upon discovery, I can perceive murder to be a viable alternative."

"Your reasoning, my dear Warloch, puts me to shame." So saying, the great man paced over to the window, where he stood pleating the curtains between his bone-white fingers.

"And, pray tell"—a smirk tugged at my lips—"what are your deductions, oh Master Mind?"

"That the Lady Sinclair was a woman born to be loved."

Such were his pearls of wisdom! The man did wonders for my fragile ego, and I began to see the advantages of having him for a guest, if not as a private detective, were I ever to find myself in dire straits. After several moments of silence, I said, in hope of encouraging him to more cerebral endeavors, "It is certainly a case one can sink one's teeth into." Upon receiving no reply, I heaved out of my chair and with a pettish clanking of glass to bottle replenished our drinks.

Batinsky bestirred himself to offer a toast. "To our first client, my friend!" Encouraging. I allowed myself to hope that we would spend the rest of the night wrapping up the affair of The Veiled Lady, but it was not to be. He immediately left the room and did not reappear, leading me to the annoying conclusion that he was hiding out in the mahogany-enclosed tub until I should be driven to my bed. Being the softhearted old codger that I am, I could readily understand his embarrassment at failing to come up a brilliant solution to the case, but I resented having to make my ablutions in the little watering hole off my dressing room. It was enough of a sacrifice to do so during the day, but if Batinsky was about to make the bathroom his night quarters, as well, I could see the need to suggest he look into taking up residence elsewhere. It was in a grim mood that I eventually retired.

Shortly before noon the next day I was met by my secretary, who was exiting the bathroom. It was irksome to be forced to speak up for my troublesome guest, but I girded my dressing-gown cords about me and did my duty.

"Miss Flittermouse, I trust you did not disturb Baron Batinsky."

" 'Course I didn't." She batted her eyes at me and raked her six-inch fingernails through her tar-black hair. "To be honest, I'd quite forgot about him when I went in to wash me hands, but it makes no matter because he weren't there."

"Weren't . . . wasn't in the bath?"

"You've got it, guv'ner." Startled by my bewilderment, she scuttled for the sitting room, all the while flapping her arms as if in some futile attempt to get airborne. To the accompaniment of a crescendo being played upon the typewriter keys, I flung open the bathroom door to see for myself . . . that Batinsky wasn't there.

Not to panic, I told myself. I should take it as a promising sign that he had overcome his aversion to daylight and ventured out, perhaps for a stroll in the park. Determined to look on the bright side—and indeed there was no escaping the sun which, in defiance of the time of year, streamed ruthlessly through the windows—I drank several cups of coffee before beginning the day's dictation of my memoirs. As the hours passed, however, and Batinsky did not return, I experienced a growing alarm.

For all I knew he could have left the flat by way of the bathroom window in the middle of the night while I was still up. No one, I think, could accuse me of being a man of conscience, but my own people have been subjected to sufficient persecution over the years that I may have become a little squeamish in my old age. The thought that Batinsky might even now be sleeping off the effects of his bloodthirsty debauchery did not sit well with my luncheon. When the afternoon was over I found myself thinking that I might have done more to aid his rehabilitation. For instance, I could have suggested he meet on a weekly basis with Miss Flittermouse and others battling their particular addiction, in an atmosphere of support and fellowship.

At six o'clock my secretary placed the cover over her typewriter and vanished from the scene, leaving me to the doubtful companionship of the decanters. The prospect of facing Lady Sinclair, alone, and without the information she sought, made me feel remarkably low. I was, however, becoming resigned to my fate, when the outer door opened and Batinsky walked into the sitting room, for all the world as if he had just been out to buy a newspaper.

"So it's you!" I sank lower in my chair, sounding very much like a shrewish wife.

"My dear Warloch." He stood unbuttoning and rebuttoning his cape with black-gloved hands. "I trust my absence did not cause you any alarm."

"You might have left a note."

"Don't pout, Warloch." A smile touched his lips. "My kind is not easily civilized, but I promise," he avowed humbly, "another time I will be more thoughtful."

"Then we will say no more on the subject."

"You must not let me off so easily." His eyes glittered with an emotion I could not read, in a face white as the walls. "And I must relieve your mind of any fears that I have suffered a relapse. The truth is I have been out and about on legitimate business, in the course of which I was able to confirm that the woman is dead."

At once my concern for his mental health reasserted itself. But before I could remind him that Lady Sinclair's state of being had never been at issue, he produced my cloak from the armoir and informed me we were going out.

"Make haste, my friend! We are off to pay a call on Mrs. Edward Browne."

"But what of . . ."

"We will be back in time to receive Lady Sinclair." Batinsky clapped my hat upon my head, draped a silk scarf about my neck, and hurried me out the door and down several flights of stairs to the pavement where he faced me under the glare of the street lamps. "It is my understanding that Mrs. Browne tonight is hosting her annual masquerade ball, an occasion not to be missed, do you not agree, Warloch?"

"Indeed!" I spoke to his back, for he was already heading past the shuttered shops and bleary-eyed dwellings towards the crossroad, his cape billowing out behind him and his feet appearing to glide at least two inches off the ground. Before I reached the corner a cab had already drawn up alongside him, whether or not of the driver's own volition I cannot say. Batinsky issued the required address to the driver, whose eyes looked ready to bolt out of his head.

"We are on our way to a fancy dress do," I said.

"Ah, that explains it!" the man replied in vast relief. "Hop aboard! And don't neither of you get any ideas of putting a hex on me if the traffic is bad and I don't make good time!" His laughter rumbled away under the turning of the wheels.

The moon poked her pale face through the window but there was little to see and nothing to hear. Batinsky did not speak a word during the short journey to the Browne residence, and by the rigidity of his posture he prevailed upon me to maintain the silence.

Upon alighting from the cab, we found ourselves facing a broad flight of marble steps leading up to what would appear from its onion domes and curlicue spires to be a tomb all in an Arabian night's work. Batinsky had barely laid a hand upon the knocker when the red lacquered door inched open with a sound like a spent sigh.

We found ourselves looking in upon a gilded cage, where flocked all manner of birds of paradise. Indeed there must have been a hundred people in the hall, whose circular walls soared two stories high to a ceiling painted with cavorting nymphs and shepherds. Immediately before us, in the light dripping from a chandelier whose spangles might have been clipped from an exotic dancer's costume, stood a plumply pretty dairymaid with very red hair and an expectant smile on her painted lips.

"Mrs. Edward Browne?" My companion raised his voice above the crowd, and her hand to his bloodless lips. "I am the Baron Batinsky and this"—a nod in my direction—"is Dr. Warloch."

"Charmed, I'm sure!" Our hostess watched in fascinated confusion as we stepped over the threshold and the door swung silently shut behind us. "You must be nice lads," she rallied, "and not mind me not recognizing you, for when all's said and done—that's the whole point of a costume party, isn't it? And your disguises are ever so good, even though you're being naughty and not wearing your masks. I'm the only one who gets to show me face round here."

She poked a finger at Batinsky's chest. "But don't think I'll be too hard on you, 'cos if I was to meet you in some dark alley, you'd scare the living daylights out of me."

"You'd have no call to worry, Madam." I made my bow. "He is in recovery."

"Now, if that don't ease my mind!" Mrs. Browne appeared not to know if she was on her head or her heels which was hardly surprising since around her the masked figures wove in and out as if in step to the formation of some vast minuet.

"My dear lady," Batinsky said, "your memory does not fail you. Neither Dr. Warloch nor myself was on your guest list."

"Well, we always have some of that, don't we—people barging in uninvited?" Eyes suddenly hostile, hands on her ample hips, she looked us up and down. "I never used to bother about it; but after what happened last year there's a new set of rules. People may say the lady killed herself, but who knows? So if it's all the same with you, then, I'll be showing you a shortcut to the door."

"It is on account of Lady Sinclair's unhappy demise that my colleague and I are here tonight." Batinsky fixed her with his compelling gaze. "We are private detectives employed by a client, whose name we are not free to divulge, to ascertain what really happened upon that balcony one year ago this day."

"Well, I never!" Mrs. Browne clapped her hands to her rouged checks. "So that's the way the wind blows! Someone thinks the lovely Elspeth didn't take matters into her own hands. And now you want me to escort you to the scene of the crime, is that it?" Without waiting for an answer she plowed through the crowd at the foot of the stairs and beckoned for us to follow her.

Up she went, always three steps ahead of us, her skirts bunched in her hands, her words rattling down upon our heads. "I was downstairs this time last year, right where we was just standing, when I heard that scream what made my blood run cold. I tried to get up the stairs, but it was jammed with people not knowing whether they was coming or going, and when I almost saw my way clear—down came some poor pirate (we always have a lot of pirates) with a swooning female in his arms. Seems she'd been overcome by the heat of the ballroom—as if I can help it getting stuffy up there!" Mrs. Browne nipped around the bend in the staircase, her feet keeping pace with her words. "It's a tragedy whatever way you slice it. Still, I must say I'd feel better knowing Elspeth Sinclair didn't take her own life."

"I have it from an unimpeachable source that she did not," Batinsky replied.

"Well, tell that to Sir Justin! Word is that he's scarcely left the house in a year. And his butler turns everyone away from the door. I went round several times myself but it weren't no use . . ."

"Was the suggestion ever made," I queried, panting, "that he might have been responsible for her death?"

"Not as I heard. And anyway, why would he want to do away with her? She was young, beautiful, and didn't have money of her own to speak of."

Spoken like a devoted mistress, former or otherwise, I thought sourly. My disposition is never improved by exercise better suited to a mountain goat, but, happily for my creaking joints, we had by now reached the fourth floor.

Proceeding down a broad corridor hung with portraits of bogus ancestors to a set of double doors, we found ourselves at the entry to the ballroom. The musicians on the dais were, at that moment, resting their instruments, but I doubt a full orchestra could have heard itself above the babble. The room was as congested with humanity as the hall had been. Curses! I unavoidably stepped on the toes of Lord Nelson and was forced to make my apologies for elbowing aside a lady from the court of Queen Elizabeth before we came to a door providing escape. It is possible that my wits had gone begging, but I gave not a passing thought to our hostess as a prime suspect in the case.

"Here we are, lads!" Mrs. Browne stepped aside to let us enter but did not follow us into the anteroom. It contained a scattering of chairs and had curtains looped aside to reveal French doors giving onto a semicircular balcony.

"What now, Batinsky?" I asked, with an attempt at nonchalance. Blame it on the stresses of the day, but my usual delight in the macabre had deserted me, and I found myself attempting to admire the paintings upon the walls. For that reason I did not see the gentleman, sans mask and unimaginatively suited in evening dress until he materialized ten feet from the backdrop of glass panes.

"Sir Justin Sinclair, I presume?" Batinsky arched a black eyebrow and, upon receiving no reply but a blind stare, continued in his most expressionless voice: "I am come to tell you that your wife was murdered."

"Do you think that I of all people need to be told that Elspeth did not take her own life?" The words came as if wrenched from the very soul of the man, and I found myself stirred to an unlikely pity when looking into that ravaged face. Once upon a time, he must have combined remarkable good looks with a well-nigh irresistible charm, but he was now an empty shell, a creature beyond hope of heaven or hell. As to whether or not Mrs. Browne had known of his presence, who can say? Women, for me, will always retain an element of mystery.

"You think me some avenging angel." Batinsky smiled grimly at the thought. "But there is no call for alarm, sir; my client wishes only your peace of mind."

"Who sends you?" The words were a hoarse cry.

"Your wife."

"That cannot be!" Sir Justin staggered backwards.

"Cannot be—because she is dead, or because you are the one who killed her?"

Here it was, the moment when self-congratulation was in order, for most assuredly I had led Batinsky to this conclusion. So how was it, then, that I wanted only to be home in my own armchair drinking the first of several glasses of port?

"I loved her!"

"I believe you." Batinsky walked forwards until he stood only a scant few feet from his quarry. "Lady Sinclair described the love between the two of you as one of the grand passions. But, being the man you are, that did not prevent your enjoying a frolic with Millie Tanner, the seamstress who came to sew Lady Sinclair's costume for the masquerade ball. She had worked for your wife once or twice before, and this time you contrived to be present at every sitting, turning the girl's head with your blandishments. A harmless diversion in your mind, no doubt, but on the night of the ball she sent you a letter . . ."

"She demanded that I meet her within the hour, or she would go to Elspeth and inform her of our liaison." Sir Justin covered his face with his hands.

"I first suspected Miss Tanner's involvement," Batinsky said, "when I learned that the seam of Lady Sinclair's costume ripped apart within moments of her entering this house. An inexperienced needlewoman might be given to such lapses, but surely not a seasoned dressmaker! I recalled your pocketing the note when it was delivered and only reading it when pressed to do so by Lady Sinclair. The whole business smacked of the surreptitious. But, tell me, how did Millie conduct herself at your rendezvous? Was she amenable to being fobbed off with a few pounds a week in return for her silence?"

"She wept, and said she was sorry for causing me embarrassment. I believed her assurances that there would be no future difficulties."

"With what a light heart you must have arrived at this house, Sir Justin," Batinsky remarked as if making polite conversation. "And what a stroke of good fortune it must have seemed when you encountered one of the guests, dressed as a pirate, heading down the house steps as you were about to mount to the front door. You had not your valet with you to assist you into your costume, but I am sure you managed the bushy beard and head scarf without undue difficulty. Your mask in place, you must have believed the evening a success and your marriage secure, until you discovered that Millie had followed you into the house. A most enterprising young lady, although, according to Mrs. Browne, others have achieved the same feat."

"I panicked," Sir Justin said drearily.

"So you took the girl up to one of the bedrooms and strangled her." Batinsky pressed on. "And when a woman dressed as Nell Gwyn pushed open the door, you had no way of knowing that she was your wife, or that she thought herself to be witnessing not a deathbed scene but a pair of lovers sharing a moment of passion. So you followed her from the room, and the very familiarity of her fragrance was against you: no warning sounded as you caught up with her upon the balcony and hurled her down four stories to the pavement. Still unknowing, you returned to the bedroom for your first victim and carried her down the stairs, informing passersby that the girl had just swooned from the heat."

Locating my voice at last, I said, "I am to understand, Batinsky, that when you spoke to me this evening of having confirmed upon investigation that the woman was dead, you were speaking of Millie Tanner."

"Who else, my dear Warloch?"

"Elspeth would have forgiven my involvement with Millie"—Sir Justin lifted his hands as if to ward off the awfulness of memory—"but I could not conceive of causing her such pain."

"I believe you," Batinsky told him, "and you may believe me that she loves you still."

"You said"—the words came in a strangled blend of bewilderment and hope—"that she sent you. Oh, if that were but true! For I would have you know that since that night a year ago I have been one of the living dead." He turned from us on the last word, and while Batinsky and I stood like two statues anchored in several feet of concrete, he walked slowly through the French doors, climbed onto the balcony railing, stood upright for a moment arms spread wide, and then leaped into night.

From the ballroom behind us came the soft strains of a Viennese waltz and from the street below the beginnings of pandemonium. "Time to go home." In a rare attempt at intimacy I reached out a hand and placed it on Batinsky's shoulder. "We must not keep Lady Sinclair waiting."

"She will not keep the appointment." He moved away from me to stand staring out at the sky, from which the moon had hidden her face, and all the stars had disappeared—as if they were handheld candles blown out by the wind.

"You are no doubt correct," I said. "But keep in mind that there will be other cases, other clients."

"But none"—he spoke in a voice of utmost wistfulness—"quite like the late lamented Lady Sinclair. She must, I think, have had a lovely neck."

Telling George

A saint, an absolute saint, is the only way to describe my husband, George. In thirty odd years of marriage, as true as I'm standing here on me own two feet, and strike me down if I tell a lie, we've never had so much as a cross word. Not a single one. The old love never raises his eyebrows let alone his voice. Oh, you know how it is, there's some as would say I'm boasting, but kind in't a good enough word for my George. At sixty-two years old, he still offers his seat to an older person on the bus. And tidy! Let me tell you I've never had to bend down and pick up one of his socks. "I'm not seeing my wife a drudge," he said the day after we come back from our honeymoon at his mother's house. "I'll do my bit around the house." Them was his very words, "And what's more I'll take on all the shopping. No call for you to go lugging home the Sunday roast and the porridge oats in a string bag, I'll see to getting in the necessaries of a Saturday."

Bless his heart, he's got his funny little ways, but if they don't bother me I haven't the foggiest why they should get in me friend Bonnie's craw. On and on she goes like a gramophone.

"Out with it, Vera," she says last week when we was having a cuppa in her front room. She stopped calling it "the lounge" when she read that was common in "Horse And Hooves" or in one of them la-de-da magazines. And she took down the picture of Her Majesty for the same silly reason. "Come on, spill the beans! When's the last time the old buzzard bought you a birthday or Christmas present? Nineteen forty eight'd be my guess, and then you'd 'ave been bloody lucky if it was a packet of piper cleaners." She always talks like that, does Bonnie, as if she's Queen of the frigging May; all because she and her Bert have a downstairs' lav and a microwave.

"What's wrong with being careful?" I says. "The way I sees it, George is good as gold to me in the ways what count."

"That's right, duck! He don't drink, he don't smoke and he don't chat up dollies on the bus, and I'll tell you for why! He's too buggering mean to part with his own spit."

She's been good to me has Bonnie, letting me use her tumble dryer during that 'orrible cold spell last winter. I turned up at her house—she lives next door but one, with me lips blue and all of a shake because for a minute when I was pegging out George's shirts I'd felt like what I was on one of them trapezes. The wind had been that fierce. Trust Bonnie to make one of her jokes about the washing looking like it was freeze-dried. She's good for a laugh is Bonnie but there's always it bit of a sting in the tail if you get my meaning.

That afternoon when we was having tea she pipes up with, "You should hear me and Bert having a laugh over the time your Jimmy, when he was a kiddy, let slip as how he thought Salvation Army was a brand name for pre-washed, ready-patched blue jeans."

"Jimmy's doing very well for his self," I says. "He just got a promotion at the jam factory, over in Stockton-On-Lea, and him and the wife are thinking about buying a house."

"And when's the last time he sent his Mum so much as twopence? Talk about a chip off the old block." Bonnie poured us both another cuppa from the pot, she swears up and down is real silver, though she got it off the market.

"It's all right for some," I said, without trying to be nasty like, "but George wasn't born with no silver spoon in his mouth."

"No more was Bert." Bonnie got that high and mighty look. "But it don't kill him to take me to the pictures of a now and then or buy me a new Hoover. You can't get so much as a new plug for yours out of the old skinflint. I'll tell you straight, Vera, it makes me see red every time I come over and see you crawling around on your hands and knees, with the dustpan and brush, like something out of bloody 'Upstairs, Downstairs.' Then again, my duck, with a bit of bloomin' luck, your carpet'll fall to pieces, or you will, and you won't have to bother."

"Unlike some," I looked at the photo of Bert on the mantelpiece (only now we call it the mantel shelf), "George believes in putting by for the future." By now, as you can probably tell, I was getting a bit rattled, same as me cup and saucer, so I took them off me knee and put them on Bonnie's spanking new coffee table. "And I've just thought as how he did give me a present once. Remember our dog Panhandler?"

"He was a stray," Bonnie wasn't about to budge an inch. "And the only reason you got to keep him was that he ate 'out.' Don't get me wrong, Vera, I'm not saying George is a monster, it's just that I wouldn't in a million years have him putting his shoes under my bed at night."

That's the trouble with Bonnie. She's the type what fancies herself, if you get my drift. Oh, she'll joke about her hour glass figure turning into a hurricane lamp, but it's the talk up and down the road as how she lives at the hairdressers. And catch her without her eyebrows on and you're as good as dead. My guess is it ticks her off that George don't hang over the garden fence of a morning, watching her bend down to pick up the milk bottles. And I know she has to be jealous as cats that he has all his hair, while old Bert is bald as a snooker ball and in't about to set any hearts beating faster when he clips tickets on the Southend to Liverpool Street train. Believe you me, I know that don't excuse me sitting there, eating jam tarts, and listening to Bonnie tear me hubby up one side and down the other. I was wrong there's no two ways about it. But, when all's said and done, it weren't as though George'd ever get wind of what we'd been saying and get all upset like. And the thing was I was pleased to go over of a now and then and 'ave a cuppa with Bonnie. You can always count on her having a baking fire soon as there's a nip in the air. And as I've said she's good to me. I call always run over to borrow a cup of sugar or a couple of eggs when I don't have any in the house. And then, there's our weekly outing.

For the last few years it's been a habit with Bonnie and me to take the bus into Romford or Ilford of a Thursday afternoon and go poking around the second hand shops. You know the sort of place, all of them with names like Good As New or The Church Mouse. And mostly selling junk—like dressing tables that'd keel over if you looked at them cross-eyed, and hat racks with all the hooks missing. But Bonnie, being a bit of a swank, liked to say she's 'into antiques.'

In the beginning I'd been a bit leary like of saying anything to George about them Thursday shopping sprees. He's always worked so hard has George, keeping the wolf from the door, that I always felt a proper criminal even though I never did more than treat meself to a few scraps of lace or a tape measure for next to nothing. Seems his mother had always got by using bits of string for measuring. Lazy people take the most pains was what she used to say, and a beautiful woman she was, may her soul rest in peace. Like mother, like son, is what they say. And in the end, I'd known I had to tell George, because sneaking around don't do a marriage no good. Not that speaking up was easy mind you. I'd had a hard enough time, way back when, telling him that I was expecting our Jimmy. We'd always agreed, you see, as how kiddies was a luxury we couldn't justify. But I'd known right off the bat I couldn't keep a child from him, and this was no different.

And can you believe it! George was a proper brick. "I've never been against you spending a bob or two here and there, Vera, old girl," them was his very words. "If it makes you happy, and don't put us in the poor house, you won't hear a word from me, should you treat yourself to some light bulbs with a bit of spark left in them."

So much for Bonnie's ideas that he hung on to every ha'pence! After picking over no end of odds and sods, I never did have no luck finding a plug for the Hoover, but I did come across a rusty cake tin, that with a bit of a scrub, wouldn't give you lockjaw. And then there was the broom what looked to me as good as new, even though Bonnie had to go and say it didn't have as many whiskers as a cat. She was all into artsy-fartsy stuff, like doily dolls and embroidered hand towels not big enough to wipe your nose, but then we're all different aren't we?

It was a nasty, wet Thursday last week, and I almost said to Bonnie we shouldn't make the rounds as per usual. But she got a bit snippy as is her way and, anything for a bit of peace, I put on me coat and scarf and went with her down to the bus. I'd got the gas bill and water rates money with me, and thought as how I could nip in and pay them on me way home.

"What about having a look at that new shop?" Bonnie says to me when we got off in Romford High Street.

"What, Yesterday's Treasures?" I looks at her, surprised like. "In't that a bit on the pricey side?"

"Oh you!" All swanky like in her leopard coat and cherry

hat. "Afraid you'll go bonkers, Vera, and break the Bank of England?"

That's the way she is sometimes, makes you feel like a right Charlie. But, when all's said and done, I can't say as how she made me walk through that door. I can't blame no one for what happened but meself. Treasures was one of them musty smelling places, with shadows that walk right up alongside of you to make sure you don't go pinching things. Give me the shivers it did. And if that weren't bad enough, there was lots of mirrors taking their turn watching, along of I dunno how many grandfather clocks standing around, with nasty looks on their faces, ready to nab you if you made a break for it.

The sales lady was at counter in the back—pinging away, sort of absentminded like, at the cash register, with one hand and flipping catalogue pages with the other. My word, she was a queer sort of woman with pink hair shaved all up one side and left flopping in a sort of page boy on the other. And if that didn't give you the creeps, she was wearing ping pong earrings and a plaid dressing gown for a jacket. I couldn't help staring and, wouldn't you know, she caught me at it.

"Afternoon, ladies!" She had a sort of ragamuffin smile.

"We're just looking," I says, all tight faced.

"I'm hooked on hooked rugs," Bonnie stuck in her two-penny worth gabbing on about no pun being intended, whatever that meant. "But you don't have to worry about Vera here buying you out lock stock and barrel: she's come without her pocket money." It was just one of her jokes. But I'd had one of me headaches all day; I've been bothered with them some since the change and I felt meself go a bit teary like.

"You wouldn't have any old vacuum cleaner plugs?" I says, sort of defiant like, and you could have knocked me down with a feather when the saleswoman said, serious as could be, that the pre-war jobbies were awfully hard to find these days.

"Sorry love, we don't have a one; they're extremely collectible. But is there anything else we can do you for?"

"What about . . ." I only said it to show off and because I was sure she wouldn't have none, the place being all wardrobes and clocks. "What about hatpins?"

"Now you're talking." The woman's smile went all curly at the corners, as—with Bonnie standing there gawping, she reached up to the shelf. "This is the only one I have, but it's a rather pretty little number, dated nineteen twelve."

"Very nice," I says, stepping back because it was very long and pokey. "But in't it a bit rusty?"

"That's why it is so affordable," a flip flop of that daft hair, not to be nasty, "a real bargain at twenty five . . ."

"Who would have thought!" I said, all la-de-da. I must have been off me rocker, for I didn't want that hat pin no more than a smack in the face, but all I could think of was putting Bonnie in her place, good and proper. "Seeing as how you've twisted me arm, I'll take it."

"Lovely!" You'd have thought I was buying a frigging tiara, the way she fished out the tissue paper, while I dug into me purse for the money. When I pushed the coins across the counter, the saleswoman looked it me all peculiar like. "What's that for, love?"

"In't it right?" I said counting out the pennies

Oh, it was embarrassing. Her face went as pink as her hair. "I meant twenty five pounds," she says, "not 25P."

I couldn't believe I was hearing straight. "What, for that?" I says.

"Now then, Vera," Bonnie had to go and chip it. "You said you'd 'ave it; so don't go making no stink." And all of a sudden like, I couldn't think straight, what with me heart bonging away like one of them bloody grandfather clocks. Would they let me out of the shop without coming after me with their pendulums cling-clanging? All me life I never could abide scenes.

"If you'll take a look here," the saleswoman's earrings started ping ponging as if someone had taken a bat to them as she edged a catalogue across the counter to me. Ever so nice and soft, she says, "This here is *Hatpin Heirlooms* and, if it isn't the strangest thing! I was checking through it when you came in. See," she thumbed through almost to the middle, "here is your hatpin and it's listed at seventy pounds. I meant to change the ticket but . . ."

She unwrapped the tissue paper and I heard meself saying, all weak and watery, "It is very pretty." And so it was—like a long stemmed silver rose. But twenty-five pounds! "Me husband would kill me!" I hung on to the counter.

"Listen to her," Bonnie says, jolly as could be. "All she talks about day in, week out, is her hubby, St. George, what hasn't said a cross word in thirty years, and now she'll have us believe he'll take the hatchet to her."

"You have to think of this sort of thing as an investment, love," the saleswoman looked at me, sort of pitying like.

"There you go," says Bonnie, "in six months or a year, that hat pin'll be worth a hundred quid and old George will be over the moon."

"You really think so?" Don't ask me to explain it. I must've gone completely barmy, because all of a sudden the shop disappeared in a sort of fog and all I could see was George with a wacking great smile on his dear old face. "Vera my girl," he was saying, "you should be Chancellor Of The Exchequer. You've made our fortune, that's what you've done."

"But I don't have the money," I says.

"Course you do, duck," Bonnie laughed. "You've got the gas and water rates money in your purse."

"And one of these days you'll be investing in a porcelain holder for your collection of hatpins." The saleswoman took the notes from me trembling hand, and rung up the sale with lots of pings that sent shivers all through me. And all at once all the clocks started booming, like they was laughing at me.

Even so, I tried to tell meself I done right. All the way down to the bus I was empty inside, while feeling like what I had the weight of the world in my handbag. I couldn't tell if it was raining or if them drops on me cheeks was tears. I couldn't hear what Bonnie was saying to me. We didn't have to wait for the bus; it come along like it had been sent to chase me down.

"You done right, Vera," says Bonnie but not quite as confident as she'd been in the shop. "We all need a fling now and then."

"And like you was saying," I managed—all choked up like, "it is an investment."

"Course it is!" She looked at me, same as Jimmy used to do when he knew he gone too far, and didn't know as what to do to put things right.

Every bounce of the bus made me feel sick, and the nearer we got to home the more I panicked. George wasn't going be pleased. The old love thought he was risking good money every time he bought a loaf of bread.

"I could say as what I had me pocket picked," I turned to Bonnie, "and not even mention the hatpin."

"Whatever suits your fancy, duck." She held me arm when we got off the bus and walked up the road. "See you, Vera," was her words as she turned in at her gate, but I didn't answer none.

I know it sounds silly, but the house acted all cold, like it wasn't pleased to see me. Even when I turned on the lights, the place stayed dark, if you get my meaning. And I hadn't got as far as the kitchen when I knew as how I couldn't tell George that rubbish about the money being pinched. You know how lies are. It would always be there, sometimes between us, sometimes off to the side, waiting to pounce like. After thirty some years of marriage things'd never be the same and that thought I couldn't abide. So when it come to the time when he always gets home of a night, I unwrapped that horrid hatpin from the tissue paper, and waited for him by the door. Poor old love! Explaining to the police would be so much easier than telling George.

The January Sale Stowaway

Who would have guessed that Cousin Hilda had a dark secret? She was tall and thin, with legs like celery stalks in their ribbed stockings. Her braided hair had faded to match the beige cardigans she wore. And once when I asked if she had been pretty when young, Cousin Hilda said she had forgotten.

"Girly dear, I was fifty before I was thirty. You'd think being an only daughter with five brothers, I'd have had my chances. But I never had a young man hold my hand. There wasn't time. I was too busy being a second mother; and by the time my parents were gone, I was married to this house."

Cousin Hilda lived in the small town of Oxham, some thirty miles northeast of London. As a child I spent quite a lot of weekends with her. She made the best shortbread in the world and kept an inexhaustible tin of lovely twisty sticks of barley sugar. One October afternoon I sat with her in the back parlor, watching the wind flatten the faces of the chrysanthemums against the window. Was this a good moment to put in my request for a Christmas present?

"Cousin Hilda, I really don't want to live if I can't have that roller-top pencil box we saw in the antique shop this afternoon—the one with its own little inkwell and dip pen inside."

"Giselle dear, thou shalt not covet."

Pooh! Her use of my hated Christian name was a rebuff in itself.

"Once upon a time I put great stock in worldly treasures and may be said to have paid a high price for my sin." Cousin Hilda stirred in her fireside chair and ferried the conversation into duller waters. "Where is that curmudgeon Albert with the tea tray?"

A reference, as I understood it, to her lodger's army rank—a curmudgeon being several stripes above a sergeant, and necessitating a snappy mustache as part of the uniform.

"Cousin Hilda," I said, "while we're waiting, why not tell me about your Dark Secret?"

"Is nothing sacred, Miss Elephant Ears?"

"Mother was talking to Aunt Lulu and I distinctly heard the words 'teapot' and 'Bossam's Department Store.' "

"Any day now I'll be reading about myself in the peephole press; but I suppose it is best you hear the whole story from the horse's mouth."

While we talked the room had darkened, throwing into ghostly relief the lace chair backs and Cousin Hilda's face. A chill tippy-toed down my back. Was I ready to rub shoulders with the truth? Did I want to know that my relation was the Jesse James of the China Department?

Hands clasped in her tweed lap, Cousin Hilda said—in the same voice she would have used to offer me a stick of barley sugar, "No two ways about it, what I did was criminal. A real turnup for the book, because beforehand I'd never done anything worse than cough in church. But there I was, Miss Hilda Finnely, hiding out in the storeroom at Bossam's, on the eve of the January Sale."

To understand, girly dear, you must know about the

teapot. On Sunday afternoons, right back to the days when my brothers and I were youngsters in this house, Mother would bring out the best china. I can still see her, sitting where you are, that teapot with its pink-and-yellow roses in her hands. Then one day—as though someone had spun the stage around, the boys had left home and my parents were gone. Father had died in March and Mother early in December. That year, all of my own choosing, I spent Christmas alone—feeling sorry for myself, you understand. For the first time in years I didn't take my nephews and nieces to see Father Christmas at Bossam's. But by Boxing Day the dyed-in-the-wool spinster suspected she had cut off her nose to spite her face. Ah, if wishes were reindeer! After a good cry and ending up with a nose like Rudolph's, I decided to jolly myself up having tea by the fire. Just like the old days. I was getting the teapot out of the cupboard when a mouse ran over my foot. Usually they don't bother me, but I was still a bit shaky—thinking that the last time I used the best china was at Mother's funeral. My hands slipped and . . . the teapot went smashing to the floor.

I was distraught. But always a silver lining. My life had purpose once more. Didn't I owe it to Mother's memory and future generations to make good the breakage? The next day I telephoned Bossam's and was told the Meadow Rose pattern had been discontinued. A blow. But not the moment to collapse. One teapot remained among the back stock. I asked that it be held for me and promised to be in on the first bus.

"I'm ever so sorry, madam, really I am. But that particular piece of china is in a batch reserved for the January Sale. And rules is rules."

"Surely they can be bent."

"What if word leaked out? We'd have a riot on our hands.

You know how it is with The Sale. The mob can turn very nasty."

Regrettably true. On the one occasion when I had attended the first day of the sale, with Mrs. McClusky, my best bargain was escaping with my life. Those scenes shown on television—of customers camping outside the West End shops and fighting for their places in the queue with pitchforks—we have the same thing at Bossam's. The merchandise may not be as ritzy. But then, the Bossam's customer is not looking for an original Leonardo to hang over the radiator in the bathroom, or a sari to wear at one's next garden party. When the bargain hunter's blood is up—whether for mink coats or tea towels, the results are the same. Oh, that dreadful morning with Mrs. McClusky! Four hours of shuddering in the wind and rain, before the doors were opened by brave Bossam personnel taking their lives in their hands. Trapped in the human avalanche, half suffocated and completely blind, I was cast up in one of the aisles. Fighting my way out, I saw once respectable women coshing each other with handbags, or throttling people as they tried to hitchhike piggyback rides. Before I could draw breath, my coat was snatched off my back, by Mrs. McClusky, of all people.

"Doesn't suit you, ducky!"

The next moment she was waving it overhead like a matador's cape, shouting, "How much?"

The dear woman is still wearing my coat to church, but back to the matter at hand. For Mother's teapot I would have braved worse terrors than the January stampede but, hanging up the telephone, I took a good look at myself in the hall mirror. To be first at the china counter on the fateful morning I needed to do better than be Hilda Jane. I'd have to be Tarzan. Impossible. But, strange to say, the face that looked back at me wasn't downcast. An idea had begun to grow and was soon as securely in place as the bun on my head.

The afternoon before The Sale I packed my handbag with the essentials of an overnight stay. In went my sponge bag, my well-worn copy of *Murder at the Vicarage*, a package of tomato sandwiches, a slice of Christmas cake, a small bottle of milk, a piece of cardboard, and a roll of adhesive tape. And mustn't forget my torch. All during the bus ride into town, I wondered whether the other passengers suspected—from the way I held my handbag—that I was up to something. Was that big woman across the aisle, in the duck-feather hat, staring? No . . . yes, there she went elbowing her companion . . . now they were both whispering. So were the people in front. And now the ones behind. I heard the words "Father Christmas" and was put in my place to realize I wasn't the subject of all the buzzing on the bus. That distinction belonged to the stocky gentleman with the mustache, now rising to get off at my stop.

He was vaguely familiar.

"Dreadfully sorry," I said as we collided in the aisle. His Bossam's carrier bag dropped with a thump as we rocked away from each other to clutch at the seat rails. My word, if looks could kill! His whole face turned into a growl.

Behind us someone muttered, "No wonder he got the sack! Imagine him and a bunch of kiddies? Enough to put the little dears off Christmas for life."

Silence came down like a butterfly net, trapping me inside along with the ex-Father Christmas. For a moment I didn't realize the bus had stopped; I was thinking that I was now in no position to throw stones and that I liked the feeling. We "Black Hats" must stick together. Stepping onto the pavement, it came to me why his face was familiar. That day last year, when I left my wallet on the counter at the fishmonger's, he had come hurrying after me . . .

His footsteps followed me now as I went in through Bossam's Market Street entrance.

Now was the moment for an attack of remorse, but I am ashamed to say I didn't feel a twinge. Familiarity cushioned me from the reality of my undertaking. The entire floor looked like a tableau from one of the display windows. The customers could have been life-sized doll folk already jerkily winding down.

Directly ahead was the Cosmetics Department, where bright-haired young women presided over glass coffins filled with a treasure trove of beauty enhancers sufficient to see Cleopatra safely into the next world.

"Can I help you, madam?"

"I don't think so, dear, unless you have any rejuvenating cream."

"You might try Softie-Boss, our double-action moisture balm."

"Another time. I really must get to the China Department."

"Straight ahead, madam; across from the Men's Department. You do know our sale starts tomorrow?"

"I keep abreast of world events."

Well done, Hilda. Cool as a cucumber.

The ex-Father Christmas headed past and I mentally wished him luck returning whatever was in his carrier bag. Probably a ho-hum present or, worse, one of the ho-ho sort . . .

Perhaps not the best time to remember the year I received my fourth umbrella and how accommodating Bossam's had been about an exchange. Rounding the perfume display, I reminded myself that no bridges had been burned or boats cast out to sea. I had a full half-hour before closing time to change my mind.

Courage, Hilda.

There is a coziness to Bossam's that ridicules the melodramatic—other than at the January Sale. It is a family-owned firm, founded after the First World War and securely anchored in a tradition of affordability and personal service. The present owner, Mr. Leslie Bossam, had kept a restraining hand on progress. Nymphs and shepherds still cavort on the plastered ceilings. The original lift, with its brass gate, still cranks its way from the basement to the first floor. No tills are located on the varnished counters of the Haberdashery Department, which comprised the first store. When you make a purchase, the salesperson reaches overhead, untwists the drum of a small container attached to a trolley wire, inserts the payment, reattaches the drum and sends it zinging down the wire to the Accounts window, where some unseen person extracts the payment and sends a receipt and possible change, zinging back. A little bit of nostalgia, which appears to operate with surprising efficiency. Perhaps if I had presented my case, in person, to Mr. Bossam . . . ?

"In need of assistance, madam?" A black moth of a saleswoman came fluttering up to me as I reached the China Department.

"Thank you, I'm just looking."

The absolute truth. I was looking to see where best to hide the next morning, so as not to be spotted by the staff before the shop doors opened, at which moment I trusted all eyes would be riveted to the in-rushing mob, permitting me to step from the shadows—in order to be first at the counter. The Ladies' Room was handy, but fraught with risk. Ditto the Stock Room; which left the stairwell, with its landing conveniently screened by glass doors. Yes, I felt confident I could manage nicely; if I didn't land in the soup before getting properly started.

Parading toward me was Mr. Leslie Bossam. His spectacles glinting, his smile as polished as his bald head under the white lights.

"Madam, may I be of service?"

One last chance to operate within the system. While the black moths fluttered around the carousel of Royal Doulton figures, I pressed my case.

"My sympathy, madam. A dreadful blow when one loses a treasured family friend. My wife and I went through much the same thing with a Willow Pattern soup tureen earlier this year. I wish I could make an exception regarding the Meadow Rose teapot, but the question then becomes, Where does one draw the line? At Bossam's every customer is a valued customer."

Standing there, wrapped in his voice, I found myself neither surprised nor bitterly disappointed. The game was afoot and I felt like a girl for the first time since I used to watch the other children playing hopscotch and hide-and-seek. My eyes escaped from Mr. Bossam across the aisle to Gentlemen's Apparel, where the ex-Father Christmas hovered among sports jackets. He still had his carrier bag and it seemed to me he held it gingerly. Did it contain something fragile . . . like a teapot? The thought brought a smile to my face; but it didn't linger.

"Rest assured, madam, we are always at your service." Mr. Bossam interrupted himself to glance at the clock mounted above the lift. Almost five-thirty. Oh, dear! Was he about to do the chivalrous thing and escort me to the exit?

"Good heavens!"

"I beg your pardon, madam?"

"I see someone I know, over in Gentlemen's Apparel. Excuse me, if I hurry over for a word with him."

"Certainly, madam!" Mr. Bossarn exhaled graciousness until he followed my gaze, whereupon he turned into a veritable teakettle, sputtering and steaming to the boil.

"Do my spectacles deceive me? That man . . . that embezzler on the premises! I warned him I would have him arrested if he set one foot . . ."

Mr. Bossam rushed across the aisle, leaving me feeling I had saved my own neck by handing a fellow human being over to the Gestapo. No, it didn't help to tell myself the man was a criminal. What I was doing was certainly illegal. Slipping through the glass doors onto the stairwell, I fully expected to be stopped dead by a voice hurled hatchet-fashion, *That's not the exit, madam*. But nothing was said; no footsteps came racing after me as I opened the door marked "Staff Only" and hurried down the flight of steps to "Storage."

Electric light spattered a room sectioned off by racks of clothing and stacks of boxes into a maze. "Better than the one at Hampton Court," my nephew Willie had enthused one afternoon when he ended up down here while looking for the Gentlemen's. When I caught up with him he was exiting the staff facility. And, if memory served, the Ladies' was right next door, to my left, on the other side of that rack of coats. No time to dawdle. As far as I could tell, I had the area to myself, but at any moment activity was bound to erupt. The staff would be working late on behalf of The Sale, and no doubt crates of merchandise would be hauled upstairs before I was able to settle down in peace with *Murder at the Vicarage*.

These old legs of mine weren't built for speed. I was within inches of the Ladies' Room door, when I heard footsteps out there . . . somewhere in that acre of storage. Footsteps that might have belonged to the Loch Ness Monster climbing out onto land for the first time. Furtive footsteps that fear magnified to giant proportions.

"Anyone there?" came a booming whisper.

Huddled among the wool folds of the coat rack, I waited.

But the voice didn't speak again. And when my heart steadied, I pictured some nervous soul tiptoeing into the bowels of the store to search through the maze for some carton required double-quick by an irritable section manager. Silence. Which might mean Whoever had located what was needed and beaten a hasty retreat? But it wouldn't do to count my chickens. Stepping out from the coats, my foot skidded on something. Jolted, I looked down to see a handbag. For a flash I thought it was mine, that I had dropped it blindly in my panic. But, no; my black hold-all was safely strung over my arm.

Stealthily entering the Ladies' Room, I supposed the bag belonged to the attendant who took care of the lavatory. I remembered her from visits to spend a penny; a bustling woman with snapping black eyes who kept you waiting forever while she polished off the toilet seat and straightened the roll of paper, then stood over you like a hawk while you washed and dried your hands—just daring you to drop coppers into the dish. Even a sixpence seemed stingy as you watched her deposit the damp towel, slow-motion, into the bin.

Fortune smiled. The Hawk wasn't inside the Ladies', buffing up the brass taps; for the moment the pink-tiled room was empty. Opening my handbag, I withdrew the piece of cardboard and roll of adhesive tape. Moments later one of the three lavatory stalls read "Out Of Order."

Installed on my porcelain throne—the door bolted and my handbag placed on the tank, I opened my book; but the words wouldn't sit still on the page. With every creak and every gurgle in the pipes I was braced to draw my knees up so that my shoes would not show under the gap. Every time I looked at my watch I could have sworn the hands had gone backward. Only six-thirty?

I had no idea how late people would stay working before The Sale. But one thing I did know—my feet were going to sleep. Surely it wasn't that much of a risk to let myself out of my cell and walk around—just in here, in the Ladies'. After I had warmed my hands on the radiator, I felt reckless. The sort of feeling, I suppose, that makes you itch to stick your finger through the bars of the lion's cage. Hovering over to the door, I pushed it open—just a crack.

Standing at the rack of coats was the Ladies' Room attendant—yes, the one I mentioned. The Hawk. Unable to move, even to squeeze the door shut, I saw her button her coat and bend to pick up a handbag and a Bossam's carrier bag. Now she was the one who stiffened; I could see it in the set of her broad shoulders and the tilt of her head. I could almost hear her thinking . . . Is someone here? Someone watching?

Shrugging, she headed around a stack of boxes taller than she.

Gone.

I was savoring the moment, when the lights went out. The dark was blacker than the Yorkshire moors on a moonless night. Believe me, I'm not usually a nervous Nellie, but there are exceptions—as when the mouse ran over my foot. Instead of celebrating the likelihood of now having the store to myself by breaking open my bottle of milk, I was suddenly intensely aware of how mousy I was in relationship to three floors of mercantile space. To my foolish fancy every cash register, every bolt of fabric, every saucepan in Housewares . . . was aware of my unlawful presence. All of them watching, waiting for me to make a move. I couldn't just stand here, I slipped out the door, then hadn't the courage to go any farther in the dark.

"Lord, forgive us our trespasses."

Opening my handbag, I dug around for my torch and felt

my hand atrophy. A light beam pierced the dark and came inchworming toward me.

I grabbed for cover among the coats in the rack, felt it sway and braced myself as it thundered to the floor.

"Ruddy hell."

The light had a voice . . . a man's voice. It was closing in on me fast. Intolerable—the thought of facing what was to be, defenseless. Somehow I got out my torch and pressed the button.

"On guard!" came the growly voice as the golden blades of light began to fence; first a parry, then a thrust until . . . there was Retribution—impaled on the end of my blade.

"What brings you here, madam?"

"I got locked in at closing."

"Herrumph! If I believe that, I'm . . ."

"Father Christmas?"

"If you know what I am," he grumped, "you can guess why I'm here."

He was prickly as a porcupine with that mustache, but my torch moved up to his eyes and they were sad. Here was a man who had done a good deal more wintering than summering during his life. How, I wondered, had he escaped the clutches of Mr. Bossam?

"So, why are you here?" My voice was the one I had used for Mother when she was failing. It came echoing back to me from the blackness beyond our golden circle, but I wasn't afraid. "You won't remember me, Mr.—?"

"Hoskins."

"Well, Mr. Hoskins, I remember you. About a year ago I left my purse on the counter at the fishmonger's and you came after me with it. So you see—whatever your reasons for being here, I cannot believe they are wholeheartedly wicked. Foolish and sentimental like mine, perhaps. I'm jumping the queue on The Sale, so to speak. I'm after a teapot in the Meadow Flower pattern . . ."

A ho-hoing laugh that would have done credit to Saint Nicholas himself.

"Don't tell me you're after it too?"

"No fears on that score, dear madam." He played his torch over my face in a way I might have taken to be flirtation if we weren't a pair of old fogies. "I came here to blow the place up."

Alone with the Mad Bomber! I admit to being taken aback by Mr. Hoskins's confession. But, having survived life with five brothers and their escapades, I managed to keep a grip on myself . . . and my torch.

"I've frightened you."

"Don't give it a thought."

He opened the door to the Ladies', and I jumped to the idea that he was about to barricade me inside, but I misjudged him. He switched on the light and propped the door open.

"All the better to see me?" I switched off my torch but kept it at the ready.

Looking as defiantly sheepish as one of my brothers after he had kicked a ball through a window, Mr. Hoskins said, "The least I can do is explain, Mrs.—"

"Miss . . . Finnely."

Dragging forward a carton, he dusted it off with his gloves and offered me a seat.

"Thank you. Now you pull up a chair, and tell me all about it."

"Very kind." A smile appeared on his face—looking a little lost. He sat down, and with the rack of coats as a backdrop, began his story.

"Thirty-five years I gave B. & L. Shipping, then one day

there it is—I'm turned out to pasture. Half kills me, but I'll get another job—part-time, temporary—anything. When I read that Bossam's was looking for a Father Christmas, I thought, why not? Wouldn't do this crusty old bachelor any harm to meet up with today's youth. Educational. But funny thing was I enjoyed myself. Felt I was doing a bit of good, especially knowing the entrance fees to the North Pole were donated by Bossam's to buy toys for needy kiddies.

"The person bringing the child would deposit two shillings in Frosty the Snowman's top hat. Each evening I took the hat to Mr. Bossam and he emptied it. A few days before Christmas I entered his office to find him foaming at the mouth. He told me he had suspected for some time that the money was coming up short and had set the store detective to count the number of visitors to the North Pole. The day's money did not tally. No reason for you to believe me, Miss Finnely, but I did not embezzle that money."

"I do believe you. Which means someone else helped themselves."

"Impossible."

"Think, Mr. Hoskins." I patted his shoulder as he sat hunched over on the carton. Dear me, he did remind me of my brother Will. "When did you leave the money unattended?"

"I didn't."

"Come now, what about your breaks?"

"Ah, there I had a system. When I left the Pole, I took the top hat with me and came down here to the Gents'. Before going off for a bite to eat, I'd hide it in the fresh towel hamper, about halfway down."

"Someone must have seen you."

"Miss Finnely"—he was pounding his fists on his knees—

"I'm neither a thief nor a complete dolt. I made sure I had the place to myself."

"Hmmmm . . ."

"My good name lost! I tell you, Miss Finnely, the injustice burned a hole in my gut. Went off my rocker. As a young chap I was in the army for a while and learned a bit about explosives. I made my bomb, put it in a Bossam's carrier bag, so it would look like I was making a return, and . . ."

Mr. Hoskins stood up. Calmly at first, then with growing agitation, he shifted aside coats on the rack, setting it rocking as he stared at the floor.

"Miss Finnely, upon my word: I put it here and . . . it's gone. Some rotter has pinched my bomb!"

"Cousin Hilda." I was bouncing about on my chair. "I know who took the deadly carrier bag."

"Who, girly dear?"

"The Ladies' Room attendant. You saw her pick one up when she put on her coat. She didn't mistake that bag for her own. Remember how she stiffened and looked all around? Crafty old thing! I'll bet you twenty chocolate biscuits she was one of those . . . what's the word?"

"Kleptomaniacs."

"She stole the Father Christmas money!"

"So Mr. Hoskins and I concluded. She must have seen him going into the Gentlemen's with the top hat and coming out empty-handed." Cousin Hilda rose to draw the curtains.

"What did you do?"

"Nothing."

"What?" I flew from my chair as though it were a trampoline.

"We agreed the woman had brought about her own punishment. A real growth experience, I would say—opening up that carrier bag to find the bomb. What she wouldn't know was that some specialized tinkering was required to set it off. And she was in no position to ring up the police."

Before I could ask the big question, the door opened and in came Albert the lodger with the tea tray. We weren't presently speaking because I had beaten him that afternoon playing Snap.

"Cousin Hilda," I whispered—not wishing to betray her Dark Secret, "do you know what happened to Mr. Hoskins?"

"Certainly." She took the tray from the curmudgeon. "Albert, I was just telling Giselle how you and I met."

"Oh!" I sat down with a thump. That was what she had meant about the high price of sin.

"One lump or two, girly dear?"

The teapot had pink and yellow roses.

The Gentleman's Gentleman

"I've been thinking, Dickie." Lady Felicity Entwhistle, known to her friends as Foof, pursed her cherry red lips and looked soulful.

"Bad idea, old thing, likely to give you a confounded headache," her twenty-four-year-old companion on the stone bench under the arbor smiled at her fondly. "Doesn't do, you know, to get yourself stirred up. Not with the wedding only three weeks away. Stupid idea of Mother's, having a house party this weekend. And she shouldn't have shown you those photos of Great Uncle Wilfred last night." Mr. Richard Ambleforth looked decidedly downcast. "The thought of any of our children inheriting his nose rather takes the icing off the cake."

"But that's the whole point, Dickie." Foof fussed with the strand of beads that hung to what would have been the waist of her green voile frock, if current fashion had not dictated that ladies' garments forgo shape in favor of showing what would once have been considered an unconscionable amount of leg.

"Can't say I see what you're getting at." Dickie reached into his pocket for his cigarette case and lit up. "Spill the beans, Foof. What is the whole point?"

"That we won't be having any children." She hung her

head so that her dark, silky hair swung over her ears, and even in the midst of feeling nervous and upset, part of her reveled in the tragedy of the moment. There was no denying that the grounds of Saxonbury Hall, with its formal rose gardens, rock pools, and darkly beckoning maze made a fitting setting for beauty in distress. The wind murmured mournfully among the trees and the sun slipped tactfully behind a cloud.

"No children?" Dickie took a moment to assimilate this piece of information. "Well, I don't suppose that matters, but are you sure?" He stubbed out his cigarette and placed an arm around his betrothed's drooping shoulders. "Been to see a doctor, have you? Things not quite right in the oven, is that it?"

"Oh, really, Dickie!" Foof could not keep the exasperation out of her voice even as a sob rose in her throat. "You do have a way of putting things, and I do still love you in a way, darling, but the reason we won't be having any children is that I can't marry you."

"Mother been at you again?" Dickie wore what was for him an unamiable expression. "Shouldn't take any notice if I were you, old thing. Won't have to see her if you don't like after we are married. The Pater has managed to avoid her for the best part of thirty years. Nothing to it in a house this size. And, anyway, most of the time we'll be living in the London flat."

"No, we won't." Foof stood up, but managed to resist stamping her foot. "You're making this most frightfully difficult, but the truth is I'm in love with someone else. One of those bolt of lightning things. I hate having to hurt you, but there it is. You will be a sport about it, won't you, Dickie? He's frightfully keen that you and I stay friends. That's the sort of person he is, absolutely noble, besides being the handsomest man alive." Foof clasped her hands together and her eyes took on a glow that would have rivaled the stars had this not been midafternoon.

Dickie was looking up at the sky. He decided it had turned remarkably chilly for July. "You must have drunk too much wine at lunch. Yes, that's it." He nodded his head vigorously. "You were trying to keep up with George, which is always a mistake. Never knew such a chap for knocking it back. Now, I don't say I blame him today, with Mrs. Bagworthy droning on about nothing and that ghastly girl, Madge, ogling him across the table, although one would think old George was used to that sort of thing. Girls tend to make the most alarming twits of themselves where he's concerned. He isn't the one, is he?" Dickie lit another cigarette with a determinedly steady hand. "You've not gone and fallen in love with George?"

"Betray you with your best friend?" Foof flushed a deep rose. "Honestly, Dickie! I understand your being cross with me and all that, but one would think you'd know I'd never sink that low. It's not as though I've been keeping things from you. I haven't known," her voice took on a dazed quality, "my beloved very long."

"*How* long?" Dickie ground out the words along with his cigarette.

Foof avoided his eyes. "Well, I know it sounds silly," she said, "but we only met this afternoon."

"You're pulling my leg!"

"I told you it was like a bolt of lightning. But you never do listen. I came out into the garden after lunch, when you were playing billiards with George. If you must know, I wanted to get away from your mother, who was buttering up to Madge like anything and making it as plain as day that she would far rather have her for a daughter-in-law. And," Foof sat back on the bench, drew up her knees and cupped her chin in her hands, "there he was, getting out of a taxi."

"A what?"

"Oh, Dickie, you're such a snob. Not everyone has to flaunt around in a chauffeur-driven car. And, looking back, I realize it was his simplicity that immediately attracted me." Foof smiled dreamily. "Our eyes met and we moved towards each other. Just like that, Dickie, we both knew that fate had brought us irrevocably together."

"Does this blackguard have a name?"

"Of course he does. You don't think I'd fall in love with just anyone, do you?" Foof reached for his hand. "His name is Lord Dunstairs."

"What?" Dickie bounced up and almost lost his balance as one foot slid sideways on the mossy path. "You can't be serious! He has to be donkey's years old. And you can forget about fate. It was Mother who invited him for the weekend. She's been curious as all get-out about Lord Dunstairs ever since he moved down here last year. All those stories about his being a miserly recluse, living alone in that rambling old house at Barton-Among-The-Reeds got her all fired-up to bag him for one of her house parties."

"He's *not* old." Foof sat spinning her beads. "If you must know, Dickie, Lord Dunstairs isn't a day over thirty-five. And he doesn't live alone in a ramshackle way as you make it sound. He has servants like everyone else. There's a housekeeper and a valet. The housekeeper is getting a bit past it, but his man is a gem. Every bit as good as your indispensable Woodcock, from the sound of it. Sometimes, you know," Foof tossed her silky head, "I've wondered why you didn't decide to marry Woodcock instead of me; but there it is, Dickie. Don't let's have any hard feelings. Lord Dunstairs isn't the old crackpot people assumed. He's a mature man who doesn't need to be always off at his club or out shooting with his friends." Foof paused to let these words sink in. "He enjoys the quiet pleasures of his library and his wine cellar. And what it comes down to, Dickie, is that there's room in his life for a woman to matter in a terribly vital sort of way. I don't mean to be cruel and go on about him, because, really, I do love you and always shall in a way. So you will," Foof squeezed his hand, "be a brick and wish me joy?"

"I'll be damned if I'll do anything of the sort." Dickie flounced to his feet. "And anyway, aren't you being a bit premature? Surely the blighter hasn't proposed to you already?"

"No, but he did kiss me under that weeping willow over there before going into the house to meet your mother and father. And I know, fantastic as it sounds, that it's just a matter of time until he does ask me to marry him. Oh, darling, don't look at me like that. You'll find someone else. Who knows, it could even be Madge Allbright. You're wrong about her making eyes at George. It's that squint of hers that's so confusing. I've known for ages that Madge is absolutely dotty about you."

"I have to get out of here, Foof, before I choke you with those beads." Dickie could feel his own face turning suffocation red. "And that would be a pretty daft thing to do when I should be saving my energy to do in the real villain of the piece."

"Wait." Foof tugged at her finger. "I must give you the ring back."

"So I can throw it into the rock pool?" Upon this surly response Dickie retreated with all the wounded dignity he could muster, and upon entering the gloomy splendor of his ancestral home encountered his mother in the hall.

Mrs. Ambleforth was one of those deceptively comfortable-looking women, rather like an overstuffed sofa that gives no hint at first glance of the springs poking up through the upholstery. "What ever is the matter, my dearest boy?" she asked as she bustled towards her one and only offspring. "Has Foof been upsetting you?"

"If you must know, Mother," Dickie addressed one of the portraits hung upon the wainscoting, "she has broken off the engagement."

"Oh, my poor love," Mrs. Ambleforth pressed a hand to her maternal bosom, "but perhaps it is all for the best. Naturally, I never said a word, but it was clear to me from the word go that Foof was not the girl for you. And your father thought exactly the same."

"Thanks for the boost, Mother." Dickie was already trudging up the oak stairs. "I'd prefer not to discuss the matter further."

"Of course, dear. Much wiser to put the whole foolish business out of your mind." Mrs. Ambleforth dabbed at her eyes. "Foof never deserved you. A willful creature if ever I saw one. Always flapping about and saying whatever silly thing came into her head. One dreads to think what your life would have been like with her. Now, a girl like Madge Allbright is a different story altogether! Impeccable manners and the gentlest nature."

"And about as much sex appeal as one of these banisters."

"Dickie! Really, you shouldn't say such things. Such a vulgar expression. But there, I do understand you are not thinking clearly at the moment."

"And neither are you, Mother," Dickie looked down at her from the top stair, "or instead of gloating you'd be planning what to say to people when word gets out that your son has been ditched by the lovely Lady Felicity Entwhistle."

"Good heavens!" Mrs. Ambleforth paled. "You don't suppose anyone could possibly concoct nasty stories suggesting *I'm* the cause of her backing out of the marriage? Oh, but surely not! No one who knows me could think I haven't done everything within my power to embrace Foof as a daughter. What did the tiresome girl say? What reason did she give for breaking the engagement?" Mrs. Ambleforth's voice followed her son along the upper gallery, and even when he closed his bedroom door behind him he still heard its distant vibrations.

"Ah, there you are, sir," Woodcock's voice was as soothing as massaging lotion without being the least bit oily. The consummate gentleman's gentleman, he could tell without turning round from the wardrobe, where he was putting away some freshly laundered shirts, that something was not right with his young master. "Shall I run you a bath, sir?"

"I should say not." Dickie flopped down on the four-poster bed and glowered up at the tapestry canopy. "It's hours until I need to change for dinner."

"I beg your pardon." Woodcock crossed the room with the aplomb of a Prime Minister. "Perhaps a glass of sherry would be in order."

"Not unless you put poison in it."

"That's one liberty you may be assured I would never take, sir."

Dickie ignored this response. "Although I don't know why," he grumbled, "I should choose to do away with myself, when it's that blasted Lord Dunstairs I should be plotting to put underground."

"The gentleman who arrived after luncheon?" Woodcock bent to remove his employer's shoes and, after a swift investigation to ascertain they had suffered no recent scuffmarks, placed them on a table designated for the purpose. "Am I to assume, sir, that you did not take to Lord Dunstairs?"

"That's rum!" Dickie vented a bitter laugh. "The taking has all been on Lord Dunstairs' part!"

"I'm afraid I don't quite follow you, sir."

"Well, it's quite simple. The blighter has stolen Lady Felicity's heart. Love at first sight and all that rot. They met in the garden, and the next thing you know she is breaking off our engagement."

"Surely not, sir," Woodcock poured whiskey from a decanter, having deemed sherry insufficient to the circumstances, and upon Dickie's sitting up, handed him the glass. "I have not seen Lord Dunstairs, but I had attained the impression of a gentleman well advanced in years."

"Not according to Lady Felicity, unless of course you view the age of thirty-five or so as being on the brink of decrepitude."

"Hardly, sir, given that I am myself no spring chicken."

"Rubbish," Dickie drained his glass and set it down, "you never get any older. *I'm* the one who's aged ten years in the last hour. Perhaps I should go ahead and shoot myself. The thought of her ladyship wallowing in guilt until the end of her days does rather cheer me up."

"Sir, if I might presume . . ."

"Oh, by all means, presume away." Dickie waved a languid hand, sending the whiskey glass onto the carpet.

"It occurs to me, sir," Woodcock retrieved the glass and removed it to safety, "that her ladyship may have fallen prey to the wiles of Lord Dunstairs during a period of uncertainty. Young ladies, as I understand it, are inclined to require reassurance by way of florid protestations of devotion from the gentlemen to whom they are affianced. And, if you will pardon the impertinence, sir, I am inclined to the opinion that, with your not being a person much given to effusion . . ."

"No need to go on like a confounded dictionary." Dickie sounded decidedly testy.

"Very well, sir. Shall I say that you may have failed to provide Lady Felicity with the desired assurance that you are one hundred percent—if you will pardon the vulgarism—" Woodcock cleared his throat, "bonkers about her?"

"But she *must* know." Dickie got off the bed and began pacing up and down, shoulders hunched, hands sunk deep in his pockets. "Dash it all, Woodcock, I asked her to marry me, didn't I? Not the sort of thing a chap does if he isn't enamored. Told her I would get her a spaniel bitch for her birthday. Not particularly keen on spaniels myself. Much rather have a bullmastiff, but what's a small sacrifice here and there? And I'll say this," Dickie gave the wardrobe a thump of his fist for emphasis, "the biggest sacrifice of all has been not kissing her as much as I would have liked. Never know where that sort of thing will lead, Woodcock. And you see," Dickie's voice reduced to a mutter, "for all she's so up-to-the-minute in lots of ways, Felicity's a complete innocent and only an out-and-out cad would take advantage of her. Damn Dunstairs! I'm back to thinking I'll have to bump him off. But if I understand you, Woodcock," Dickie sank down on the wing chair by the window, "your advice is that I try to win Lady Felicity back by fair means."

"I wouldn't go that far, sir." Woodcock smoothed out the bedspread and adjusted the angle of a reading lamp. "Certainly I would suggest that you present yourself in the most appealing light when next encountering her ladyship, but I see nothing amiss in attempting to discover if Lord Dunstairs may not be all that is desirable in a suitor. Happily, it occurs to me that the new gardener, a man by the name of Williams, came to us after working for his lordship and I will be happy to have a tactful word with him, if you should wish, sir."

"Sounds a topping idea." Dickie bounded to his feet like a man rejuvenated. "You're the best of good chaps, Woodcock. And I don't know what I would do without you. Now tell me if I have this straight. I'm to let Felicity know that I'm dashed miserable. Perhaps have a bunch of flowers sent up to her room?"

"An admirable start, sir, but I do suggest going the extra mile. Poetry, I have been given to understand, has a remarkably softening effect on the female, and if you were to exert yourself to pen a few verses . . ."

"I suppose I could try," Dickie looked doubtful, "but I've always been most awfully thick when it comes to that sort of thing. And anyway, other people have already bagged most of the best lines. I suppose it would be cheating to write 'Come into the garden, Foof, I am here at the gate alone'?"

"I am afraid so, sir."

"I can't help thinking that it might be simpler to order Lord Dunstairs from the house."

"Unwise, if I may say so, sir. Far better to trust that, during his visit here, his lordship will show himself up in such a way as to lower him in Lady Felicity's esteem."

"Yes, there is always that." With this, Dickie took himself from the room, intent on retreating to the library and thumbing through volumes of poetry in hopes of inspiration. However, he was circumvented in this plan by colliding with his friend George Stodders at the top of the stairs.

"By gad," said that gentleman, looking very sporting in knickerbockers and knee-length socks, "don't seem to be able to get away from you, old chap."

"What's that supposed to mean?" Dickie suddenly bore a striking resemblance to the portrait of his grim-faced great-grandfather hanging on the wall to his left.

"Keep your shirt on," answered George. "All I meant is that I've been stuck with the impossible Madge for the last half hour, listening to her rant on about what a sublime fellow you are. The poor girl is in a bad way for you, Dickie. Thinks it's her little secret. But head over heels in love with you."

"Well, I suppose I should be glad someone is."

"I say, what's this all about?" George's pale blue eyes narrowed. "Can see now you look a bit glum. Problems with Foof?"

"She's broken off the engagement." Dickie had always considered himself the reticent sort, and here he was spilling the beans for the third time since entering the house.

"You must be joking!" George leaned against the banister rail and produced his cigarette case.

"Only wish I were," Dickie reached for his lighter, they both lit up, and even as he determined not to say any more, the words tumbled out. "Foof has fallen hook, line, and sinker for Lord Dunstairs."

"Don't think I know him."

"Neither did Foof until just after lunch. He's here for the weekend at Mother's invitation."

"And you're telling me that he and Foof hadn't laid eyes on each other until an hour or so ago?"

"Precisely."

George's lips parted in a soundless whistle, but after a few seconds he managed to ask if Dickie had broken the news to his mother that she had invited a serpent into their midst.

"I told her the engagement was off but I didn't explain why, and she was so relieved she forgot to ask." Dickie puffed resolutely on his cigarette. "And after talking with Woodcock just now, I'm glad I didn't give Mother the full story, because even though she's not overly keen on Foof, I'm sure she wouldn't appreciate having me, and herself in the process, made ridiculous and would insist on Father giving Lord Dunstairs the boot."

"And what would be so bad about that?" George tapped out his cigarette in a potted plant.

"Let's say I prefer to handle Lord Dunstairs in my own way."

"Going to call him out?"

"I haven't made up my mind what I'm going to do." Dickie's expression now made his great-grandfather's painted physiognomy look positively amiable by comparison. "But let me assure you," Dickie ground out his cigarette, "I intend to do whatever it takes to get Foof back."

"That's the spirit, old man!" George beamed at him. "And as your best friend, I'll do my damnedest to help out. How would it be if I suggest a game of poker after dinner and fleece the lining out of Lord Dunstairs' pockets?"

"Decent of you. But I'd rather you left things to me."

"No, no! I insist on doing my bit."

Deciding it was pointless to argue, Dickie said he was in need of solitude and wended his way downstairs to the library where he pored over the *Oxford Book of English Verse* for a full minute before tossing it aside and himself down on the leather sofa under the window. What he should be doing, he realized, was seeking out Lord Dunstairs and sizing up the opposition, but Dickie had the sinking feeling that so doing would only succeed in making him wish that he were taller, with a thicker head of hair and the daunting manner of a man to whom Latin and women came easily. Rather than face his rival in person, Dickie settled for an imaginary conversation in which he wiped the floor with Lord Dunstairs and afterwards turned to find Foof tearfully repentant and positively desperate to become re-engaged to him. After replaying this scenario a half dozen times, Dickie dozed off and was awakened by the chiming of the carriage clock on the mantelpiece to the realization that he had less than ten minutes in which to change for dinner.

Woodcock sped him into his dinner jacket with a minimum of commentary and Dickie set off for the dining room looking slightly more cheerful than a man about to be hanged. His palms were sweating as he pushed open the door, and it took a few seconds for the roaring inside his head to sort itself out into the voices of the people gathered in the room. Then came the necessity of shuffling the faces out of deck to get a clear view of who was present.

His mother, wearing a puce-colored frock, was standing at the far end of the table talking to the large woman in black brocade and pearls who was Mrs. Bagworthy. His father, looking rumpled and distracted as always, was endeavoring to attend to whatever George was saying to him. And, Dickie's throat tightened, there by the fireplace was Foof, looking unquestionably ravishing in a silvery frock with fringe at the hem and a glittering band encircling her forehead. It required a couple of gulps for Dickie to steady himself sufficiently to size up the man engaged in animated conversation with Lady Felicity. On the bright side, Lord Dunstairs was neither possessed of great height nor an imposing physique, but the most critical observer would have been obliged to concede that he was a not a man ever to be overlooked in a crowd. He had the dark good looks of a film star and, Dickie decided bleakly, all the assurance of a man who could charm the birds off the trees. There are times when it is good to feel invisible, and Dickie was savoring the heartwarming realization that no one appeared to have noticed his entrance, when the door banged into him from behind, shooting him several feet into the room, and Madge Allbright's voice ripped through the hum of conversation.

"I'm late again, aren't I?" She was addressing the group at large but looking at Dickie, her squint very much in evidence. "Really, I don't know why you put up with me, I'm quite impossible. Yesterday I kept you waiting and the soup was cold because I couldn't find the sash to my frock, and today it was my amber beads."

Poor Madge, thought Dickie. She's so thoroughly irritating, the kind of girl who seems to go to great lengths to make herself look as unappealing as possible. That lank hair and the frumpy frock! But she looks almost as unhappy as I am, and that makes us temporarily kindred spirits.

"Don't worry, Madge dear," Mrs. Ambleforth said in her oozy voice, "we're having a chilled soup this evening. Ah, there you are, Dickie!" She crossed the room towards her son and, under the guise of planting a kiss on his cheek, whispered to him, "I was worried, son, when you didn't come to the drawing room for drinks. And I haven't known how to behave to Foof. So difficult trying to put a brave face on things and not spoil Lord Dunstairs' visit after waiting so long to meet him. Oh, I don't think," Mrs. Ambleforth's voice returned to normal levels, "that you two have met. Lord Dunstairs!"

His lordship responded instantly to her beckoning finger. And Dickie put on his bravest face as he uncurled his fist and shook hands. "Good to have you at Saxonbury." The words were forced out between his teeth. It was impossible not to glance at Foof. "Everything to your liking, Lord Dunstairs?"

"Couldn't be better." His lordship produced what Dickie deemed a well-oiled smile, providing a glimpse of excellent teeth. "Having a bang-up time. Such a pleasure to meet everyone. And Lady Felicity was kind enough to take me through the maze."

"Don't suppose you found that a dead end."

"Meaning?" His lordship's smile now appeared decidedly malicious.

"Yes, exactly what are you getting at, Dickie?" Foof came up alongside him, a rhinestone-studded cigarette holder tucked between two fingers and her dark hair dancing about her chin.

"Just a joke." He had been effectively reduced to the status of petulant schoolboy, and his discomfiture was only increased when Madge piped up.

"You've always been such a wit, Dickie."

"Absolutely," George had to stick in his oar. "Would keep a barrel of monkeys laughing."

"There, my dearest," Mrs. Ambleforth squeezed her son's elbow, "isn't it nice to know how fond everyone, or, I should say," shooting a furious look at Foof, "*most* people are of you?"

"What I'm fond of," Mr. Ambleforth spoke up from across the room, "is having dinner served on time." His untidy appearance, capped by hair better suited to a mad scientist, would not have created the impression that he was a slave to routine. Sometimes it seemed that the passion in his life was neither his wife nor his son but his bee-keeping activities; any unnecessary time spent away from his hives was torture. "Allow me, Mrs. Bagworthy," he said, offering his arm to that lady, "to see you to your place at table, and if the rest will be seated, my wife will ring for Mercer to bring in the first course."

There followed a scraping back of chairs and a settling of damask napkins on knees. Dickie, seated across from Foof, tried to take a particle of solace in the fact that she was still wearing her engagement ring and that Lord Dunstairs was on his side of the table, between Madge and Mrs. Bagworthy. His mother gave the bell rope a tug before assuming her place and almost instantly the door opened and a trolley was wheeled into the dining room by Woodcock.

"My goodness." Mrs. Ambleforth turned an inquiring look upon him. "Where is Mercer?"

"He is unwell, Madam. A sudden attack of lumbago. And he hopes it will not be inconvenient for me to take his place this evening." Woodcock removed the lid from the soup tureen, and while giving the contents a stir with the ladle, briefly caught Dickie's eye.

"I wouldn't put up with that kind of thing," boomed Mrs. Bagworthy before Mr. or Mrs. Ambleforth could respond. "A butler giving in to twinges! Where is this world headed? My late husband was a stickler when it came to the servants. And I still refuse to have any slacking at Cobblestone Manor."

"Have you lived there long, Mrs. Bagworthy?" Lord Dunstairs crumbled the roll on his bread and butter plate. "I've had the feeling ever since being introduced to you that I know you from somewhere. You don't by any chance originate from Butterfield, a village just outside Reading? I know the place quite well. There's quite a decent pub, The Black Horse, where I've stopped in for a drink on occasion."

"Well, I'm sure you didn't see *me* there." Mrs. Bagworthy flushed all the way down her neck and shifted in her chair, with the result that Woodcock narrowly missed spilling her soup into her lap. "I don't frequent public houses and I'm sure I've never been anywhere near," she took a deep breath, "Buttergate or whatever the place is called."

"I say! Isn't life full of surprises?" George reached for the pepper pot. "It seems people around here have had you pegged all wrong, Lord Dunstairs. I heard you didn't get out and about much and that you were . . ."

"A bit of a nutter?" His lordship smiled over the rim of his soup spoon. "Quite true, I'm afraid. I'm a regular Bluebeard, with a dozen or more wives buried under my cellar floor."

"Oh, how horrible!" Madge shrank into her chair.

"Don't be such a goose," said Foof.

"What's that?" Mr. Ambleforth started as if stung by his

bees. "Goose, you say? I thought we were having rack of lamb."

"So we are, dear." His wife's laugh vibrated on the edge of irritation. "My husband has his head in the clouds half the time," she told Lord Dunstairs.

"Happens to all of us as we advance in years." His smile was exclusively for Foof. "I could have sworn I sent a note accepting your gracious invitation, Mrs. Ambleforth, and I arrive to find everyone amazed to see me."

"You really mustn't worry about it."

"But I do. I am not usually an oblivious man." Lord Dunstairs was again looking at Foof, who blushed rosily.

"I'm sure there is some perfectly simple explanation," Mrs. Ambleforth said, sounding as though she had just discovered she was sitting on a pin. "There usually is."

"Nice of you to let me off the hook so easily." Lord Dunstairs dipped his spoon into his soup and drew it to his lips. "And I do suppose the likeliest explanation is that my housekeeper forgot to post the letter. She's not the brightest woman alive, but as I'm sure you'll all agree," looking around the table, "it's almost impossible to get decent servants these days."

Dickie felt himself go hot under the collar, and was about to speak when Woodcock appeared at his side and, in handing him another roll, placed discreet pressure on his arm. The room was thus left for a few moments in uncomfortable silence, and the mood of those seated around the table never seemed to pick up during the rest of the meal. George made the liveliest attempt at conversation, but nobody paid him much attention, so with equal goodwill he began concentrating his energies on his wineglass. Madge sat fidgeting with the front of her frock as if feeling for the amber beads she had misplaced. Mrs. Bagworthy's usually unassailable appetite seemed to have failed her. Mr. Ambleforth was mainly silent, and his wife a little disjointed in her conversation. Dickie didn't want to think about what Foof had on her mind as she pushed her food around on her plate. As for Lord Dunstairs, Dickie ground his teeth and pictured what the man would look like with an egg custard sitting on his head.

At last the ladies withdrew, leaving the gentlemen to their port, and after staring glumly at the unlit cigar in his hand, Dickie excused himself, saying he had the most confounded headache. Over George's protestations that he would feel better for a game of cards, Dickie went up to his room. Twenty minutes later Woodcock joined him.

"Very clever of you," Dickie looked up from the chair in which he was reclining, "persuading Mercer that he didn't feel up to snuff so that you could take his place at dinner."

"A liberty, sir."

"So, what did you think of his lordship?"

"A remarkably good-looking man." Woodcock poured his employer a glass of brandy.

"That's all you can say?" Dickie glowered. "I felt like tearing his tongue out when he made that remark about it being impossible to find good help, and I would have done so if you hadn't pinched my arm."

"It was not my place to take offence, sir," Woodcock handed over the glass, "and I intended only to brush a fly off your sleeve. I do, however, most humbly beg your pardon."

"Oh, cut the cackle, you old poser!" Dickie downed half the brandy and leaned back in his chair. "If you saw nothing amiss with his lordship I'm sure I'm no end delighted. I've obviously been overreacting to his pursuit of my fiancée, and I suppose it was my blasted imagination that made me think that every time he looked at me he did so with the most gloating of expressions. Get me a refill, Woodcock," he said, handing back his glass, "while I make a mental note not to make snap decisions about people in future."

"Very wise, sir."

"Well, I wonder what his lordship is up to at this moment. Kissing Lady Felicity in the garden springs to mind, but I'm such a pessimist."

"I believe, sir," said Woodcock lifting the decanter, "that he has engaged to play cards with Mr. Stodders. But at the moment, he may be in discussion with Mrs. Bagworthy. I saw his lordship talking with her in the alcove to the right of the stairs as I was proceeding down the gallery to this room, sir."

"Always said you're a positive mine of information." Dickie forced a smile.

"I endeavor to be of use." Woodcock dabbed around the rim of the brandy glass with a white cloth before returning it to his employer. "Is there anything more you will be needing? Because if not, sir, I would very much appreciate your permission to use the telephone. You have my assurance that I will leave fourpence in the box on the table."

"I suppose you had better," said Dickie, "even though I've never known you to use the phone before. Father often gets a bee in his bonnet (goes with the hobby), and now he's come up with the idea of making everyone—including myself and Mother—pay for our calls. Oh, stuff, perhaps it's as well Felicity won't marry me. What with Uncle Wilfred's nose and Father's nutty episodes, our children could be a sorry bunch."

During the rest of the evening, Dickie endeavored to resign himself to his lot by looking for other reasons that would indicate that being jilted was a cause for celebration. By the time he retired for the night he had drunk sufficient brandy to enable him to fall asleep after only half an hour of tossing from one side to the other. He woke once or twice during the small hours to a feeling of uneasiness, but each time fell back asleep before sorting his way through the layers of consciousness to the source. And when he sat up in bed the next morning, the only thing that was crystal clear to him was that he had the worst headache.

"Woodcock!" Dickie bellowed, but there was no response. And when he rang the bell it was one of the chambermaids, a cheeky girl by the name of Gladys, or it might have been Daisy, who popped her head round the door.

"No, I haven't seen Woodcock, sir," she responded in answer to his inquiry. "But I'll have a look and send him right up."

"No need," said Dickie. Feeling abandoned on all sides and heartily sorry for himself, he descended half an hour later to the dining room, where he found his parents sitting in state at the long table with their breakfast of bacon, kidneys, and fried mushrooms on their plates.

"Your father is in one of his moods and I can't get out of him what's the matter," said Mrs. Ambleforth as Dickie, after an unenthusiastic glance at the dishes set out on the sideboard, took his seat.

"Not keen on some of our guests." Mr. Ambleforth glowered at his wife.

"So you keep saying, dear," his wife buttered a slice of toast, "but that's not very specific, is it?"

"Well, I'm not talking about Foof. Like that girl, always have. Dickie's lucky to get her, and I won't stand for your becoming the heavy-handed mother-in-law, Alice."

Before Mrs. Ambleforth could respond to this admonition the door opened and George Stodders slunk into the room. From his unearthly pallor, Dickie concluded that his friend had a devil of a hangover, and this was borne out when George collapsed into a chair and gripped the table edge as if in hope he could stop it from spinning.

"Is there any black coffee?" he asked in a croak and, when Dickie obliged by fetching him a cup, said, "I don't know whether to drink this or drown myself in it."

"It looks to me," said Mrs. Ambleforth in her deceptively cozy voice, "that you stayed up till all hours, George, playing cards and drinking more than was good for you."

"Spot on!"

"Oh, I'm late again!" bleated a voice from the doorway, and Madge blundered into the room—all elbows and darting eyes. "May I sit next to you, Dickie, since Foof isn't here?"

"Delighted."

No sooner was Madge in her seat than the door opened again to admit Mrs. Bagworthy, and coming in right behind her was Foof, looking so desperately pale that Dickie did not need to hear her whisper his name to leap to his feet and follow her out into the hall.

"Not here." She gripped his arm so tightly that her nails dug through his jacket sleeve. "Come into the library, where no one can hear us. And don't you dare say anything," she told him through quivering lips when they entered that room and she had closed the door as if bolting them in against an enemy army. "Not a word, Dickie, until I'm finished talking, unless . . ." tears spilled down Foof's cheek, "you can find it in your heart to tell me you still love me."

"Of course I do. Always have and always will." Dickie's voice sounded ludicrously high-pitched, but it was necessary to speak up in order to be heard over the pounding of his heart. "Don't cry, you silly goose." He pulled her into his arms and kissed her fiercely. "You had me worried yesterday, but I needed to be brought to my senses. Woodcock said as much. And he was right, as he almost always is. I haven't let you know, not properly," he kissed her again, "that I'm absolutely nuts about you, Foof. And my mother can go to perdition if she doesn't like it."

"I'll make her like me, I'll do anything, Dickie! Oh, if ever a girl was born a fool, it was me! It's true I wanted to shake you up, darling. Make you jealous. As if it wasn't enough to know you're the dearest man alive. Well, I've been punished." Foof stepped back from him and pressed her hands to her throat in an attempt to hold back a sob. "He has to be the most evil creature alive . . ."

"Did he," Dickie strove for some measure of control, because the last thing his beloved needed was for him to go to pieces, "did Lord Dunstairs . . . ?"

"No," said Foof, "he didn't take advantage of me, at least not in the way you mean. But oh, it was horrible. I got up early, you see, and went out into the garden. I had to clear my head after not sleeping hardly at all for wishing I hadn't been so silly—letting him kiss me after talking to him for five minutes, and then talking all that rubbish to you about being in love with him. He is handsome and—I'll admit it, Dickie—I *did* get in a bit of a flutter over him at first. But at dinner I realized I didn't like him at all, and when I saw him in the garden this morning, I felt sick remembering I'd let him kiss me like that. I kept thinking about what he'd said about being a Bluebeard and burying numerous wives in the cellar. And perhaps he read all that in my face, because . . ."

"Because what, Foof darling?"

She shuddered and clung to him for a moment before straightening up. "It was as though he'd finished playing one game and had started on another. He said he was leaving and asked me to thank your parents and the rest for providing him with a most amusing time. And then, Dickie, it got to be really horrible. He started ticking off on his fingers what he called the high points of his visit."

"Which were?" Dickie held Foof's hands tight but could not stop their trembling.

"Fleecing George at cards last night. He got several hundred pounds out of him. And he also got a nice little sum out of Mrs. Bagworthy, playing what he called another sort of game."

"Meaning?"

"Blackmail." Foof sat down on the nearest chair. "That's what anyone but him would call it. It seems he recognized her and knew that before she came here, having come into a large legacy, she used to be a barmaid at a pub. He said she cried when he asked how she would feel if people found out she was a 'jumped-up' and she begged him to let her write him out a cheque."

"My God!"

"And he stuck his claws into Madge in a different way. He got her alone and told her it stuck out a mile that she was in love with you, and asked if she could imagine how people were laughing behind her back at her."

"Damnable."

"Dickie, remember how she said she couldn't find her amber beads? Well, he had them in his pocket. He pulled them out and showed them to me. And that's not all. He said he'd even helped himself to the telephone money from that little box your father put on the table. And then he laughed in a way that made me wish I could be sick. 'Wouldn't you say I've made the most of my visit to Saxonbury Hall?' That's what he said. I told him he'd be laughing on the other side of his face when we sent for the police."

"That was very brave of you," said Dickie, "but awfully risky, Foof. What if he'd hit you over the head with a brick? It doesn't bear thinking about."

"I was afraid for a minute that he would go for me, because

it was as clear as day that he was completely wicked. But do you know, Dickie, I think what he did was just as scary. He just smiled and said nobody was going to ring up the police because doing so would mean all those nasty little secrets coming out, and we wouldn't want that, would we?"

"So now we know," said Dickie, "why his lordship doesn't get out and about much. Who'd want him for a houseguest? And I'm willing to bet that those servants of his are employed by some relative or other to keep him under lock and key." He was about to say more when a disturbance was heard in the corridor outside: upraised voices, and a screech that sounded as if it could have come from Madge. Seconds later, the door burst open and a wild-eyed George brought Dickie and Foof to their feet.

"You won't believe it," he cried. "The gardener just came running into the house to say that he was doing a bit of trimming and found Lord Dunstairs, dead as a doornail, inside the maze. Your father's ringing up the police, because," George took a deep breath, "it appears his lordship was strangled. Oh, I say! What's wrong with Foof?"

"She fainted, you clot!" Dickie had caught his beloved before she could slump to the floor. "Get out of here, George, and don't let anyone in here, least of all my mother."

"Aye, aye, sir!"

The door closed and Foof opened her eyes as Dickie lowered her onto the leather sofa. "I didn't," she clutched at his jacket lapel, "truly, I didn't kill him."

"Of course you didn't, darling!"

"But the police will think I did! They're fiendishly clever, Dickie. They'll ask all sorts of innocent-sounding questions and get it out of me that Lord Dunstairs played me for a silly little fool."

"He made monkeys out of everyone here. And one of them

killed him. Oh, my God! What if it was my father, Foof? He's got a few spokes missing when it comes to such things as his bees and the telephone money. He could have seen Dunstairs emptying the box and gone after him in a blind rage. And there's my mother! I'm sure she noticed the looks he was giving you last night! What if she suddenly saw herself as a lioness protecting her one and only cub?"

"Oh, you poor darling!" Foof sat up and reached for his hand. "What a fix to be in, because of course we can't spill the beans about everyone having a motive to do away with that monster. It simply isn't done, turning in one's friends. I'll just have to let them take me away and hope like anything the judge is a kind old man, with a soft spot for pretty young women. It would be quite awful to be hanged; but, God willing," her voice broke, "I suppose I would get used to prison food in time, even though I am the most dreadfully picky eater."

"You're trying to make me laugh." Dickie kissed her cherry lips and stroked her silky dark hair back from her forehead. "And I adore you for being brave, but there's really no need. Don't you see, my treasure, I am the obvious suspect. I've talked about wanting to kill Lord Dunstairs for tampering with your affections."

"Oh, darling." Foof clung to him as if fearing he would be torn away from her by the arms of the law at any moment. "I don't believe any sensible person could seriously suspect you. And it would be too cruel, when I so desperately want us to get married and have a dozen children, even if they all have Uncle Wilfred's nose. Surely the real murderer will own up. It would be the only decent thing to do."

"I beg your pardon for the intrusion," Woodcock's voice jerked them apart, "but I thought you would wish to know that the body, covered with some sacking so as not to alarm the ladies, has been brought into the house and placed in the study. And I thought, sir," he said, looking keenly at Dickie, "that you might wish to make a positive identification before the police arrive. They tend to be sticklers, and might deem the gardener to be a man who flusters easily and not, therefore, to be entirely relied on in such a matter."

"Oh, for heaven's sake," Dickie said crossly, "isn't it abundantly clear that I have to stay with Lady Felicity?"

"I'll come with you. No, really." Foof got to her feet. "I think I need to see him to convince myself that he really is dead and not just pretending."

"If you will excuse the liberty, your ladyship," Woodcock looked at her with troubled eyes, "I do believe it would be wiser to leave this to Mr. Ambleforth."

"Rubbish," she retorted roundly, and Dickie knew she would only stay put if he tied her to the sofa—an impossibility given that he had no rope handy. So he took her arm and led her in Woodcock's wake to the study. He felt her sway against him for a fraction of a second before standing up very straight and staring unflinchingly at the desk, which was sufficiently sizable for the body (covered in sacking, as Woodcock had described) to have been laid out on its leather top.

"Pull that stuff back, please, Woodcock," she said in a tight little voice, "and let us take a look."

"As you wish, my lady." He moved to one end of the desk and turned back a corner, sufficient for them to view the face of the dead man.

"But it isn't him." Foof and Dickie almost fell over each other as they leaned closer.

"Isn't whom?" responded Woodcock.

"Lord Dunstairs."

"If you will pardon the impertinence, I have to disagree with you. This *is* his lordship."

"But he is an old man." Foof looked quite exasperated. "And I have most certainly never seen him before in my life."

"But Williams the gardener has, and as I mentioned to Mr. Ambleforth last night, he worked for his lordship until recently, before coming here, and he was in no doubt as to this gentleman's identity."

"Then who . . . ?" Dickie watched, spellbound, as Woodcock replaced the triangle of sacking.

"Who was the so-called gentleman who came here under false pretenses? It is my belief, sir, that he was Lord Dunstairs' valet. A man by the name of Villers. I had my suspicions that he was not the genuine article when you mentioned to me that he had arrived in a taxi. That struck me as decidedly odd. Gentlemen of Lord Dunstairs' sort do not usually arrive in taxis. And then last night, when I was serving dinner, I was struck by the way the supposed Lord Dunstairs partook of his soup. Rather than lifting his spoon away from him in a backwards motion, as is considered proper, he lifted it directly to his lips as," Woodcock smiled without amusement, "I myself might do. Given my suspicions, I asked your permission, sir, to make a telephone call."

"So, you did," said Dickie.

"I was able to reach Lord Dunstairs' housekeeper. A sensible and quick-witted woman from the sound of her. And in the course of our conversation I ascertained that his lordship had that afternoon given his valet notice, after discovering that the man had not been dealing honestly with him."

"So that's who turned up here." Foof stood very still. "Yes, I can imagine him delighting in pulling such a stunt for the sheer malicious thrill of it. All that talk at dinner about his letter accepting your parents' invitation going astray, Dickie. I don't suppose his lordship ever wrote a response."

"The housekeeper was quite sure he hadn't," said Woodcock. "She explained to me that her employer had been in failing health for some time, and was besides of a reclusive nature, who rarely opened any of his post. She told me she would not wake him to relay my suspicions as he was already in bed for the night, but would speak to him first thing in the morning. I must assume she did so, and that, thoroughly outraged, his lordship got into his car, a risky business in his infirm state, and drove over here at the crack of dawn."

"Where he met Villers in the garden after I went back into the house." Flora looked sadly at the desk. "Oh, how I hope the police catch up with your murderer, Lord Dunstairs."

"I am convinced they will, your ladyship," said Woodcock. "I just now took the liberty of telephoning Police Constable Jones, an acquaintance of mine, and put him in possession of the facts. One of which is that there is no sign of his lordship's car, which would indicate that Villers made away in it after hiding the body in the maze, where it might not have been discovered for some time had the gardener not been working on it."

"You never cease to amaze me." Dickie managed a smile while wondering if Foof was inwardly doing battle with the realization that, among her other woes, she had been kissed by a valet, but he decided he had in all likelihood done her an injustice when she left his side to press her bright lips against Woodcock's cheek.

"I know you feel awful about Lord Dunstairs," she said, "but you mustn't blame yourself in any way for his death, and I want you to know that if I weren't promised to Dickie I would definitely set my cap at you, dearest Woodcock."

"Thank you, my lady." The usually imperturbable gentleman's gentleman looked suspiciously moist around the eyes. "I feel entirely undeserving of your appreciation, given the fact that this morning I overslept, not having slept well last night, and for the first time failed in my morning duties to Mr. Ambleforth."

"Shocking," said Dickie with a severe expression and a wink at Foof. "I think I may have to replace you, Woodcock, but not for thirty or forty years. It's not easy these days to find help who can save a chap from being sent up on a charge of murder."

Come to Grandma

Emma Richwoods had never adored her mother-in-law, but she would have proffered a polite welcome, had circumstances been different. At thirty-five, Emma had just given birth to her first child, and now comes the heart of the problem: mother-in-law Mildred had been dead almost six years.

Emma, a successful C.P.A., in partnership with her husband, Howard, was not subject to imagination. Her appearance—trim, tailored, dark hair brought up in a smooth knot, horn-rimmed glasses—bespoke her dislike of excess. Spiritualism was the stuff of which late-night horror movies were made, and the Richwoods always turned off the TV immediately following the ten-o'clock news in order to spend quality time with their portfolios. One of the oddest things about the situation was that rational Emma never considered the rational explanation—that her visitor was a manifestation of postpartum depression.

Mildred had made herself quite at home in the white-on-white apartment when the Richwoods returned from Community Hospital with baby Kathleen. She was camped in front of the TV watching a game show. Her hair—still done in spit curls—needed a tint, and her glasses—those vulgar checkerboard frames—were held together at one temple with masking tape. The only visible difference from her former self appeared to be that she wasn't breathing.

"Surprise! It's me, the late Mildred." She uncrossed her polyester legs, revealing that she had helped herself to a pair of Howard's designer socks. "And to think I was never late—not once in my whole damn life! Strange . . . !" She squinted around. "Seem to remember leaving you my grade-school and high-school perfect attendance diplomas. Don't see them prominently displayed, Em. Guess they don't go with that picture of tire tracks!"

The artwork was *Rumination*, by a sound-investment artist.

Howard stared at the TV. "This is appalling. Forgive me, dear! To leave the apartment without turning off the set! All I can say in my defense is that becoming a father so suddenly must have unsettled me more than I realized."

Transfixed, Emma felt him remove her coat. Seeing . . . hearing Mildred was like being given another spinal.

"Shucks, Howie, was it too much to hope that my only grandchild get named for me?" The . . . ghost began making goo-goo faces over the carry crib.

At that moment two aspects of the situation became clear to Emma. One, Howard could not see or hear his mother; his unobtrusive face, under the precision-cut auburn hair, did not change expression. Two, death had not improved Mildred.

"Some welcome this!" Mildred straightened up to her full four foot eleven. "Think it didn't take some wangling for me to get here? And I'd have been in the delivery room if old Pete had gotten dug out sooner from the paperwork." Sun, breaking through the wide windows, flashed on her breastplate of bowling "200" pins. A heaveless sigh. "Don't know why I thought things'd be any different on this happy occasion. But dumb bunny did. 'I'll be wanted,' says I to the gals in the choir. Begged to come and help out."

"Have you forgotten you are dead?" Emma moved close to the carry crib. Howard was off putting their coats away.

"And that makes me useless?"

"Unavailable."

"Don't give me that!" Mildred was bouncing the side of the carry crib so that it rocked like a boat in a storm. Odd, Kathleen didn't scream a protest. If anything, her tiny face seemed less scrunched up than usual. "You always did put your family first! Your mom and dad. Your sister! Aunts, uncles, and the rest of the stuffed *'shits.'* Know why the pill was invented, don't we?"

Mildred plugged a Winston between her lips, plopped down on one of the chairs that went with the smoked-glass dining table. Her eyes said, "Want to try making me sit out on the patio?"

"Your entire family is dead." Emma sounded as though she were evaluating a file. "No one left."

"Imprecise, Emma. I have you and Kathleen." Howard had come in soundlessly, and was turning the crib so that the baby was not in the sun's glare.

Emma slid down on a tubular steel chair, omitting to smooth her clerical gray skirt under her. A warm iron and a damp cloth would remove any wrinkles; but would anything remove Mildred?

"You are pale." Howard rested a hand briefly on Emma's shoulder before saying he would fetch her a glass of water.

Mildred dropped her cigarette into a vase containing roses sent by the rival grandparents. "Before we get down to picking up the pieces, Em—I'll get a few things off my chest. I wasn't thrilled with being cremated."

Emma fingered her black-and-white bow tie. "Mildred,

it seemed best for all concerned."

"It seemed cheap."

"How long do you intend to stay?"

"That depends on . . . which way the wind blows." A gentle smile that made Emma wish to break the checkerboard glasses. What was happening to her—the woman who thought a raised voice on a par with blowing one's nose in public. If Mildred had manifested as a floating white sheet uttering mournful cries, could she have been blamed on hormones and dismissed with two Tylenol and an early night?

"Have you been talking to the baby, dear?"

Emma responded to Howard's popping up beside her by knocking the glass of water out of his hand. Upsetting. But the incident had its positive aspect. Emma realized she had been sliding out of control and put on the brakes. While Howard blotted up the wet spot in such a way as not to disturb the pile, she calculated her options and decided the soundest course would be to wait Mildred out. Shouldn't take her long to take the huff. Hadn't she divorced Howard's father (ten years before his death) because one night he had mentioned, conversationally, that the fried chicken was a little greasy? Incidentally, Mildred had not prepared that chicken. She had purchased it from Cluck Cluck's Carry-Out.

As of now she was back to making kitchi-coo over the carry crib. "A face only a grandma could love! Stuck with your nose, Em, but makes up for it with my red hair."

Emma's face remained smooth as ice.

"Naughty old Gran." Mildred went smack-smack to her own hand before lighting up another cigarette. Had she forgotten that smoking had killed her?

"Can't go saying I'm *breathing* germs over Kathleen." The bowling pins flashed along with Mildred's dentures—purchased, extravagantly, only weeks before her death.

"Emma, are you all right?"

"Perfect, Howard, thank you. I see clearly what must be done. We will think of her as a television set that won't turn off but can be tuned out." The words escaped before Emma could stop them.

Howard looked at her as though she were a balance sheet that . . . didn't.

Mildred wore her most motherly smile as she parked herself in a corner. "Woo me with rudeness, why don't you, Em?"

"I don't think I can agree to tuning Kathleen out, dear"—Howard brought his fingers together and assumed his pensive mien—"not until she is of an age when"—nervous laugh—"she begins to tune a guitar."

That night Emma went to bed before the ten-o'clock news, wishful, if not hopeful, of waking to a void—in the family circle. She sat up in her bed, called to account by Kathleen's demands for a night feeding and . . . other noises. Someone was clumping around the apartment. How could Howard continue to be deaf to his mother's invasion? Emma sent the other twin bed a displeased look and opened the door.

"For crying out loud, Em, you look like death warmed over. And me full of beans!"

This was going to be hell! Mildred kept getting between Emma and Kathleen during the diaper change—shaking talcum powder where it wasn't wanted and patting the small tummy. She wore a sweatshirt over a pair of men's long johns, and her head was a metal cap of bobby pins.

"What me, cause my boy to lose his beauty sleep? I hope I'm not that kind of mother! The excitement of having me back would cause Howie's blood pressure to skyrocket. I saw that soon enough and kept the barriers up. Can't promise him that I'm here to stay." Mildred looked upward. "Ours is a very uncertain world."

What about my blood pressure? Emma could feel her skin tightening. *What about my sanity?* She knew she was not currently mentally impaired, but even lacking statistical data, she was prepared to predict she would soon find she had crossed the line. She clung to Kathleen's tiny hand and . . . that equally tiny hope. The visit sounded temporary. Was Mildred subject to recall at a moment's notice?

Mildred touched Kathleen's hair. "Ain't it a shame, red not being a favorite color with accountants."

Why was this happening? Was the answer as simple as . . . spite? Mildred had said frankly, when Howard first introduced the two women, that she had no time for anyone who didn't know the bowling meaning of *strike,* looked down on Early American furniture, and read books with appendices longer than their texts. For relaxation Mildred read romances set on lush tropical islands. For culture, real-life accounts of the inner world of boxing.

Emma, about to pick Kathleen up from the changing table, found her eyes fixed on her mother-in-law, outlined by the window frame. A good-sized window . . . and open. Temptation did not come easily to Emma. Every act was carefully premeasured. But how exhilarating, how therapeutic, to push Mildred out into the half-light. One snag: It would have meant leaving Kathleen unattended on the table.

Morning fetched another idea. Emma telephoned a woman, Selina Brown, a resident two floors down in Apartment 321, and asked if she could stop by at—yes, ten-thirty would be fine. Almost out the door, when . . . there was Mildred, adding her assurances to Howard's that the baby was in excellent hands.

Nerves shredded Emma's voice; she even lunged forward, hands clawing. "You think I want to leave my baby with you?"

"*Our* baby, dear." Howard backed up, his face a wall of hurt. The Richwoods had arranged on the night of conception that they would both work at home for three weeks post-delivery.

"Forgive me, I was joking, Howard." How false the words sounded. Emma never joked until after her seven p.m. cocktail.

Selina Brown was not a person Emma had ever wished to know, other than as an elevator acquaintance. The woman had a face that might have been tie-dyed. She wore cannonball earrings, lots of fringe, and reeked of incense. Several of the residents had accused her of moving furniture around in the middle of the night, her defense being that the occurrences were "involuntary."

Emma passed through the jangle of beads into a room of black draperies, gauzy fumes, and an atmosphere of peace. And somehow . . . she was in the midst of her account before she knew she had begun.

Selina leaned back in her woven grass chair, spread her Indian silk skirts across her mammoth lap, and wheezed. "Tell me, sugar, what's so hard in being a little giving, a little open? Think you've got a copyright on mother-in-law troubles? So she wants to make nice with her grandkid!"

"She is dead."

"So, Mrs. Richwoods, are most of my best friends." Selina lit up a thin black cigarette from a candle.

Emma pressed her feet and her hands together. "I try not to be emotional in my judgment, but Mildred was never my kind of person, never close. I disliked the way she ate, the way she spoke."

"Liked the way she made Howard, did you, sugar?" A wheezing laugh that caused the draperies to swirl.

"She swears, she smokes . . ." Emma repressed a blush as Selina tapped away ash. "She talks endlessly and unintelligently about her operations and the . . . constipation that followed."

"And now"—Selina held her smoking hand still, eyes closed—"you foresee listening to endless how-I-died stories. I begin to find it in my rocky heart to sympathize with you. The woman is a bore. Something a ghost should never be. See here"—another wheeze, and she flicked ash into the palm of her hand—"I have a friend; he's a parapsych prof at the junior college. I'll get in touch with him. Soon. He's off camping now with his kids. Tread water, Mrs. Richwoods, I'll get back to you."

Emma lifted her chin. "I am grateful. Thank you."

Her empty living room welcomed her back, and she saw nothing odd in ascribing it a personality—a day had made many changes. Howard must be in the nursery. As for Mildred . . . Emma determined not to get her hopes up. She sat on the nubby white sofa, drawing calm from the atmosphere of tubular steel and nude wood. She had not brought this unpleasantness on herself. Nothing here invited the . . . unusual.

Time to go to the nursery. Through the partially open door she could see Howard feeding the baby, the bottle held at the appropriate angle. The door to the guestroom was also ajar. Hope seeped away. Mildred was lying on the bed, reading a magazine that must have forced its way in there with her. *Male Marvels*. Depraved. A jar of generic cold cream was on the bedside table.

The telephone in the hallway shrilled, and Emma picked it up. Top marks for efficiency—if Selina had located her Authority.

"Emmie?" The voice coming through the receiver was Ruth's. Her sister. Those two had never been compatible. But time alters cases.

"How things going, Sis? Mind if I bring some of the kids along to see their new cousin?"

Emma removed the receiver an inch from her ear and smoothed her hair. "That would be nice, Ruth; however, I am getting somewhat housebound. I would prefer Howard and I to bring Kathleen over to you."

"Whatever. Sure you're up to the drive?"

"I hardly think," Emma snapped, a novelty with her, "that a fifteen-minute ride will exhaust me. We will come now, if that suits you."

She had barely hung up when there came the dreaded voice. "And if that ain't enough to make a pig shit! Taking my granddaughter away from me before we've gotten ourselves acquainted." Mildred had her arms akimbo. "Know what your problem is, Em? You head's too stuffed with schooling to have room for sense."

A soundless scream tore apart Emma's lips. "How often must I keep saying—your family is dead! Everyone. Dead . . . dead . . . dead and buried." She drew a racking breath. Her throat hurt. My God, she rarely raised her voice. As for screaming . . . what must Howard think of her?

He stood rigid in the doorway, his face set in pacifying lines. "Relax, Emma." He sounded as frightened as that time when he found a decimal point in the wrong place. "You've been overdoing."

"Not on account of me, she hasn't." Mildred positioned herself inches from Emma. An ingratiating smile for the son who couldn't see her. "Never could understand, Em, why your mom and dad—the Bobbsey Twins—rate so high above me. Not here doing their bit, are they? 'Course not! Off on some fancy-dancy cruise to the Parakeet Isles. How I do remember that first Christmas after you and Howie were married. Your mom gets a black silk nightdress. Me—I get an umbrella. And know what? It leaked the first time a bird pissed on it. Didn't matter. I already had three—still in their boxes."

Emma's eyes went wild. Worse, she hurled herself at Mildred. "You never would have worn a black silk nightgown."

"Certainly not, dear." Howard backed into the nursery. "Mind if I have a few moments quiet time with Kathleen?" He closed the door. There was a telephone in there. Was he about to phone Dr. Hubner, the gynecologist, requesting a referral to a psychiatrist?

Mildred adjusted her glasses. "Seems to me, hon, you and Howie aren't communicating like you should. Secrets hurt, not heal, a marriage—as you would know, Em, if you took time to watch the soaps. Best if I go to my room. Last thing on earth I want is to be a cause of friction."

Emma closed her eyes. When she opened them, she was alone. Entering the nursery, she found Howard holding the baby—not the phone. Kathleen was crying, which hopefully had kept him from turning in a report on his wife's unnerving behavior.

Is that what she wants, Emma questioned, *me out of the way in the psychiatric ward, and Howard and Kathleen all to herself? How I wish I had pushed her out the window . . .* Her hands clenched as the futility struck her. Mildred couldn't be made to die twice.

"Howard." Emma opened the nursery door and crept up behind him, very much as Mildred had done to her. "Excuse my behavior out in the hallway—due, I believe, to some sort of waking nightmare." She grabbed at his arms.

"Careful!" He sidestepped her, his arms protecting the baby. Emma had lost sight of the fact that he was holding

Kathleen. The baby's cries ripped through her.

"I will go and freshen up." Her smile, meant to be appeasing, appeared to frighten father and child. "I told Ruth we would go over for a little while."

"Emma"—Howard was frowning—"the baby is distressed."

"She'll be fine."

Escaping into the bathroom, Emma pondered what Howard would say to Ruth and her husband, Joe. Then all thought was drowned out by Mildred's singing—in a rusty voice, a ribald song about a monk and a cow. She was there—under the spurting shower, all lathered up and wearing a pink plastic cap.

"Shucks! Never a moment's privacy around here!" A snatched washcloth and the shower curtain swished shut.

Ruth's house became an oasis. Emma, while getting Kathleen wrapped up, fought the fear that her mother-in-law would decide to intrude along. Could Mildred . . . manifest away from the apartment?

So far . . . so good, they were out the door. Howard held on to her arm as they crossed the car park. Hurry . . . ! And then she almost caused him to trip, along with the carrying crib, when she twisted around to look back up at the apartment window. There it was—the reproachful silhouette.

Howard frowned. "Emma, please—did you forget something?"

"I thought I might have . . . then remembered I hadn't."

Kathleen fussed during the short drive. A relief to pull into Ruth's toy-strewn driveway. Before Emma could get her door open, her nieces and nephews spilled out onto the porch, seven-year-old Sean yelling, "Aunt Emma, you won't believe who is here!"

She swayed against Howard. Logic should have told her

that Mildred did not need a car for transportation. The children dragged Emma out of the car, and next she was in Ruth's burlap living room—where cereal bowls were stuck in among bookcases and jigsaw pieces made a broken mosaic on the floor.

"Who is here?" she managed.

Ruth was scooping up magazines and tossing them in a corner. "Uncle Mo and Aunt Vin; they called just after you and I spoke. The more the merrier, I said. Joe has them out back showing off his tomatoes. We're being taken over by them." She straightened up. "Jeez, Emma! You look wrung out! Here—take a load off." She dusted off a chair with a T-shirt. Always a slob, Ruth. Howard was afraid to eat in this house. So much for Mildred's accusations that she had been pushed out in favor of Emma's side.

"Hello, young Kath." Ruth took the carry crib from Howard. "You all want to stay for supper? Won't beat the socks off your gourmet fare, just a hot-dog casserole . . ."

"Are you making reference to the sort Mom used to make?" Emma squeezed the arms of her chair, ignoring Howard's pained expression.

"The same." Ruth gathered in Kathleen with practiced ease. "Want to bet there's not a hot dog on that cruise?"

The eyes of the sisters met, both seeing their mother squeezed into blue satin, prepared to eat a real live dog rather than admit she didn't understand the French menu. How would their father survive if they wouldn't let him have beer with his breakfast?

In came the children, followed by Joe, Uncle Mo, and Aunt Vin. And, totally unexpectedly, Emma wanted to be part of the warm muddle of this . . . her family. She wanted Kathleen to become the adored little cousin. She wanted Howard to stop looking as if he wished to reprogram everyone. What waited back at the apartment made this all seem . . . so structured. Emma knew she would have to regain control, with or without Selina Brown's help.

"Thank you, Ruth, we will stay for dinner," she said

Back at the apartment, the air was stinky with cigarette smoke. How could Howard not notice? Hadn't he admitted once that his mother had controlled his childhood thoughts but that it had taken him years to untie the apron strings? Emma stood in the living room, holding onto the baby for strength. No clumping of feet. No sound at all; but Emma knew Mildred was in the guestroom.

"Nice," she whispered against Kathleen's downy hair. "Granny may pout all she wishes if I can get through your night feeding without her help."

And, amazingly, things worked out that way. At two a.m. Emma found herself straining for any movement from her house ghost. A giggle escaped her. Embarrassing. And now an odd feeling came—a kind of . . . something verging on . . . pity for Mildred. Had she come back, hoping to repair their relationship? Emma stuck herself with a diaper pin, annoyance with herself welling up with the drop of blood. Mildred had come back to be a thorn in the flesh of the woman who had taken Howard away. And now she was using silence. But not for long . . .

Mildred did not appear at the smoked-glass breakfast table the following morning. Emma heard the shower going . . . and going. Howard was in excellent spirits, dancing a rattle over Kathleen. "Daddy's so proud of his little girl." He straightened up from the carry crib. "Emma, that visit to Ruth does seem to have put you back on the path to stabil—full strength. Mind if I go down to the office for an hour? Unless you object to being alone?"

"I will not be alone."

"No offense." He smiled ruefully at the baby.

Emma was glad when he left. She wished to assess her situation without wondering if he was still wondering about her state of mind. No sounds from the guestroom. Emma tucked Kathleen back into her crib proper, and then . . . surrendered to the urge to open that door and look in on Mildred. She was lying on the bed, a washcloth wadded up on her forehead and a bottle of generic aspirin displayed alongside the pot of cold cream. Surely they could only be visual aids.

"Do you feel all right?" Emma asked.

Silence. A very negative silence.

Emma almost squeezed off the doorknob. How lovely and peaceful it would be to creep up and move that cloth down over Mildred's nose and press down . . . down. What would that make her—a murderess in name only?

She fell away from the door when the telephone rang.

"Greetings," came Selina Brown's voice. "My parapsych prof called, we picked at the bones of your situation, and he says he'll see you this afternoon."

"Not this morning?"

"Think you're the only one with problems, sugar?" A pause, and Selina's voice became a little less tepid. "So you say easy for him, right? How's 'bout if I come tell you the guts of what he said?"

"I would prefer that you did not," Emma whispered. "She might be listening."

"Then you hustle down here."

"I'm not sure . . . Howard is at the office and the baby is sleeping . . ."

"So?" Selina wheezed. "Who's to have you up for neglect with Grandma baby-sitting?"

"Very well, but I will not remain more than a couple of minutes." Emma hung up. If she went to take Kathleen, Mildred was bound to appear and demand to know where they were going. Emma squared her shoulders and smoothed her hair. She was being overprotective. For all her faults, Mildred wouldn't do anything to hurt Kathleen; the love of a real live grandma had been visible in those goo-goo faces.

"And so does Mommy love you." Emma felt self-conscious saying the words. Bending over the crib, she touched the fingers to the warm, round form under the quilt with its geometric shapes. Which matched those of the gently turning mobile.

The journey, down three floors in the elevator, was stifling. Selina was standing outside her own apartment door.

"Tell me," Emma said. Was she mad to believe in this woman wearing a purple turban and magician's robes?

"Sugar, you tell your mother-in-law to leave. You heard me. Subtlety isn't something she understands. She won't up and out until she's been sufficiently insulted. That way she can go tell her kindred spirits what a hellish time she's had of it."

Emma became her old self again. Each problem to its own solution, one need only look for the answer in the right column. How could she have been so slow-witted?

"Thank you, Selina. And do convey my appreciation to the professor. When she was alive, Mildred's visits always ended in her slamming out of the apartment. She would accuse us of kicking her out. And nothing else about her has changed. She still has a mouth like a sewer, is insatiably jealous of my family. Excuse me, I must hurry . . ."

The elevator would not hurry. It stopped at each floor, then took its time opening its door. Emma hurried along the hallway, opened the apartment door, and then, slowing her pace and breathing, headed for the guestroom. She was determined not to feel sorry for Mildred. This bon voyage must be final.

The guestroom was empty. The bedspread neat and smooth. The pillow plumped up. The jar of cold cream and the bottle of aspirin gone from the nightstand . . . as was the pink shower cap from the hook behind the bathroom door. Emma stood in the hallway. This was perfect. She must telephone Selina with the good news. Mildred had already been sufficiently insulted.

Not a whiff of cigarette smoke. As for the whiff of . . . regret, Emma did ask herself: If she had known her mother-in-law's visit was to be so short, would she have been a little more welcoming?

Too late now, and if she did not hurry, she would be late for Kathleen's feeding.

She entered the nursery, her heart lifting at the sight of the geometric mobile spinning above the crib.

An empty crib. Pinned to the quilt was a note:

Dear Em,

Guess I'm not cut to be a backseat driver. Never thought to ask me to go to Ruth's, did you? Well, two can play at that game. I'm taking my redheaded granddaughter, Mildred, Junior, to show off to my side of the family. Howie will know she's in excellent hands.

Mom

Fetch

"I'm sorry, old bean, but every once in a donkey's age a husband has to take a stand, and what it comes right down to—putting the matter in the proverbial nutshell, so to speak—is that I will not have a notorious thief under this roof." Mr. Richard Ambleforth, aged twenty-five, but looking more like an earnest six former home for the hols, felt rather good about this masterful speech addressed to his bride of two days.

"Honestly, Dickie! How can you be so stuffy!" The former Lady Felicity Entwhistle, known to her intimate circle as Foof, tossed her silky black bob, stamped her dainty foot, and flounced over to the window seat. There she sat balefully eyeing the ceiling and addressed the crown molding. "Your mother was right. You should never have married me; I was bound to let on sooner rather than later that I prefer hobnobbing with criminals to having afternoon tea with the vicar."

"I say." Dickie glanced nervously over his shoulder as if expecting his formidable parent to materialize and clasp him to the maternal bosom. "Shouldn't bring the mater into this, tempting fate, don't you know! Before we can duck behind the curtains there'll be a knock at the door. And in she'll march with a list of all the foods I'm not supposed to eat on the honeymoon."

"Oh, more the merrier!" Foof gave a hollow laugh. "After

all, we are taking Woodcock with us. Heaven forbid he should be left behind looking sadly at his bucket and spade!"

At this less than propitious moment a large man with iron gray hair, in unequivocal butler's garb, entered the book-lined sitting room of what had been Dickie's London bachelor digs. Despite his size he moved with a lightness of step that verged on the ethereal as he placed a silver tray with a decanter and two glasses on the table behind the worn leather sofa.

"Oh, jolly good fun! It's time for sherry!" Foof sat swinging her lengthy rope of pearls in an arc that threatened to lasso the clock off the mantelpiece. "How about a toast, Dickie? To life on the streets for that miserable miscreant I so regrettably brought home because"—her voice broke—"I'm sure Woodcock followed your orders and turfed the poor fellow out onto the fire escape."

"I must confess to having fallen short in that regard." The butler addressed the sherry glass he handed to her. "After forty years in the service of Mr. Ambleforth's family I am wont to take the occasional liberty of making certain modifications to the instructions bestowed upon me, when I deem it in the best interest of continued harmony within the household. If in so doing on this occasion I have transgressed beyond the bounds of leniency, then I shall respectfully hand in my notice and repair to my room to pack my travel bag."

"I thought it was already packed for the honeymoon." Such was Dickie's state of alarm that he could pick up only on this trivial point.

"I stand corrected, sir." Woodcock's austere demeanor was belied by the twinkle in his eye and Foof sprang to her feet, dribbling sherry down the front of her elegant frock to bestow a kiss on his cheek.

"You treasure of a man! How horrid of me to think for a

moment that you would not see the matter precisely as I do. Haven't I always been certain that Dickie only got up the courage to propose to me after you told him what to say and prodded him out the door with one of his mother's hatpins? Now, if you can only persuade him"—Foof put what was left of her drink down on a table and clasped her hands imploringly—"that it is his Christian duty to help reclaim a wayward soul, I will be an exemplary wife to Dickie, and the perfect mistress to you, darling Woodcock."

"Sorry, Foof! But I refuse to budge on this." Dickie wandered over to the sofa table and picked up his sherry glass. "If I allowed my heart to soften and agreed to let the fellow remain here, we'd be letting ourselves in for the most beastly time. Before we'd know it not one of our chums would be willing to set foot inside the flat for fear of having their coat pockets picked or their handbags raided."

"Fiddlesticks!" His bride returned to the window seat in a swirl of skirts. "I explained to him that he was lucky not to be in prison with the wicked man who got him into a life of crime. Had you seen the remorse in his soft brown eyes you would know that he has truly seen the error of his ways and is intent on becoming a pillar of society."

"Even the most hardened of hearts do, upon occasion, see the light and henceforth embark upon lives of unblemished spirituality." Woodcock proffered this pronouncement along with a plate of wafer-thin almond biscuits, which he had procured from the interior of the sideboard. "I am thinking, Mr. Ambleforth, most particularly of my cousin Bert who led a ribald youth consorting with women of an unsavory nature. He had not attended a church service in many years until one Sunday morning, when feeling the effects of the night before, he entered a Plymouth Brethren meeting hall. Merely in search of a place to sit down. But whilst there he came to realize in a blinding flash—as he described it to me—that his previous life had been nothing but wickedness and sin."

"What a lovely story," enthused Foof. "I suppose he was embraced back into the bosom of the family."

"An attempt was made," responded Woodcock, "but resentment was felt by some at his attempts to dissuade them from engaging in such unholy practices as walking down to the village green to watch Sunday cricket matches. However, such a complete and sustained conversion is not, from what I have gleaned of life, in any way uncommon. Such was my thinking, Mr. Ambleforth, as I prepared a light repast for the personage presently in the kitchen. And sensing a willingness on his part to rethink the manner of his days, agreed to add my voice to Lady Felicity's in pleading his cause."

"Oh, bring him in here! It's clear I'll have no peace until you do." Dickie flopped back down in his chair, refusing to meet his bride's eyes while Woodcock retreated out into the hall and seconds later wafted back into the room with what looked like shamed humility itself tiptoeing in his wake.

"Darling, Dickie! Does he look like a cutthroat cur?" asked Foof in her most wheedling voice.

"No, I suppose not, but he wouldn't have been much good at his job if he did. Oh, very well, let's hear what he has to say for himself."

"Woof!" came the ingratiating response.

"There," cried Foof, dancing across the room to scoop the small black-and-brown dog with a face like a floor mop into her arms. "Fetch is saying he's ever so sorry that he got into bad company and was led wickedly astray. But if you will be his new master, Dickie, he will never again steal so much as a matchstick. Isn't that so"—kissing the furry forehead—"my adorable precious?" The animal looked over her shoulder and woofed with a great deal of conviction.

Dickie wasn't entirely mollified. "Yes, he sounds sorry, old bean. But we can't lose sight of the fact that he's a confidence trickster."

"Very true, sir," concurred Woodcock. "Were such not the case, Lady Felicity might have been less sympathetic when she found him in an alleyway, after being informed by her milliner that he had been rendered homeless when his master, Lord Bentbrook, was recently made a guest of His Majesty. But one should perhaps bear in mind, Mr. Ambleforth, that in all walks of life, four-footed or otherwise, there are those who are induced to live by their wits because life's contrivances against them."

"Miss Honeywell pined to take Fetch in herself but she could not risk getting dog hair on her adorable hats. And anyway, darling Dickie, I am sure he will be much happier with us. A honeymoon is just what he needs to help banish the past and—"

"Now there I do draw the line," protested Dickie, "that dog is not, I repeat not, coming with us."

His words were still ringing in his ears an hour later when he, Foof, Woodcock, and Fetch sat in a train heading out of London Bridge Station for Little Biddlington-on-Sea. They had decided against driving the car and had selected a third-class carriage because Dickie harbored the not unvalid fear that his mother might have instructed her innumerable acquaintances to be on the lookout for them. And at the first report of a sighting she would be on their track. Possibly even waiting for them when they arrived at the honeymoon suite. Because what mother worthy of the name would allow her son to go off on his very first honeymoon without her being there to make sure that he did fail to attend to his health by eating regular meals and getting a good night's sleep?

"Little Biddlington-on-Sea sounds absolutely topping!"

Foof looked delectable in a slim brown suit, buttoned shoes, with one of Miss Honeywell's demurest hats cupping her face. Fetch sat beside her like a small furry package as she gazed dreamily out the window at the rows of sooty faced houses whizzing past on the embankment.

"Yes, it should be perfect." What Dickie meant was that it was the last place on earth his mother would look for them. It was known to be a pretty resort, but one favored by working-class people who wanted to enjoy a quiet holiday without crowded promenades, fun fairs, and young people belting out songs as they came wavering home from the neatest pub. He was still feeling a bit glum about Fetch's presence, but he had to admit that so far the dog had not misbehaved an inch. True, the little beast kept glancing at the communication cord as if considering the possibility of leaping up and giving it a tug. But Foof's soothing hand upon his wiry back kept him in place. Until, that is, the train pulled into a station and a woman entered the carriage, which so far they'd had to themselves.

She was a nondescript person of medium build in a gray flannel coat and a serviceable hat secured to the bun at the back of her head with a small-tipped pin. Foof, who was wondering aloud how much farther it was to Little Biddlington-on-Sea, barely looked at her. But Dickie had the uneasy feeling that he might have seen the woman somewhere before. Could she be one of the mater's spies, cleverly disguised to look like somebody's housekeeper? Woodcock, who had been perusing a periodical providing advice on the proper maintenance of a gentleman's wine cellar, rose and placed the woman's small suitcase on the overhead rack. He resumed his seat at the opposite window from his employers. She took hers across from him and, as the train rumbled back to life, opened her handbag, withdrew a darning bobbin, and was just about to pull a black sock over its mushroom-shaped head when Fetch leaped into action. Scrambling across the floor, he attacked the woman's shoes in a blur of brown-and-black fur, tearing at her laces while barking out the side of his mouth.

Dickie's mother would have denounced it as a common bark, definitely cockney. But there was worse to come. When the woman bent down, dropping her darning in the process, Fetch leaped with the speed of light onto the seat and was rummaging inside her handbag when Woodcock, rising to ominous proportions, hauled him up by the scruff of the neck. And continued to dangle him in the air.

"I trust the animal did not inflict an injury, Madam." This was Woodcock at his most butlerish, concerned but unflustered and Foof silently vowed that she would never go on a honeymoon without him.

"It's all right, he hasn't hurt me." The woman looked down at her tangled shoelaces. And Dickie, who wasn't known amongst fellow members of his club to be uncannily astute, got the odd feeling that she did so to avoid meeting Woodcock's eyes. Almost as if she were the one to feel embarrassment.

"It was frightfully naughty of him." Foof still had her hands clapped to her face—which was as white as Dickie's was red. "I should have had him on his lead. My husband and I are most awfully sorry."

"More than we can possibly say," croaked Dickie.

"Fetch, I want you to apologize to the lady," instructed Foof.

A decidedly hangdog woof resulted. Woodcock returned the animal to its appropriate seat and handed the woman's darning back to her.

She replaced it to her handbag, saying, "I think I'll have a sleep. That'll help me get over the scare." Whereupon she proceeded to sit with eyes resolutely closed for the next hour and a half. At which time the train chuffed into the station displaying a sign reading Little Biddlington-on-Sea. Instantly, the woman became alert, and took down her suitcase before Woodcock could help her with it. Foof and Dickie voiced renewed apologies as she stepped down onto the platform ahead of them. The evening was cloudy, but they felt considerably brighter when she disappeared from view. Even Fetch displayed a renewed perkiness as he trotted alongside them on his lead. Woodcock located a porter to assist with the suitcases and they soon found themselves outside the station, looking hopefully around for their taxi.

"My profound apologies, Mr. Ambleforth and Lady Felicity. I telephoned to arrange for one to be waiting for us upon our arrival." Woodcock shook his head. It was rare that his organization skills did not meet with impeccable results and beneath his imperturbable exterior he felt the matter keenly.

"I think I can guess what happened, sir," offered the porter. "Smith was here with his taxi, fifteen minutes ago. Likes to be ahead of himself when possible and have a cheese sandwich and a cup of cocoa from his Thermos. We had another train come in, the three-fifty from Nottingham, and just one gentleman got out. Anyways, to cut a long story shorter he talked Smith into taking him where he needed to go."

"Well, of all the cheek!" said Foof.

"Always one to make an extra five bob, is Smith. But I did hear the man say he was feeling poorly, so it could be Smith's heart was touched and he wasn't just thinking about the tip he'd get out of it." The porter was sympathetic to their plight, but unable to come up with a solution to the problem of transportation. There wasn't another taxi service or a bus that went to the Sea Breeze Guest House. It seemed they would have to walk.

"It can't be far." Endeavoring to console Woodcock, Dickie picked up a suitcase before he could be prevented.

"One would assume not, sir. When I telephoned to make inquiries into the nature of the premises I was informed that they are located not five minutes' walk from the railway station, and within a stone's throw of the sea."

"Exactly what I was told by my friend Binkie Harbottle, whose landlady always comes here on her holiday. Chin up Woodcock! Never say die, Foof. Let's be on our way. We can even sing 'Ten Green Bottles' to help pick up the tempo."

Dickie, having manfully decided that he wouldn't let Fetch's lapse ruin things, began to hum as he strutted forward along the road that rose into a hill. A hill that shortly began to seem part of a mountain range. Up and up they puffed, afraid to stop unless they slid backwards to the bottom. Had they perhaps misunderstood the porter's directions when he told them to turn right on leaving the station and continue straight ahead until they reached the Sea Breeze? It was a chilly evening for June, but Foof had never felt hotter in her life. She was gasping for a cup of tea.

They passed no one, although a couple of times Dickie thought he saw a figure a considerable distance ahead of them making the same interminable trudge. Then, just as Foof whispered that she couldn't go on, she would have to lie down and die, they saw a gate. It bore the sign SEA BREEZE GUEST HOUSE and stood blissfully open. With renewed energy they all, including Fetch, who long ago had looked as though his paws had given out, hobbled down the short path to the door. While Woodcock rang the bell Dickie strove to regain his voice.

"Old Binkie's landlady told a whopper about the Sea

Breeze being a short walk from the station, but she didn't misrepresent about it being a stone's throw from the sea. We're on top a beastly cliff. I expect that if we go around the back we'll be able to stand on the brink of the precipice and toss pebbles into the surf to our hearts' content."

"The Sea Breeze had better have other attractions or I'm leaving first thing tomorrow morning." Foof sagged against the door just as it was opened by a cozy-looking woman in a hair net, who ushered them into the dark varnished hall with a strip of Turkish-red carpet and bade them welcome. As Mr. and Mrs. Ambleforth. Woodcock, in accordance with his employers' desire to avoid an excess of bowing and scraping, had not mentioned Foof's title when booking them in.

"I'm Mrs. Roscombe. Leave your cases here and the hubby will bring them up. Me and him have run this place for years. So we know how to make our guests comfortable. Had a pleasant journey did you? Well, isn't that nice! And already feeling the benefit of our good salt air from the looks of you." She dug into her overalls pocket for a bunch of keys and hurried ahead of them up a flight of steep narrow stairs as Dickie and Foof produced incoherent replies. Woodcock and Fetch vouchsafed nothing at all.

"You young marrieds are to have this room." Mrs. Roscombe unlocked the door and handed Dickie the key. "There's a basin and wash jug, but you shouldn't have to wait over long to use the bathroom. We've only got three other guests booked in at the moment. There's Mr. and Mrs. Samuels that comes from the midlands, two doors down from you. They were here last year. And her cousin Miss Hastings is at the end of the hall. She just arrived. We often gets families here." Mrs. Roscombe beamed with pride. "We make things easy. That's what they like. The front door's always open so you never have to worry about taking a key out with you. And we don't fuss if people come down late for breakfast or get back late for the evening meal. You can have yours to-night as soon as you're ready."

"You don't object to our dog?" Dickie asked her.

"Not a bit! The hubby and I are proper softies when it comes to animals."

Fetch showed his appreciation by woofing in a manner that would have done credit to Uriah Heep. And Mrs. Roscombe pronounced him a dear little fellow, before saying she would show Woodcock to his room, which was directly across the hall from that of his employers. Foof and Dickie went inside to study their surroundings with determined cheerfulness. It wasn't what they were used to, but it was spotlessly clean with a mock-silk bedspread in the same dusky rose as the curtains, two elderly wardrobes, and a decent sized dressing table whose mirror made the room look a little larger than was actually the case. Moments later a stooped but smiling Mr. Roscombe appeared with their suitcases and the instant he departed Woodcock tapped and, upon entering, suggested that Mr. Ambleforth and Lady Felicity might wish to go downstairs while he unpacked for them.

"I expressed to Mrs. Roscombe my belief that you might not be adverse to a pot of tea, my lady."

"Dearest Woodcock!" Foof stood up from removing Fetch's lead. "You are a paragon among men."

"I've always known that," said Dickie, "but what I don't know—and what has my mind in a tweak, Woodcock, is who was that woman in the train? I'll be blowed if I haven't seen her somewhere before, and from the glint in your eye when you looked at her you were wondering the same thing."

"Her identity was not what had me in a quandary, sir. I recognized her when she entered the carriage. She is a Miss Hastings. Housekeeper to Sir Isaac Gusterstone. When he is in town, which is not often of late due to his advancing years, he resides in one of the flats across the street from your own. You have possibly noticed the woman at one time or another upon her entering or departing the building."

"I say!" Dickie exclaimed. "You're spot on, Woodcock! I have seen her. Passed her in the street a couple of times. Remember thinking she looked like someone who'd always lived a confoundedly dreary life, without a spark of happiness to call her very own. But if you weren't trying to remember who she was, Woodcock, what was it about her that had you puzzled in the train?"

"Only, sir, that she showed no sign of recognition on seeing me. And, although we are not well acquainted, we have spoken upon occasion."

"Perhaps she was startled to the point of confusion at seeing Dickie and me in a third-class compartment," suggested Foof.

"That is possible, my lady." Woodcock trod soundlessly across the floor to the suitcases. "However, I do not intend to repine upon the matter, especially as it is always possible that I may discover the reason during the course of our stay at the Sea Breeze."

"And just how is that likely?" Dickie asked him.

"Because, sir, as Mrs. Roscombe informed us Miss Hastings is also staying here. She is certainly a fast walker to have moved so far ahead of us up the hill. Of course, it is also possible that factors unknown to us lent wings to her feet. And now if you and your ladyship will excuse me, I will not further delay the unpacking."

Taking the hint, the honeymooners departed the room with Fetch at their heels. But when they reached the bottom of the stairs and Foof turned to remind the dog to be on his best behavior, meaning he was not to get any ideas about silver teaspoons, they discovered that he was gone. Racing back to their room, Dickie found Woodcock placidly stowing shirts in the gentleman's chest of drawers. The butler had not readmitted Fetch to the room, and he voiced the conviction that the door had been closed until Mr. Ambleforth reappeared. Even so, he searched under the bed and behind the curtains along with every other place where it was remotely possible that the dog might be hiding.

Woodcock then accompanied Dickie out into the hallway. All the other doors were shut except for the one at the far end. Assuming, correctly, that here was the bathroom, they went inside to discover a likely solution to Fetch's disappearance. The window overlooked a veranda, making it simplicity itself for Fetch to have jumped down onto its roof and from thence to the ground.

"A bit thick, wouldn't you say, Woodcock, for the little beggar to repay all Lady Felicity's kindness to him by bunking off at the first opportunity?" Dickie heaved a sigh. "But then again it's undoubtedly for the best. We would never have known what he would be up to next. One of these days we could have found ourselves charged as accessories before or after the fact when the police came banging on the door looking for the 'goods.' "

"There is that, sir."

"Yes, well, I'd better go down and break the news to the poor old bean. She wasn't particularly worried. Thought, like I did, that he'd gone back to our room. I wouldn't be surprised if she has an attack of the weeps when I spill the beans. That we are back to being a dogless couple after a day and a half of marriage."

Having geared himself up to break the news that would break his bride's heart, Dickie entered the sitting room with its seaweed colored chairs to find himself temporarily unable to get Foof's attention. She was being talked at by a middle-aged woman with bleached ash-blonde hair and protruding eyes seated across from her. Miss Hastings was also present and, but for the black sock she was darning, faded conveniently into the beige wallpaper.

"My husband—Mr. Samuels"—the woman's voice declared her to be from the midlands—"is a commercial traveler for Hartwoods' Hairbrushes. Their top seller. Of course it means he's gone from home a lot. And he's been complaining lately that he's not as young as he used to be. Says he's been getting some bad headaches. But as I keep telling him he only has to keep going for another fifteen years. After that he can sit back and enjoy the results of what we've accomplished during our very happy marriage." Mrs. Samuels paused just long enough for Foof to open her mouth, then was back in full flood. "And as I sometimes have to remind him, I've done my share in building us a nice little nest egg. Right from day one I've always handled the money. Paid all the bills. Bought his clothes, from suits to handkerchiefs. Decided what we could afford to spend on holiday. It means a lot being able to say—right down to the last safety pin—what's ours and what isn't."

Foof, catching sight of Dickie hovering in the doorway, was about to break in and introduce him, but Mrs. Samuels was off again, as relentless as a train that would not have attempted to stop had thirty people jumped on the line.

"But, as I like to say, there's a big difference between being careful and being mean. I've always seen that Mr. Samuels takes a packet of biscuits and a Thermos with him on his trips so that he doesn't have to bother about stopping in at some cafe where you don't know what the food's like. And I've always encouraged him to let my cousin Miss Hastings come on holiday with us each year to a nice place like this and help her out a bit with the price of the room. Isn't that right, Ethel?"

Mrs. Samuels finally drew a proper breath.

"What's that, Mavis?" Miss Hastings jerked forward in her chair, jabbing her finger with the darning needle.

"I was telling the young lady that we always take you on holiday with us."

"Not always." Miss Hastings dropped the darning bobbin and sock into the lap of her gray skirt and sucked at her injured finger. "If you remember, dear, you went to Margate without me twice." Her eyes shied away from her cousin's suddenly accusing glance. "But I am grateful, of course I am, for everything you and Leonard have done for me over the years."

"As you've tried to demonstrate, in your own funny way!" Mrs. Samuels gave a barking laugh that reminded Dickie that he still had to break the news to Foof about Fetch's disappearance. But the awful woman had finally spotted him. "Ah, here comes your husband by the looks of him, Mrs. Ambleforth. Mine still isn't back from having to go up to the head office this morning. Like as not it'll be late when he shows up. But you can't keep a man on a string all the time, can you? And I hope that years from now you're as happy with your man as I've been with Mr. Samuels. Not a morning gone by, including this one, that he doesn't say how he worships the ground I walk on."

"How lovely." Foof got to her feet, introduced Dickie to the two women (Miss Hastings displaying no sign of having seen him on the train), and after he had shaken their hands, she said that it looked as though her husband wanted a word with her. Following him out into the hall, she closed the door, tiptoed away from it, then put her arms around his neck and kissed him passionately. "Darling, promise you won't let me turn into that sort of wife. Wasn't she too ghastly for words? No wonder poor Miss Hastings looks like everyone's poor relation. I'm sure Mrs. Samuels only brings her on holiday so she can rub her nose in the fact that she doesn't have a husband who is a top-selling commercial traveler."

"And woe betide Miss Hastings if she doesn't act properly grateful." Dickie kissed Foof back. "But let's forget about them, old bean! There is something I have to tell you. A blot on the old honeymoon I'm afraid." Whilst speaking he produced an impeccable white handkerchief from his pocket and Foof made full use of it upon being gently informed that Fetch would seem to have disappeared from their lives as speedily as he had entered them.

"Oh, the poor darling! How we must have failed him!"

"Fudge!" Dickie placed a husbandly arm around her quivering shoulders. "That dog knew we expected him to turn his life around and he probably thought we would make him go to the sort of meetings that helped Woodcock's cousin Bert see the light."

"But I was sure he was growing fond of us." Foof sobbed harder.

"We'll get you another dog."

"There'll never be another Fetch."

"Chin up, old bean!" Dickie returned the drenched handkerchief to his pocket. "Let's go and find Mrs. Roscombe. You'll feel better after you've eaten, and then we'll go for a walk before it gets too dark for us to find our way back."

Unable to offer an alternative to this sensible scheme, Foof agreed with wifely submission. In the dining room at the back of the house they partook of cold beef, salad, thick bread and butter and cheeses. Afterwards Dickie went back to their room to fetch a coat for her. And they set out to walk along the cliffs under silky gray skies, upon which the moon appeared to be pinned like a crescent-shaped brooch. Now that Foof had rallied from the immediate shock of losing Fetch she became annoyed with herself and Dickie.

"We should have gone looking for him at once."

"What would have been the point? He would only have run off again at the first opportunity."

"Perhaps you didn't want to find him."

"That's not true." To his surprise Dickie realized he meant what he said. It was a rum go, but there it was. In a few meager hours he had developed a sneaking fondness for the little dog. Being a stuffy sort of fellow himself he couldn't help but admire Fetch's audacity. "You never know, he may still come back," he said, upon their walking back to the house.

Neither of them held out any real hope. And when they returned to their room there was no Fetch. Foof picked up her sponge bag from the dressing table where Woodcock had placed it, draped a towel and her dressing gown over her arm, and went along to the bathroom to wallow in a good cry and, mindful that she must not keep the other guests waiting, a quick soak. On her way back to her room she passed Miss Hastings, who was in her turn heading for the bathroom. Her face was puffy as if she too, had been crying. Another indication that the woman was in an agitated state of mind was that she had not properly closed the door to her room. Let alone lock it. But of course this wasn't London where people were inclined to be more cautious in safekeeping their property. Also, besides herself, Dickie, and Woodcock, the only other guests were Miss Hastings's cousin. And the husband who had possibly yet to return.

Telling herself that if she didn't watch out she would turn into a meddlesome matron, Foof entered her room to find Woodcock pouring Dickie a brandy from the bottle he had brought with him and listening to his employers detailed account of what Mrs. Samuels had been saying in the sitting room.

"A fiercely controlling woman, sir, by the sound of it." The butler turned to inquire if her ladyship also desired a nightcap. He was interrupted when the door that Foof, like Miss Hastings, had left ajar was nudged open. Fetch came scurrying into the room with a mushroom-shaped object clamped between his teeth and a black sock dangling to the ground. Sitting back on his haunches, he dropped his loot at Foof's feet and uttering a prideful bark, cocked his head to one side, the better to view her appreciation.

"I say!" Dickie looked stricken. "He's well and truly gone back to his old tricks."

"It would appear so." Woodcock bent to pick up the darning bobbin and sock. "But one does find cause to wonder, sir, why—when the dog has been trained to snatch gentlemen's wallets, ladies' purses, and other commodities of value—he would present these homely items to her ladyship. And look so proud of himself."

"Perhaps he couldn't find Miss Hastings's purse," Foof felt compelled to say.

"I would think it doubtful she has any jewelry worth the taking lying around in her room," said Dickie. "And, potty as it sounds, I haven't a doubt in the world that Fetch knows the difference between the real article and paste."

"It is indeed a puzzle." Woodcock continued to stand with the bobbin and sock in his hands.

"Well, no real harm is done," Foof scooped Fetch into her arms. "Surely Miss Hastings won't make too much fuss when we return her property and explain that Fetch can be a little mischievous at times." She was prevented from continuing when a scream erupted from somewhere close-by. Such was its volume that the bed seemed to lift off the ground and Fetch wrapped his paws around Foof's neck, as she exclaimed, "Miss Hastings is going to make a fuss after all."

Woodcock put the bobbin and sock into his jacket pocket. Then the four of them—Fetch being still attached to Foof like a fox stole—poured out into the hallway and found themselves moments later standing not in Miss Hastings's room, but that of her cousin, Mrs. Samuels. A man wearing a business suit lay on the bed. Face down. And if he wasn't a corpse, he was doing a very good job of acting the part. Miss Hastings was cowering by the foot rail, whilst Mrs. Samuels stood in the middle of the room, her face as bleached out as her ash-blond hair. Swaying like a tree in winter.

"Somebody get a doctor," she shouted as Mr. and Mrs. Roscombe arrived. "I think my husband's dead. I just walked in to find him like that. And I started screaming. It's such a shock. He was perfectly well this morning. But I suppose he must have felt ill, come back early, and lain down and had a heart attack."

"Yes, that must be it. Our poor, dear Leonard." Miss Hastings wept into her hands.

"You telephone for the doctor," Mrs. Roscombe told her husband, flapping him out of the room with her skirts. "And while we're waiting, how about I make a pot of tea? A cuppa will do you good, Mrs. Samuels, and you too, Miss Hastings."

"If I may be pardoned the liberty of making the suggestion." Woodcock inclined his head toward Dickie. "I believe it advisable that the police also be summoned."

"Now why do you say that?" Mrs. Roscombe sounded all of a splutter.

"Because of the possibility that Mr. Samuels did not meet his death from natural causes."

"But what else could it have been?" His widow looked suitably bewildered. "I told you that it must have been his heart."

"Indeed, Madam." Woodcock wore his most impassive face. "You voiced your view of the situation in a remarkably articulated manner for a woman in the full force of grief. I think we all received a clear picture of your husband returning to the premises and letting himself in through the unlocked front door. At an hour earlier than you had expected him. So that you were unaware until moments ago of his presence. But, for reasons that I would prefer not to discuss until the arrival of the police, I believe that something more sinister than a heart attack is afoot here."

"I'm sure I don't know what you can be getting at," said Mrs. Roscombe. "Poor Mrs. Samuels, as if you aren't going through enough as it is! Still, there's no choice is there? When there's talk of foul play—even if it's from someone that maybe just wants to make himself feel important." She gave Woodcock a doubtful look. "We've got to send for the police."

After hustling her husband through the door with a barrage of instructions on what to say when he got through to the station, Mrs. Roscombe went to stand alongside Mrs. Samuels. Not budging until some ten minutes later, when the door again opened and the doctor and a uniformed policeman crowded in upon them.

"Now, now! What's all this?" rumbled the constable.

"Some amateur trying to do my job for me?" The doctor cocked an irritated eyebrow.

"I am Mr. Richard Ambleforth and this is my wife, Lady Felicity." Dickie spoke out with the full force of a man who only travels in third-class train carriages by choice. "This is our butler," Dickie continued, clapping a hand on Woodcock's shoulder. "And I strongly urge you to listen to what he has to say because he is a man of vast mental resources."

"Is that so?" The doctor looked up from examining the body. "Go on, enlighten us. Explain how this man died."

"Very good, sir. It is possible I am grievously in error." Woodcock did not sound or look as though he thought this likely. "However, it is my supposition that Mr. Samuels has been stabbed. Most likely in the back."

"I don't see a carving knife sticking out of him." The constable was becoming more visibly annoyed by the second.

"Assuming I am correct in my suspicions, the murder weapon wasn't a knife. It was something much daintier. Most likely a hat pin. And it would have been removed from the body to be concealed here." Woodcock reached into his pocket and withdrew the darning bobbin.

"I don't understand." Foof clutched Fetch to her heart, which had begun to pound uncomfortably at the thought that the man Dickie most revered in the world was making an idiot of himself.

"You wouldn't, my lady," the butter spoke gently, "because you have never darned socks. But the majority of women have and, therefore, know that the handle unscrews." He proceeded to demonstrate. "It is hollow inside for the purpose of keeping the darning needles. And in this case"—looking down at the object he had shaken into his palm—"has been used as a receptacle for the weapon that was used to stab Mr. Samuels. It is either rusty, or still coated with his blood."

The widow screamed. "That's not just your darning bobbin, Ethel! The hat pin is yours, too. Why"—sagging into Mrs. Roscombe's arms—"would you take my husband's life, when we've both been so good to you?"

"Because she was in love with him," explained Woodcock at his most inexorable. "I venture to suggest that Mr.

Samuels has been expending quite a few nights with her when you thought he was on the road. Her employer, Sir Isaac Gusterstone, is not often at his London residence, so they would have had the place to themselves."

"It's all true!" Miss Hastings wrung her hands.

"And then this evening Mrs. Samuels mentioned in your presence and that of my employers that her husband never left home without telling her how much she meant to him. Words which understandably would be a blow to your pride, along with your faith in Mr. Samuel's affections."

"Leonard told me his home life was wretched. And why wouldn't I believe him, Mavis, after seeing how you treated him. Always pushing him to work harder, never caring that he was already worn to the bone." Miss Hastings lifted her head even as tears continued to ooze down her cheeks. "At first he would only come to the flat for a bite to eat, that wouldn't take money out of Mavis's pocket, but little by little it all came out. His feelings for me. That they'd been there for years. Building up stronger every time we went on holiday, which was only so you could have me to lug the deck chairs down to the beach, but I'd try to see that Leonard got a little peace. And even some happiness."

"And when you found out he'd been filling your head with lies you crept up here and stabbed him." At that moment Mrs. Samuels's face was not one that most men would have loved. She looked ready to wrestle her way out of Mrs. Roscombe's arms and charge across the room at her cousin. Fetch gave a whimper, indicating he was not nearly as hardened a soul as might be believed, and burrowed his face into Foof's neck.

"I've located the puncture wound." The doctor straightened up.

"You haven't explained where you found the bobbin."

The police constable scratched at his chin as he looked at Woodcock. "But it's lucky you did."

"Thank you." The butler inclined his head. "But it would have been introduced upon the scene without my participation. Am I not correct in that assumption, Mrs. Samuels?"

The room became very still.

"I don't know what you are talking about," she said at last.

"Ah, but I think you do." His voice rolled over her. "You used your cousin's hat pin to murder your husband and hid it in her darning bobbin, because not only did you want him dead, you wanted her to pay for the crime. Being a woman of enormous ego, I doubt you realized until tonight that the two of them were engaged in an affair. It was when you suddenly recognized the sock she was darning as his that you were assaulted with the truth. I imagine that you went up to your room shortly afterwards, possibly without addressing the issue with Miss Hastings, and found your husband lying face down asleep on the bed. I had arranged for a taxi to be waiting when my employers arrived at the railway station, but we were informed by a porter that a gentleman had arrived on an earlier train from Nottingham. He told the taxi driver that he was feeling unwell and was given a lift in our place. And given the fact that Mr. Samuels had been in Nottingham today it would appear probable that he was the gentleman in question."

"He always had a headache," his widow ground out the words.

"A problem that will not afflict Mr. Samuels in future," responded Woodcock mildly. "It is even to be hoped that he died instantly after you went into your cousin's room while she was still downstairs and appropriated her hat pin, which conveniently for you was smallish in size, providing you the idea of hiding it in the bobbin."

The widow didn't have it in her to attempt a denial. "He deserved to die," she spoke in a monotone, "after all I did to make us a decent life together. And I'm glad you will have time to suffer, Ethel."

"I think I'd better go and phone the station," said the constable. "Detective Inspector Wilcox is going to be fascinated." Scratching at his chin as he looked at Woodcock. "To hear all the ins and outs of how you put all the pieces of evidence together."

"It wasn't difficult." The butler reached out to stroke Fetch between the ears. "I was fortunate, you see, in having the able assistance of someone who located the evidence and literally dropped it at our feet, isn't that so, Lady Felicity?"

"There's no other explanation, is there, Dickie?"

"None at all," he said, repressing the faint smile that didn't seem quite the thing under the circumstance. And then, horror of horrors, he heard what sounded ominously like his mother's voice down in the hall. Even Woodcock paled, but Foof rose to the occasion in wifely fashion.

"Last one out the bathroom window buys the first round at the pub," she whispered, to which Fetch responded with a delighted woof before diving between the constable's legs and out the door.

Poor Lincoln

"Barbara, darling! What a marvelous surprise!"

I was waiting to be seated for lunch at Harrods, no doubt looking conspicuously dowdy in my old navy blue coat, when I heard the rumble of an all-too-familiar voice and turned to see my ex-mother-in-law bearing down upon me. To my admittedly jaundiced eye she was a five-foot troglodyte, swaddled in a mink coat that, like the voice, was a couple of sizes too big for her. Several people, who were probably thinking about roast beef and Yorkshire pudding, stepped smartly aside to avoid being enveloped in her furry arms.

"It's been an age since I last saw you!" She took hold of my elbow, effectively preventing escape. "Darling!" The word vibrated off her tongue. "You must tell me every single, tiny detail of what's been happening in your life since you and Gerald went your separate ways." She elbowed aside two pleasant-faced women in tweeds who were having a nice talk about doing the flowers for their church altar. "It seems only yesterday, sweetie, but I suppose it must be three or . . . could it possibly be four? . . . years since the divorce."

"There's not a lot to tell, Cassandra," I replied, feeling like a talking wooden soldier.

"Mumsie, darling!" She clasped a pudgy hand (which flashed with enough diamonds to light up London during a power cut) to her mink bosom. "You really must go back to calling me Mumsie."

"I'm working at an art supplies and framing shop in Chelmsford," I told her. "Today is early closing, so I came up to have a browse around the shops." Then quickly, in order to forestall her asking whether there was a new man in my life, I inquired after her husband.

"Popsie? Rubbing along much as usual. He misses you, of course, quite dreadfully." Her voice throbbed with emotion. "Only this morning he said to me, 'I do hope that gal Gerald was married to finds some decent chap to . . .' "

"And what about your mother, how is she doing?" Here my interest was not entirely fabricated. I had been rather fond of the old lady, who was a kindly, comfortable sort of person who looked the way grandmothers used to look before they started joining health clubs and wearing miniskirts.

"I'm sorry to say, Barbara, darling"—emotion played havoc with the lines on Mumsie's face—"that Grandma began to let herself go after turning eighty last year. It was quite a shock, really, when Popsie and I realized she couldn't continue living alone in that house in Warley."

"Oh, I am sorry," I said. "Did you bring her to live with you?"

"Darling, much as I longed to do so, it just wouldn't have worked." Monumental sigh. "Popsie and I are always on the go, a month or two in the London flat, then off to the house in Devon, and after that away to our sweet little villa in Florence. All things considered, I'm sure we made the best possible decision about Grandma."

"Which was?" I asked, hoping I wasn't going to hear that Grandma had been put to sleep.

"To have Lincoln move in with her, darling!" Mumsie patted my arm. "I don't suppose Gerald talked about him much. We're only distantly related, cousins two or three times removed. You know the sort of thing. And of course Lincoln is older than Gerald. In his fifties at least. Rather a shy sort of man, which naturally wasn't helped by his getting into that spot of bother."

"No, I don't suppose so!" I didn't try very hard to sound interested. Five minutes in Mumsie's company had always been more than enough for me, and I was now determined not to get stuck lunching with her. I would have to escape to the powder room, before the dreaded words "A table for two?" rang in my ears.

"People tend to be so judgmental. Don't you think so, Barbara?" Mumsie gave a lighthearted chuckle. "As if we all haven't made the occasional mistake along the way. Really, one's heart breaks for Lincoln. I'm sure it must be the easiest thing in the world for an accountant to make a mistake with his adding up or taking away and be accused of fiddling the books. To send a man to prison for a little slip of the pencil—well, it doesn't seem right, does it, darling?"

I was speechless, but that was all to the good. Mumsie was now in full flood. "As I said to Popsie and Gerald, it's like living under the Gestapo. But thanks to some exertion on my part, things have worked out. Grandma couldn't be happier having Lincoln in the house, he is devoted to her, and my mind is at ease."

"It's certainly a solution," I agreed.

"The ideal one, if I do say so myself." Mumsie removed a powder compact from her alligator handbag and snapped it open to inspect her face in the mirror. "There's no need for you to worry, sweetie, that Grandma's fondness for Lincoln might lead her to do something silly like leaving everything to him, and us in the lurch. It can't happen—trust me, Barbara!" Her voice dropped several octaves and she popped the compact back into her bag. "The money, the house, and all important pieces of jewelry come to me by way of a trust my father set up years before he died. The only items Grandma has leave to dispose of as she chooses are the household furnishings. Believe me, there are no valuable antiques, darling! Absolutely nothing I'd want from that house in Warley. Indeed, I encouraged Grandma to leave the lot to Lincoln." Mumsie did an excellent job of looking magnanimous. "He can sell everything when the time comes or take some of it with him when he moves into a boardinghouse, or wherever he goes."

I took the dismissive tone in Mumsie's voice to indicate that she was done with the topic of Lincoln. But I quickly realized that, having succeeded in claiming my full—one might say stunned—attention, she was also done with me. In the twinkling of an eye she had spotted a tall woman in a flowerpot hat and lots of flowing scarves exiting the restaurant.

"Darling, it's been delightful—indeed, one might say it was meant to be. Fate and all that sort of thing! But I mustn't be selfish and keep you when I'm sure you're meeting someone." So saying, Mumsie blew me a haphazard kiss and charged toward her new prey, furry arms extended, diamonds flashing. "Lady Worksop-Smythe! How absolutely marvelous!"

From the back Mumsie looked more than ever like a bear who had escaped from the zoo, and I was left with the disoriented feeling that comes with abruptly imposed freedom. Should I proceed to have lunch here as planned and risk hearing rumbles of that familiar voice emanating from behind every potted plant? Or should I plan on an early-afternoon tea and meanwhile take a look around the housewares department?

It wouldn't have surprised Gerald, who had often criticized me for acting on impulse, that ten minutes later I was in my car edging out into bumper-to-bumper traffic. I told myself that I was simply no longer in the mood for an afternoon at Harrods, that I would go directly home to Chelmsford and share a boiled egg with my cat, Sunny. But before I had gone through the first traffic light I knew that I was going to see Grandma.

She lived in a house called Swallows Nest, set well back from the road behind a tall hedge, in Warley, which was no distance at all from where I lived. Unfortunately, I took a couple of wrong turns after exiting the motorway, and relief was uppermost in my mind when I negotiated the last bend in the tree-shaded drive. But as I climbed from the car onto the broad concrete sweep, I did have second thoughts about appearing in true long-lost-relative fashion on the doorstep.

It would have been politer and made more sense to phone in a day or two, if I still felt the urge. Why had I conjured up a picture of Grandma wilting away in bed while this Lincoln person who was supposed to be looking after her sat frozen in an armchair, mourning his fall from grace? Probably because Gerald had been right in accusing me of having too much imagination. In all likelihood, Lincoln was a perfectly sensible man who enjoyed living a normal life once more. And in appreciation, he would always make sure that Grandma knew where to find her slippers and never lacked for a hot meal or was left to sit by a dying fire.

The house certainly looked reassuring. Autumn flowers bloomed in the well-tended beds and, although a stiff breeze rustled the trees, the sky was clear. Afternoon sunlight stippled the rose-colored bricks with gold and sparkled on the latticed panes of the dormer windows that jutted out from the steeply pitched roof. Slipping the car keys into my coat pocket, I squared my shoulders and mounted the stone steps to the front door. The knocker was in the shape of a swallow, and I rapped it briskly, suddenly eager to see Grandma again and make Lincoln's acquaintance.

Several moments passed, and I was about to beat another tattoo when the door opened a cautious crack.

"Who is it?" came the hesitant inquiry.

"Barbara," I replied in my most non-threatening voice. "Do you remember? I was married to your grandson Gerald."

"Oh, what a lovely surprise." Grandma opened the door wide and ushered me into a hall with a dark oak staircase running up one side. "And how very kind of you to come and see me." She looked the way I remembered, a solidly built, white-haired old lady. The intervening four years had taken no visible toll, I thought as she hung my coat on the hall tree. If anything, she seemed to move more briskly. Really, she was amazing for over eighty. I explained about meeting her daughter at Harrods and apologized for coming on the spur of the moment.

"I'm glad you did, dear. I've often thought of you." She smiled kindly at me. "Tell me, did Gerald let you keep the cat when you divorced?"

"Yes, I have her," I said, feeling extremely touched that she remembered Sunny.

"Isn't that good!" She squeezed my hand. "I must say I've always been fond of cats myself. But I couldn't possibly have one now. It's a pity"—her voice dropped to a whisper—"but poor Lincoln is afraid of cats. And it's important to consider his feelings after everything he's been through."

Before I could respond, Grandma turned from me to glance over at the staircase. There was no one standing on its oak treads. But when my eye shifted to the open gallery above, I thought I saw a shadow edge around a corner of the back wall.

"I hope you'll get to meet Lincoln, he's such a dear." Grandma's face creased into a fond smile. "But you'll understand if he stays out of sight while you're here, won't you? He's such a sensitive man, shy to the point of being timid, one might say. But I'm sure my daughter told you all about him."

"Not a lot," I said. Which was true. Mumsie hadn't gone into details, such as on which side Lincoln parted his hair or whether he preferred cricket to soccer.

"Really it was very kind of Cassandra," Grandma was still looking up the stairs. "I mean—suggesting that Lincoln move in here so I wouldn't be alone if I ever needed a little help."

"Very thoughtful," I said.

"So much nicer than putting me in a home."

And probably a lot cheaper, I thought, as Grandma took hold of my elbow and shepherded me down the hall.

"I've told my daughter I bless the day she came up with the idea. Dear Lincoln has been such a gem. Nothing is ever too much trouble. Would you believe he went out this afternoon even with that nasty wind blowing? Just to buy some pots of paint because he wants to give the dormer windows a fresh coat inside and out. I told him it wasn't necessary and we don't have a ladder, but I'm sure he's hanging out of a window painting away for dear life at this very moment." There was a suspicion of a break in her voice as Grandma led the way into a large sitting room.

This was made cozy by dusky-rose walls and faded mole-colored velvet curtains. The furnishings were comfortably old-fashioned, with lots of dark wood and plenty of roomy seating.

"Why don't you take this one, Barbara?" She patted the back of an armchair and while she was settling herself across from me I looked at the picture of horses pulling a hay cart along a country lane above the mantelpiece, very much aware that on the bookcase to my left there were several photos of Mumsie and Popsie and, inevitably, my ex-husband. "I'm so sorry about the divorce," said Grandma.

"Don't be." I undid the top buttons of my cardigan because the central heating at Swallows Nest was more than adequate. "Gerald and I weren't at all suited, and I'm enjoying my new life."

"That's good to hear. And, you know, Barbara, I've always been inclined to think that bad things so often happen for a reason." Grandma sat comfortably, hands folded in her wide lap, nodding her head wisely. "It's like that problem with the car, just a few months back."

"Really?" I said.

"Lincoln had taken me into town—he's so good about that sort of thing. Always so willing. I'd wanted to do a little shopping and decided we should stop at the bank first. It's right at the top of Queen Street, which is very steep. Always has been. Children used to go sledding down it in winter years ago." Grandma's face clouded. "Dear Lincoln, ever the gentleman! He leaped out of the car the moment it was at a standstill so as to race around and open my door. And I don't know how it happened (perhaps the hand brake slipped), but suddenly the car took off at breakneck speed down the hill."

"What a dreadful thing!" My hand went to my throat as I pictured the scene.

"Dreadful is the word. Poor, dear Lincoln! He was absolutely beside himself when he reached me. Couldn't hold back the tears even though I kept telling him I was as right as rain. Not so much as a bump or a scrape because, miraculously, the car had swung into a curve at the bottom of the hill and come to a standstill within inches of a shop window. I told Lincoln he had absolutely nothing to reproach himself for; accidents, as we all know, will happen."

"Absolutely," I agreed, letting out a breath.

"It seems to me that what we must do is learn from these experiences." Grandma looked pensive. "And of course what I discovered that day is that I have never known, will never know, anyone of Lincoln's sweetness and deep sensitivity. And does he ever put me to shame." She got to her feet. "Here I am talking your ear off, Barbara, when you must be longing for a cup of tea."

I protested that I wasn't in need of refreshment, but Grandma took off, back into the hall, and I found myself trotting at her heels. The kitchen, like the sitting room, had obviously not been done up in years—the appliances were at least thirty years old—but there was the same feeling of easy livability. Grandma soon had the kettle filled and began rattling about with cups and saucers. "Such a nasty drive down from London, all that heavy traffic and never knowing when it might come on to rain." She added a sugar bowl and milk jug to the tea tray. "And sometimes when you're shopping there isn't time to stop and eat. I often used to plan on having lunch at Harrods when I went up to town, but something always seemed to get in the way."

"It so often does," I replied.

"Meaning you haven't had a thing to eat since setting out this morning." Grandma made soft clucking noises as she filled the teapot. "And I'm sure a piece of fruitcake won't bridge the gap. How would it be," she said, peering into a cupboard, "if I opened a tin of soup and heated that up for you? I've got tomato if you like that."

"It's my favorite," I assured her, knowing I shouldn't put her to the trouble but suddenly aware that I was very hungry.

"Mushroom was always my favorite." Grandma had produced a saucepan and was making headway with the tin opener, her expression intent. "But of course I could never have it in the house again, not after what happened. Oh, it was the saddest thing! Seeing poor Lincoln so upset. Of course I told him he mustn't blame himself, but there was no getting through to him."

"What happened?" I asked, availing myself of a chair.

"It was all out of the goodness of his heart." Grandma paused in the act of putting the saucepan on the stove to wipe away a tear that plopped down on her cheek. "Knowing how fond I was of mushroom soup—really, it was my fault for always going on about it—he went to all the trouble of making some, using proper stock and everything. You wouldn't believe the hours he spent stirring away. And the dear man doesn't even like mushrooms, never eats anything with them in it. You would have been so touched, Barbara, if you had seen Lincoln ladling that soup into my bowl and hovering over me like an anxious mother as I took my first spoonful."

"Was it good?" I didn't know what else to say.

"Oh, delicious, so much better than the tinned stuff!" Grandma came round to the table with my tomato soup. "And really, when my tummy started hurting afterward it wasn't all that bad. It just seemed to make sense to send for the doctor and by the time he got here I was in bed. Well, I'm never one to stay up late at the best of times, but of course Lincoln got himself worked up to a froth, even though Doctor Wicker said I was the most resilient old woman he'd ever looked after. A positively amazing constitution, is what he said, and that I would be as right as rain in the morning." Grandma interrupted herself to ask if I would like a slice of bread and butter with my soup, but I declined, no longer feeling quite as hungry. "Poor Lincoln, he just couldn't restrain his sobs," she continued, "and it was days before I saw the glimmer of a smile from him. Doesn't that just break your heart?" She sat down across from me.

I managed to nod my head and continued spooning away at my soup, without really tasting it, until the bowl was empty. After that, I asked Grandma how long it had been since Mumsie, Popsie, or Gerald had come down to see her. But it was clear she didn't want to discuss them, either because I had rubbed a nerve or because she wanted to get back to talking about Lincoln.

"I do wish he'd come down for a cup of tea." Grandma glanced upwards as if hoping a foot would tentatively appear through the ceiling. "But he's just so shy. I think it comes," she smiled mistily, "from his once having spent quite a time cooped up with strangers."

"Cassandra did mention something about that," I began, only to be kindly but firmly cut off.

"Yes," Grandma permitted herself a grimace as she gave the contents of the teapot a stir before filling our cups, "I'm sure Cassandra has told a whole lot of people, but I can't see that poor Lincoln has any reason to feel ashamed. A lot of boys can't settle at boarding school and want to go home to their mothers. He told me all about it. I remember the evening." Her voice grew reminiscent. "We had such a lovely time chatting by the fire. It was the perfect night for that sort of thing. The rain hadn't stopped all day and it was so cozy with the curtains drawn and our mugs of cocoa in our hands. Such a shame that afterward there was that unfortunate little incident with the lift."

"The what?" I was beginning to think that there was no keeping up with Grandma.

"Dear Lincoln had suggested we have one put in." She spooned sugar into her tea. "He was so worried about my using the stairs, especially the ones down to the cellar—even after I told him I never go down there anymore. Luckily, we didn't have to knock the house about when having the lift installed. There was an alcove in the hall and another directly above it on the landing, right next to my bedroom, just suited to the purpose. And there was loads of room in the cellar, seeing that I only use it to store odds and ends. Even so, I'm sure it would have been a much more expensive proposition if Lincoln hadn't worn himself to the bone doing most of the work himself." Grandma's eyes had misted over. "Was there ever anyone more thoughtful?"

"Probably not." I knew I didn't sound one hundred percent convinced.

"Despite everything Dr. Wicker said, about my being as healthy as a woman half my age, there was no talking away Lincoln's anxieties, and so I agreed to the lift. And I must say I really did enjoy the luxury of being taken up and down in style, until that night—the one when we had such a lovely fireside chat." Her voice cracked. "Lincoln was pushing me in the wheelchair . . ."

"Why the wheelchair?"

"Again, that was dear Lincoln being protective." Grandma refilled my cup. "He decided I would recover faster from that business with the mushroom soup if I kept right off my feet. Dr. Wicker said I had bounced back like a two-year-old and what I needed was more, not less, exercise. But the important thing in my eyes was to make sure Lincoln didn't make himself ill worrying about me."

"You were saying," I prompted, "that he was pushing you in the wheelchair one evening . . ."

"Yes, across the hall to the lift." Grandma nodded. "The doors opened, just like always, and Lincoln sang out, 'Heave Ho!' as he always did. Only this time the lift wasn't there—or the floor wasn't—if you know what I mean, Barbara!"

"I think I get the picture!"

"I'm ashamed to say I screamed." Grandma gave a rueful

shake of her head. "The panic of the moment! And really it was nothing more than a moment, because the instant the front wheels started to tip, I reached up and grabbed hold of the rim, or whatever you call it, above the doors. It was like clinging to the mast of a tiny boat that was being blown about in high winds. Really, rather a thrill for a woman of my age." Grandma smoothed back a strand of white hair that had inched over her left eye. "It so happens, Barbara, that I was quite a gymnast in my youth, so there wasn't any real danger of my falling. All it took was a good swing, forward and back, and then a jump to the safety of the hall floor."

"You could have been killed!"

"Oh, no, there was never any danger of that, I'm sure," Grandma replied briskly. "What bothered me was realizing that while everything was happening I didn't give a thought to poor Lincoln and how awful it must have been for his nerves when he heard the wheelchair crash into the cellar. It made the most unholy noise, although I can't say I was fully tuned in at the time. And then, of course, being Lincoln, he became so distressed that I thought I should have to send for an ambulance. Such a state he was in! Oh, it was piteous to hear him sob." Grandma dabbed at her eyes with her hanky. "And nothing I said could comfort him, not even when I told him that far from blaming him because the lift didn't work once in a while, I owed him more than I could ever hope to repay. His coming to live with me has given me a whole new lease on life."

"But Grandma . . ." I began.

"Oh, dear, I have been droning on, Barbara," she said, sounding thoroughly embarrassed. "Keeping you sitting on a hard kitchen chair when you must be tired out from all the driving you've done today. Let's go back into the sitting room where it's comfortable." She was already bustling towards the hall door. "You can tell me more about what's been happening to you. Did you say you have a job?"

I wasn't sure whether I had or not, but I explained that I was working in a picture-framing and art supplies shop, and she responded with great enthusiasm.

"Well, if that isn't a coincidence, Barbara," she said as I followed her into the sitting room. "I've a picture that I think would look better in a different frame. It's that one with the hay cart, hanging over the mantelpiece. Cassandra can't stand it; she calls it chocolate box art, but I've always liked Constable. And Lincoln is an ardent admirer."

"It is a nice print," I replied, looking up at the picture from the hearth rug.

"Oh, but it isn't a copy, dear." Grandma spoke matter-of-factly. "It's a proper painting. I had to sell all the family jewelry to pay for it. I suppose you could say that was wrong of me, because according to my late husband's will each and every bauble was to go to Cassandra after my day. But with all the jewelry she has accumulated I can't see how she could possibly wear any more. No, I really don't think I have to worry about Cassandra." Grandma settled herself comfortably in a chair. "She will do very well when my time comes."

"And she doesn't know that the Constable is genuine?" I remained standing motionless on the hearth rug.

"Not a suspicion." Grandma now sounded a little anxious. "And you won't say anything, will you, Barbara? I know it's an old lady's failing, talking too much. I haven't stopped since you got here, but I know I can trust you, dear, because you know my daughter and how she can be, well . . . a little difficult at times. That's why I had copies of the jewelry made—so that if Cassandra ever asked to see it there wouldn't be a scene. You do promise, dear, you won't let slip a word?"

"Of course," I replied, feeling like a villain, because surely it was my duty to make haste and report to Mumsie that not only had her mother recently suffered three life-threatening accidents, she also owned an extremely valuable painting that she just might have been persuaded to will, along the rest of the furnishings at Swallows Nest, to her faithful companion. Or was it possible Gerald had been right when he accused me of having an overactive imagination?

Grandma, seeing me still standing as if rooted to the spot, leaped to the conclusion that I was studying the clock on the mantelpiece. And she hastened to assure me that whilst she would have loved me to remain for hours, she did realize I had to drive home and was probably getting jumpy at the thought of leaving my cat unattended for so long. We therefore proceeded back into the hall and when passing alongside the staircase I again thought I saw a shadow figure go crouching around a corner of the open gallery above.

"Oh, I do so wish you'd got to meet Lincoln," Grandma said as we went out the front door and down the steps. "I just know the two of you would have hit it off like a house afire, but you'll understand from everything I've said, Barbara, that being so painfully shy and sensitive, he prefers to stay in the background."

We were now standing alongside my car and I, at a loss for words, nodded agreement while looking back towards the house that presented such a safe and cheerful face to the world. Following my glance, Grandma perhaps thought I was admiring the flowerbed under the sitting room window. At any rate, she asked if I could spare a few moments to take a look at her chrysanthemums, which had been extraordinary this year. And after that, everything happened in a rush of merging shapes and colors.

One of the dormer windows set in the steeply pitched roof

opened, and within its framework appeared the top half of a man holding something in his hands. The chill that crept down my spine was explained by the breeze that was already plucking at my hair. I can't say I experienced a sense of impending disaster. It wasn't until I saw the figure squeeze itself half out of the window and drop a gallon pot of paint, that I dredged up speed I did not know I possessed, threw my arms around Grandma, and dragged her to safety before the thing landed on her head. What came next seemed to happen in comic slow motion. The figure at the window had leaned out too far for personal safety and now came sliding spread-eagled, and without making a sound, down the roof to land face down on the concrete.

And I stood there in my dowdy navy blue coat, staring at the inert huddle, waiting for a foot to move or a hand to twitch. But even his hair lay perfectly still. At last Grandma freed herself from my protective arm and took half a dozen tottering steps to stand looking down at him. "Oh," she said in a broken voice, "poor Lincoln!"

The High Cost of Living

"They're not coming!" Cecil said for the fourth time, peering out into the rain-soaked night. The gale had whipped itself into a frenzy, buffeting trees and shaking the stone house like a dog with a rag doll. On that Saturday evening the Willoughbys—Cecil and his sister, Amanda—were in the front room, waiting for guests who were an hour late. The fire had died down and the canapés on their silver tray were beginning to look bored.

"They're not coming!" mimicked Amanda from the sofa, thrusting back her silver-blonde hair with an irritable hand. "Repeating oneself is an early sign of insanity . . . remember?"

Her eyes, and those of her brother, shifted ceilingward.

"Cecil, I regret not strangling you at birth. Stop hovering like a leper at the gate. Every time you lift the curtain an icy blast shoots up my skirt."

A shrug. "I've been looking forward to company. The Thompsons and Bumbells lack polish, but it doesn't take much to break the monotony in this morgue."

"Really, Pickle Face!" Amanda eyed a chip in her pearl pink manicure with disfavor. "Is that kind?"

"Speaking of kind"—Cecil let the curtain drop and adjusted his gold-rimmed spectacles—"I didn't much care for that crack about insanity. I take exception to jibes at Mother."

"Amazing!" Amanda wielded an emery board, her eyes on the prying tongues of flame loosening the wood fibers and sending showers of sparks up the chimney. "Where did I get the idea that but for the money, you would have shoved the old girl in a cage months ago? Don't hang your head. All she does is eat and—"

"You always were vulgar."

"And you always were forty-five, Cecily dear. How you love to angst, but spare me the bit about this being Mother's house and our being a pair of hyenas feasting off decaying flesh. That woman is not our mother. Father remarried because we motherless brats drove off every housekeeper within a week."

"Mary was good to us." Drawing on a cigarette with a shaking hand, Cecil sank into a chair.

"Brother, you have such a way with words. Mary had every reason to count her blessings. She acquired a roof over her head and a man to keep her warm in bed. Not bad for someone who was always less bright than a twenty-watt bulb."

"I still think some respect . . ." The cigarette got flung into the fire.

"Sweet Cecily"—Amanda buffed away at her nails—"you have deception refined to an art. I admit to living in Stepmother's house because it's free. Come on! These walls don't have ears. The only reason Mad Mary isn't shut up in a cracker box is because we're not wasting her money on one."

"I won't listen to this."

"Your sensitivity be damned. You'd trade her in for a used set of golf clubs any day of the week. Who led the way, brother, to see what could be done about opening up Father's trust? Who swore with his hand on the certificates of stock that Mary was *non compos mentis?* Spare me your avowals of being here to keep Mary company in her second childhood." Amanda tossed the emery board aside. "You wanted a share in Daddy's pot of gold while still young enough to fritter it away."

Cecil grabbed for the table lighter and ducked a cigarette toward the flame. "I believe he would have wished—"

"And I wish him in hell." Amanda tapped back a yawn. "Leaving his money tied up in that woman for life . . ."

"Mary was halfway normal when Father died. Her sister was the fly in the ointment in those days. Always meddling in money matters."

"Hush, brother dear." Amanda prowled toward the window and gave the curtain a twitch. "Is the storm unnerving you? I'm amazed we haven't had the old lady down to look for her paper dolls. For the record, I've done my turn of nursemaid drill this week. Mrs. Bridger didn't come in the last couple of days, and if I have to carry another tray upstairs I will need locking up."

Her brother stared into the fire.

"No pouting." Peppermint-pink smile. "Beginning to think, dear Cecily, that the world might be a better place if we treated old people the way we do our dogs? When they become a bother, shouldn't we put them out of everyone's misery? Nothing painful! I hate cruelty. A whiff of a damp rag and then deep, deep sleep . . . Oh, never mind! Isn't that the doorbell?"

Cecil stopped cringing to listen. "Can it be the Thompsons or the Bumbells?"

"Either them or the Moonlight Strangler." Amanda's voice chased him from the room. Hitching her skirt above the knee, she perched on the sofa arm. From the hall came voices.

"Terrible night! Sorry we're late. Visibility nil." A thud as the wind took the front door. Moments later an arctic chill preceded Cecil and the Thompsons into the room. Mrs. Thompson was shivering like a blancmange about to slide off the plate. Her husband, as thin as she was stout, was blue around the gills.

"Welcome." Amanda, crisp and sprightly, stepped forward. "I see you've let Cecil rob you of your coats. What sports to turn out on such a wicked night."

Mr. Thompson thawed. This was one hell of a pretty woman. He accepted a brandy snifter and a seat by the fire. His wife took sherry and stretched her thick legs close to the flames. That popping sound was probably her varicose veins.

"The Bumbells didn't make it." Norman Thompson spoke the obvious. "I told Gerty you wouldn't expect us, but she would have it that you'd be waiting and wondering."

"Our phone was dead," Gerty Thompson defended herself. "Heavens above!" Cheeks creasing into a smile. "Only listen to that wind and rain rattling the windows. Almost like someone trying to get in. I won't sleep tonight if it keeps up."

"She could sleep on a clothesline," came her husband's response.

"Refills?" Cecil hovered with the decanters.

Gerty held out her glass without looking at him. Staring at the closed door, she gave a squeaky gasp. "There's someone out in the hall. I saw the doorknob turn." Sherry slopped from glass.

Norman snorted. "You've been reading too many spookhouse thrillers."

"I tell you I saw—"

The door opened a wedge.

"Damn! Not now." Almost dropping the decanter, Cecil

grimaced at Amanda. "Did you forget her sleeping pills?"

An old lady progressed unsteadily into the room. Both Thompsons thought she looked like a gray flannel rabbit. She had pumice-stone skin and her nightdress was without color. Wisps of wintry hair escaped from a net and she was clutching something tightly to her chest. A child terrified of having her treasures snatched away.

"How do you do?" Gerty felt a fool. She had heard that old Mrs. Willoughby's mind had failed. On prior occasions when she and Norman had been guests here, the poor soul had not been mentioned, let alone seen. Meeting her husband's eye, she looked away. Amanda wore a faint smirk, as though she had caught someone drinking his finger bowl. Most uncomfortable. Gerty wished Norman would say something. He was the one who had thought the Willoughbys worth getting to know. The old lady remained marooned in the center of the room. A rag doll. One nudge and she would fold over. Why didn't someone say something?

Cecil almost tripped on the hearth rug. "Gerty and Norman, I present my stepmother, Mary Willoughby. She hasn't been herself lately. Not up to parties, I'm afraid. You never did like them, did you, Mother?" Awkwardly he patted Mrs. Willoughby's shoulder, then propelled her toward the Thompsons.

Gerty began shivering worse than when she was on the doorstep. "What's that you're holding, dear?" She had to say something—anything. The old lady's eyes looked dead.

An unreal laugh from Cecil. "A photo of her twin sister, Martha. They were very close; in fact, it was after Martha passed on last year that Mother began slipping. She always was the more dependent of the two. They lived together here after my father was taken."

"Sad, extremely sad." Mr. Thompson would have liked to

sit back down, but while the old lady stood there . . .

Nudging Cecil aside, Amanda slid an arm around Mrs. Willoughby. "Nighty-night, Mary, dear!" she crooned. "Up the bye-bye stairs we go."

"No." The old lady's face remained closed, tight as a safe. But her voice rose shrill as a child's. A child demanding the impossible. "I want Martha. I won't go to sleep without Martha."

"Poor lost soul!" Ready tears welled in Gerty Thompson's eyes. "What can we do? There must be something."

"Mind our own business," supplied her husband. He was regretting not keeping his relationship with the Willoughbys strictly business. They had been a catch as investors, money having flowed from their pockets this last year.

The old lady did not say another word. But everyone sensed it would take a tow truck to remove her from the room.

"I give up," Amanda said. "Let's skate the sweet lamb over to that chair in the bookcase corner. She won't want to be too near the fire and get overheated. I expect she feels crowded and needs breathing space. Look, she's coming quite happily now, aren't you, Mary?"

"Ah!" Gerty dabbed at her eyes with a cocktail napkin as Amanda tossed a rug over Mrs. Willoughby's knees. "She didn't want to be sent upstairs and left out of things. Being with the ones she loves is all she has left, I suppose."

"Yes, we are devoted to Mother," responded Amanda.

Mrs. Willoughby rocked mindlessly, her pale lips slack, the photo of her dead sister locked in her bony hands.

The others regrouped about the fire. Cecil poured fresh drinks and Amanda produced the tray of thaw-and-serve hors d'oeuvres. Rain continued to beat against the windows and the mantel clock ticked on self-consciously.

"We could play bridge, or do I hear any suggestions from

the floor?" Amanda popped an olive into her mouth, eyes on Norman Thompson.

"How about . . ." Gerty's face grew plumper and she fussed with the pleats of her skirt. Everyone waited with bated breath, for her to suggest Monopoly. ". . . How about a seance? Don't look at me like that, Norman. You don't have to be a crazy person to believe in the Other Side. And the weather couldn't be more perfect!"

Amanda set her glass down on the coffee table. "What fun! My last gentleman friend suspected me of having psychic powers when I knew exactly what he liked in the way of . . . white wine."

Cecil broke in. "I don't like dabbling in the Unseen. We wouldn't throw our doors open to a bunch of strangers were they alive—"

"Coward!" His sister wagged a finger at him. "How can you disappoint Gerty and Norman?"

Mr. Thompson forced a smile.

Gerty was thrilled. "Everything's right for communication. This house—with the wind wrapped all about it! What could be more ghostly? And those marvelous ceiling beams and that portrait of the old gentleman with side whiskers . . ." While she enthused the others decided the game table in the window alcove would serve the purpose. Amanda fetched a brass candlestick.

"Perfect!" Fearless leader Gerty took her seat. "All other lights must be extinguished and the curtains tightly drawn."

"I trust this experiment will not unsettle Mrs. Willoughby." Norman Thompson glanced over at the old lady seated in the corner.

"Let's get this over." Cecil was tugging at his collar.

"Lead on, Gerty." Amanda smiled.

"Very well. Into the driver's seat. All aboard and hold on

tight! Everyone at his own risk. Are we holding hands? Does our blood flow as one? Feel it tingling through the veins—or do I mean the arteries? I can never remember."

"My dear, lay an egg or get off the perch," ordered her husband.

Gerty ignored him. She was drawing upon the persona of her favorite fictional medium, the one in that lovely book *Ammie Come Home*. "Keep those eyes closed. No peeking! Let your minds float . . . drift, sway a little."

"I can't feel a damn thing," said Norman. "My leg's gone to sleep."

"The change in temperature! We're moving into a different atmosphere. We are becoming lighter. Buoyant! Are we together, still united in our quest? The spirits don't like ridicule, Norman."

"They'll have to lump it."

Amanda wiggled a foot against his. *Let's see if the old coyote is numb from the waist down.*

"Is anybody out there?" Madame Gerty cooed. "We are all friends here. With outstretched arms we await your coming."

Sounds of heavy breathing . . . the spluttering of the fire and a muffled snoring from the bookcase corner.

"Is there a message?" Gerty called. Only the wind and rain answered. The room was still, except for Norman, who was trying to shake his leg free of the cramp—or Amanda's teasing foot. The clock struck eleven. From outside, close to the front wall of the house, came the blistering crack of lightning. The whole house took a step backward. The table lurched toward the window. For a moment they all imagined themselves smashing through the glass to be swept away by the wind. Gerty went over with her chair, dragging Cecil down with her. The candle, still standing, went out.

It was agreed to call a halt to the proceedings.

"We must try another time." Gerty hoisted herself onto one knee and reached for her husband's hand. "I am sure someone was trying to reach me."

Amanda shivered. "My God, this place is an igloo."

"The fire's out." Cecil righted the chairs.

"Well, get it going again! I'm freezing solid. Someone stick a cigarette between my lips so I can inhale some heat."

"The trouble with your generation is, you have been much indulged. A little cold never hurt anyone. Leave those logs alone. They must last all winter. I am not throwing money on a woodpile."

The voice cracked through the room like another bolt of lightning, turning the Willoughbys—brother and sister—into a pair of dummies in a shop window. Norman Thompson sat down without meaning to, while Gerty resembled a fish trying to unswallow the hook. Otherwise the only movement came from the old lady in the corner. Even seated, she appeared to have grown. Her eyes burned in the parchment face. Glancing at the photo in her hands, she laid it down on the bookcase, tossed off her blanket, and stood up. "There has been a great deal of waste in this house lately." The voice dropped to a whisper but carried deep into the shadows.

"This extravagance will stop. When one is old, people tend to take advantage. It appears I must come out of retirement, get back in harness and pull this team."

Her face as ashen as her hair, Amanda stood hunched like an old woman. She and Cecil looked like brother and sister for once. They wore matching looks of horror—the way they had worn matching coats as children. As for the Thompsons, they resembled a pair of missionaries who, having wandered into a brothel, are unable to find the exit.

"Norman, dear, I think we should be running along; it is getting late . . ."

"We can get our own coats . . . Good night!" Husband and wife backed out the door. Never again would Gerty Thompson lift the mystic veil.

"Good night," echoed the voice of Mary Willoughby. "A pedestrian pair . . ." A pause, filled by the banging of the front door. "In future the decision as to who comes into this house is mine. I certainly do not enjoy entertaining in my nightdress, and more to the point . . ." The pale lips flared back. "You, Amanda and Cecil, are uninvited guests here. Don't forget. Whether you go or stay will depend on how we all get on together. A pity, but I don't think either of you can afford to live anywhere else at present. Gambling is your vice, Cecil. The corruption of the weak and indolent. I remember how you never wanted a birthday cake because you'd have to share it. As for you, Amanda, all you're good for is painting your nails and throwing up your skirts." A smile that turned the parchment face colder. "Neither of you are talking and I won't say much more tonight. I don't want to strain my voice. Tomorrow I will telephone lawyer Henry Morbeck and invite him out here—for the record. Your year of playing Monopoly is over. Your father left me control of his money and I want it back in my hands. The capital will come to you both one day, but bear in mind you may have quite a wait." Smoothing a hand over her forehead, Mrs. Willoughby removed the hair net and dropped it in the grate. "Good night, children. Don't stay up late; I won't have electricity wasted."

She was gone. They stood listening to her footsteps mounting the stairs. Finally a door on the second floor closed.

"It's not her!" Amanda pummeled a fist into her palm. "That creature—that monster—is not Mary."

Cecil grabbed for a cigarette, then could not hold his hand steady to light it. "That fool Thompson woman and her fun-

and-games seances. She unearthed this horror. We're talking possession. Someone else looked out of Mother's eyes. Something has appropriated her voice."

"We have to think." Amanda hugged herself for warmth. "We gave it entree, now we must find a way to be rid of it before it sucks the life out of us all. It will bleed the bank accounts dry. We'll be paupers at the mercy of an avenging spirit. We're to be made to pay for every unkind word and deed Mary has experienced at our hands."

"What do you suggest?" Cecil still had not lit the cigarette. "Do we tell the bank manager that should Mary Willoughby ask to see him, she is really a ghost in disguise?"

"We'll talk to Dr. Denver." Amanda was pulling at her nails. "He saw the condition Mother was in last week. He'll know something is crazy. He'll come up with a diagnosis of split personality or . . . some newfangled disorder. Who cares, so long as he declares her incompetent."

"He won't." With a wild laugh Cecil broke his cigarette into little pieces and tossed them onto the dead fire. "He'll opt for a miracle, and why shouldn't he? Is anything less believable than the truth?"

"Do you never stop kidding yourself?" The words were screamed. "We all know who she is, and we know why she has come back. So if you can't answer the question how to be rid of her, kindly shut up. I'll die of cold if I remain in this ice chest. Let's go to bed."

"I'll sleep in a chair in your room," offered Cecil.

"Some protection you'd be. At the first whisper of her nightdress down the hall you'd turn into a giant goose bump." Amanda opened the door. "Remember, she's seeing Morbeck tomorrow."

They huddled up the stairs like sheep, making more than

usual of saying good night before separating into their rooms. After a while the murmur of footsteps died away and the lights went out, leaving the house to itself and the rasping breath of the storm. The stair treads creaked and settled, while the grandfather clock in the hall locked away the minutes . . . the hours. The house listened and waited. Only the shadows moved until, at a little after three, came the sound of an upstairs door opening . . . then another . . .

Early the next morning Dr. Denver received a phone call at his home.

"Doctor, this is Amanda Willoughby!" Hysteria threatened to break through her control. "There's been the most dreadful accident. It's Mother! She's fallen down the stairs. God knows when it happened . . . sometime during the night! We think she may have been sleepwalking! She was very worked up earlier in the evening . . . Please, please hurry!"

The doctor found the door of Stone House open and entered the hall, pajama legs showing under his raincoat. Dripping water and spilling instruments from his bag, he brushed aside the brother and sister to kneel by the gray-haired woman sprawled at the foot of the stairs.

"Oh, Lord!" Cecil pressed his knuckles to his eyes. "I can't bear to look. I've never seen anyone dead before. This bloody storm. If she screamed, we would have thought it the wind! I did hear a . . . thump around three a.m. but thought it must be a tree going down in the lane . . ."

"These Victorian staircases are murder." The doctor raised one of Mrs. Willoughby's eyelids and dangled a limp wrist between his fingers. "One wrong step and down you go."

Amanda's eyes were bright with tears. "Our one hope, Dr. Denver, is that she died instantly."

"My dear girl." He straightened up. "Mrs. Willoughby is not dead."

"What?" Cecil staggered onto a chair that wasn't there and had to grip the banister to save himself from going down. His sister looked ready to burst into mad laughter.

"Your stepmother is in a coma; there is the possibility of internal injuries and the risk of shock." The doctor folded away his stethoscope. "Shall we say I am cautiously optimistic? Her heart has always been strong. Mr. Willoughby, fetch your sister a brandy. And how about taking this photo. Careful, old chap, the glass is smashed."

"She was holding on to it for dear life when she fell . . . I suppose," Cecil said in an expressionless voice.

Denver stood up. "Get a new frame and put it by her bed. Amazing what the will to live can accomplish. Ah, here comes the ambulance . . ."

Two weeks later the setting was a hospital corridor. "Often the way with these will-o'-the-wisp old ladies!" Henry Morbeck, lawyer, ignored the no-smoking sign and puffed on his pipe. "They harbor constitutions of steel. Had a word with Dr. Denver this morning and he gave me to understand that barring any major setbacks, Mrs. Willoughby will live."

Amanda tapped unvarnished nails against her folded arms. "Did he tell you she has joined the ranks of the living dead?"

Mr. Morbeck puffed harder on his pipe. "I understand your frustration. She remains unconscious, even though the neurologists have been unable to pinpoint a cause. Small comfort to say that such cases . . . happen. The patient lapses into a coma from which not even the most advanced medical treatment can rouse him."

"They say Mary could linger for years." Cecil's voice barely rose above a whisper. "She looked older, but she is only in her early sixties. What do you think, Henry?" Desperate for some crumb of doubt.

"My friend, I am not a doctor. And remember, doctors are not God. With careful nursing and prayers for a miracle . . . well, let's wait and see." Mr. Morbeck cleared his throat and got down to business. "Since this hospital does not provide chronic patient care, the time comes to find the very best nursing home. Such places are extraordinarily expensive, but not to worry. Mrs. Willoughby is secure. Your far-seeing father provided for such a contingency as this."

Silence.

"The bank, as co-trustee, is empowered to arrange for her comfort and care no matter what the cost. The house and other properties will be sold."

"Oh, quite, quite." Cecil knew he was babbling. "We had hoped to take Mother back to Stone House and care for her ourselves."

"I love nursing." Amanda knew she was begging.

"Out of the question." The lawyer tapped out his pipe in a plant stand and left it stuck there. "Your devotion to Mrs. Willoughby is inspiring, but you must now leave her and the finances in the hands of the professionals. Take comfort that the money is there. She keeps her dignity and you are not burdened. You have my assurance I will keep in close touch with the bank." He pushed against a door to his left. "I'll go in with you and . . . take a look at her."

The three of them entered a white, sunlit room. The woman in the railed bed could have been a china doll hooked up to a giant feeding bottle.

"She would seem at peace," Mr. Morbeck said.

There must be something we can do, Amanda thought. It

always sounds so easy. Someone yanks out the plug and that's that.

Nothing to pull, Cecil thought wearily. She's existing on her own. No artificial support system other than the IV and no damned doctor is going to starve a helpless old woman.

She has no business being alive, Amanda thought as she gripped the rail. She should be ten feet under, feeding the grubs instead of feeding off us. "Cecil, let's get out of here." She didn't care what the lawyer thought. "And if I ever suggest coming back, have me committed."

Alone with the patient, Mr. Morbeck quelled a shiver and clasped the leaden hand. "Mary Willoughby, are you in there?" His voice hung in the air like a bell pull, ready to start jangling again if anyone breathed on it. And Mary Willoughby was breathing—with relish. Had Mr. Morbeck been a man of imagination he would have thought the pale lips smiled mischievously. Eager to be gone, he turned and saw that the woman in the photo by the bed seemed to be laughing back. Mary's twin sister, Martha. Or was it . . . ? Mr. Morbeck had always had trouble telling the two of them apart.

The Family Jewels
A Moral Tale

Emmelina Woodcroft, handsome, healthy, and by no means unmodishly clever, had attained the age of one and twenty with much to vex and distress her. She was the only child of a most indifferent father and a mother who, upon her wedding night, had succumbed to a fit of the vapors from which she had yet to recover. The affections of a powdered and painted maiden aunt, whose days were spent pounding away on a Tudor breakfront in belief that it was a pianoforte, did little to alleviate Emmalina's natural turn toward melancholy. Her one reliance was upon Jim, the youthful coachman, and she lived in hourly dread that his sanguine companionship would be lost to her, were the family fortunes to plummet to new lows.

Hartshorn Hall, having at its inception combined the best blessings of nature, and architectural curiosity, had long since adopted the dissolute appearance of its male inhabitants past and present. The chimney pots were angled, one and all, at an inebriated tilt, and candlelight invariably transformed the windows into a multitude of liverish eyes, peering blearily out into the night. It may truly be said that a young lady of sound moral constitution might have rejoiced in the deprivations that were her appointed portion, but, as it has already been intimated, Emmalina was of that singular turn of mind that finds no delight in the absence of cotillions and liveried footmen.

It was on a raw March morning that she entered the winter parlor and arrived at a realization of the true evils of her situation. Squire Woodcroft stood before the window, which looked out upon the ruined rose garden, a pistol directed to his graying temple.

"Why, Papa," Emmalina's golden ringlets trembled as she pressed a hand to her muslin bosom, "is something amiss?"

"You do well to ask, Daughter," he said, taking a firmer grip on the trigger and squeezing his eyes shut.

"Were the breakfast ham and eggs perhaps not to your liking, sir?" Emmalina roused herself from a contemplation of her fingernails to make this inquiry.

"Do you women never think of ought but such fripperies as food?" The squire's face turned puce to match his smoking jacket.

"Unjust, Papa!" Emmalina's magnificent magenta eyes flashed. Her thoughts were indeed presently fastened upon coachman Jim, who could be glimpsed, flexing his muscles, if not his scythe, out on the ill kempt lawn. On his days off Jim made a very shapely gardener.

"Forgive me, my child." The squire's shoulders drooped. "I have ever been a sad excuse for a father, but I am not beyond remorse and my heart quakes when I tell you that last evening I lost at cards again in this very room." He waved a weary hand toward the table strewn with bottles and in so doing shot a couple of bullets into one of ancestors hanging upon the wainscoted wall.

"You always lose, Papa." Emmalina gave a wan smile. "It is a time-honored tradition."

A scowl darkened her parent's physiognomy. "Have you no maidenly sense of outrage, my girl? Must I go from excess to excess to rouse in you a sense of what is fitting? Tush! Let us see if this will ruffle your petticoats. At the break of day, I gambled away your hand in marriage to the Earl of Witherington."

"No!" Emmalina felt a constriction of her person that had nothing to do with the tightness of her stays. "You cannot mean it!" Perversity, her most winning characteristic, forbade her taking pleasure in this change of fortune. "His lordship is known throughout the county to be insufferably handsome and fiendishly plump in the pocket. I could never in a million years give my heart to such a monster."

"Me! Me! Let him take me!" Until that moment Emmalina had failed to notice that her Aunt Jane was seated at the breakfront pounding away on the knives and forks, which she had laid out to do duty as pianoforte keys.

"Silence!" Mr. Woodcroft bellowed, rounding on the older woman and shooting down a flurry of plaster doves from the ceiling in the process. "I can't take Mozart at this hour of the morning."

Oblivious, Aunt Jane, who had possessed a fondness for foot soldiers and law clerks in her youth, threw off her shawls with vulgar abandon and continued to shout, "Why does she get to marry him? Why am I always the bridesmaid?" before breaking down into discordant sobs.

Unable to bear more, Emmalina fled up the stairs to her mamma's bedchamber, where she found Mrs. Woodcroft reclining, as was her wont, upon her couch, a bottle of laudanum to hand and a glass of medicinal ratafia to her lips.

"I might have known," sighed the good lady. "Your papa has spilled the beans. And upon my word there was no need of so wanton a haste, for you are not to marry the earl until tomorrow morn."

"So soon!" Emmalina sank in a graceful swirl of skirts beside the chaise. "Dearest Mamma, you must know that my heart sinks at the thought of marriage to such a rake."

"All men are rakes when the bedroom door closes." Mrs. Woodcroft took a sip of ratafia before bravely setting her glass down and fixing her maternal gaze upon her daughter's visage. "Distasteful as it is for me to speak of such matters and for you to hear the revelations from my lips, the moment I have dreaded these long years is upon us. The bleak truth, my dear child, is that a husband views as his entitlement certain encroachments upon the person of his wife, which, while repellent to the female sex . . ."

Emmalina's mind, never her best feature, was in a whirl. What Mamma was describing sounded uncommonly like the ministrations Jim Coachman had provided after she, Emmalina, fell from her horse in the home wood. He had insisted that such was the most efficacious way of preventing deep bruising. Fie upon the man! She had looked up from the bracken into his eyes—one of midnight blue, the other emerald green—and assured him that this was better than any of Nanny's heat poultices any day. There had been no sense of horror or revulsion, but that might be explained by the fact that Emmalina—not usually one to pay homage to Mother Nature—had found herself, for those spine-tingling moments, transported by the glories of earth and tree, sun and sky to a rainbow of delight unlike anything she had ever experienced, which left her gasping and moaning in wonderment at the pretty little flowers that she had crushed to purple pulp in her hands.

An awareness of deep betrayal seized poor Emmelina. For years her mamma had warned her never to let a member of the susceptible male sex glimpse her creamy ankles. Therefore, being of a biddable nature, she had dutifully arranged her garments over those tempting regions while Jim

Coachman ministered to other parts of her person. And now she must discover such circumspection had all been for naught. She was deflowered. Worse, if she correctly comprehended the epilogue to her mother's narrative, she might even now be with child.

Wearied at having performed her maternal duty, Mrs. Woodcroft drifted into a doze, which prevented her from witnessing Emmalina's left hand fluttering sideways to appropriate the laudanum bottle and pocket it, even as she dipped into a dutiful curtsy. A nunnery being denied her—the good ladies of the cloth being unlikely to welcome an unmarried woman expecting shortly to be confined—Emmalina set her heart upon putting a period to her existence the moment she reached the seclusion of her own chamber.

She was hindered in this object because she had failed to place the map delineating the maze of Hartshorn's corridors in her reticule and thus, by taking three false turns, found herself in the stables. There she encountered the errant Jim Coachman and, upon signally failing to sweep him aside with her muslins, found herself seized and crushed to his manly breast. Wondering if she would ever more inhale the sweet scent of ripe manure without a remembrance of grievous ill usage, Emmalina pictured Jim weeping copious tears over her tombstone. Yes, he must be made to repine, and at once.

"Have you heard, my dear one?" Emmalina lowered her lashes and smiled her most wayward smile. "This morning the Earl of Witherington waited upon dearest Papa and solicited my hand in marriage."

The coachman dutifully touched his forelock before planting an impassioned kiss upon her inclement lips. "Aye! The devil in his many caped riding cloak made boast of his good fortune. T'was as much as I could do not to send him off upon his horse with a flea in his ear, along of . . ." holding her closer, ". . . along of a burr under his saddle."

"Avail yourself of no false hopes," Emmalina cried archly, "for the bridal documents are signed and sealed. His lordship and I wed tomorrow daybreak and depart immediately thereafter for his estate in the wilds of Yorkshire."

An anguished "Nay," broke from coachman Jim's lips, to be echoed by an equally gusty "Neigh," from the brood mare in the third stall. "Be of stout heart, my pretty peahen. What say we take this night by the coattails and elope to Gretna Green?"

"My dear one, I would like it of all things," Emmalina tossed her golden ringlets, "but you must know we have not a ladder tall enough to reach my chamber window."

A frown furrowed the coachman's brow as the truth of her words struck him most forcibly. Then a gleam appeared in his blue eye, or it may have been the green, and his lips thinned into a thoughtful smile. "I do be forgetting," he looked across the ebb and flow of the manor's park land, "that the bridal path do not always run smooth, and there do be many a slip twix . . ."

Desirous as she might be to harden her sensibilities against Jim, Emmalina could not but avail herself of the temptation to ease his suffering by offering a parting glimpse of both her ankles as she gathered up her skirts and returned to the house. There, in the confines of her chamber, she did savor the evils of her situation.

No benevolence intruding to prevent the coming of the morrow, Emmalina awakened at first light to the less-than-sanguine realization that in a few short hours she would be inexorably wed to a nobleman on whom she had yet to fasten her magenta eyes. Her dependence must be on the bottle of laudanum, for the elegance of her mind determined her against succumbing to her bridegroom's broad shoulders and well molded calves.

"Are you awake, my love?" Aunt Jane drifted into the room, her red wig as askew as any of Hartshorn's chimney pots, and her painted face atwitch with trepidation. "You are not about to throw a candlestick at me, are you, dear one? For I should not like that above half." Receiving no response but a lachrymose look from Emmalina, the good lady proceeded to bustle about, fetching forth stays and petticoats, all the while rattling on about the sad affliction of nerves that prevented Mrs. Woodcroft's attending the nuptials.

"But you must not think her unmindful of the felicity of the occasion, for she has instructed Cook to serve only a strengthening gruel at the breakfast. Rich food, my dear Emmalina, does not adjust well to the rigors of travel. And the earl's estates are sufficiently removed as to require several changes of horses."

"Are you then acquainted with his lordship's place in Yorkshire?" Emmalina permitted her tears to flow unchecked because they dampened her muslin gown so that it clung to her bosom as was the daring mode. Being absorbed in the perusal of her fair face in the looking glass, she failed to see Aunt Jane's face turn as waxen as the bedside candle.

"Indeed, I know that accursed place well. I visited at the time the late earl's wife was brought to bed with the son and heir."

"How vastly dull."

"Evil was in that house. I was threatened with the lunatic asylum if I e'er revealed to a living soul what untoward doings I witnessed at dead of night through a crack in the master bedroom door."

Emmalina, with her bridal night looming, had no inclination to reflect upon the untoward doings between men and women. She was still of a mind that it was the delights of Mother Nature which had imparted a degree of complacency to Jim's impositions in the woodland glade. A blue sky and the singing of a lark must always bid fair to banish the most grievous of ills, but doubtless a gentleman, most particularly an earl, would not choose to take his ease outside the bedchamber.

Happily, Aunt Jane said no more to vex her, removing instead to pound away madly on the invisible keys of the Henry VII breakfront, whose carved spindles were highly evocative of the pipes of the organ at St. Egret's church, whither Emmalina was shortly destined to direct her lagging steps. She found, on descending to the hall, that Mr. Woodcroft's paternal sensibilities, while not prevailing upon him to attend her to church, had led him to write a most affectionate benediction, informing her he was gone hunting.

Upon traversing the path alongside the stables Emmalina permitted herself the hope of one last sight of Jim, but this was not to be, and perchance it was as well. During her sleepless night she had reached an understanding of her own heart. While neither pride nor prejudice might preclude the bestowing of her affections upon her father's coachman, she mostly certainly was not, so far unmindful of what was owing a young lady of her quality as to wed such a lowbrow.

A soft rain having molded her muslins even more closely to her dainty bosom, Emmalina entered the chill gloom of the Norman church, to the swell of organ music and a weary acceptance of her fate. It would have been folly indeed, when she could not find the way to her own bedchamber without aid of a map, to attempt a flight to parts unknown. And surely in time she would learn to endure the earl's insufferable good looks and oppressive wealth. As she wended her way up the flagstone aisle, she made out his shadowy form, and it did not seem to her timorous gaze that he was excessively tall. Indeed he would appear to be a head shorter than the vicar, who was not known for his commanding presence. The earl was also, she realized upon drawing ever closer to the altar, decidedly stout and what gray hair he had was combed over a mostly bald head.

"Dear beloved . . ." The clergyman's voice went shivering out into the farthest reaches of the church, but Emmalina failed to bestow on him so much as a glance. She beheld only her bridegroom, whose fat purple cheeks spilled over his cravat and whose gooseberry eyes bulged with terror.

"You, sir, are not the Earl of Witherington!" Emmalina, mindful of where she was, gave her satin-shod foot the demurest of stamps.

"But I am, dear lady." The gentleman endeavored to control his apoplexy before he burst forth from his corsets. "Your mistake perhaps was in expecting the fifth earl, and I am the sixth. Pray accept my assurances that I find myself almost as afflicted by this truth as your gentle self, having come into the title only yesterday, upon the lamentable demise of my cousin Hugh."

"Who?"

"Hugh, who suffered a fatal riding accident before reaching the outskirts of your father's park."

"How exceedingly provoking," said Emmalina seriously. "And how kind of you, My Lord, to avail yourself of this opportunity to advise me I am widowed before being wed. Now if you and the revered vicar will permit," she picked up her skirts in readiness to quit the scene, "I must hasten to convey the intelligence to Papa that he has lost a son-in-law and gained back a daughter."

"You misapprehend the situation, Miss Emmalina." The earl was now wringing his plump hands and his complexion had paled from puce to lavender. "The Witherington code of honor demands that I fulfill my cousin's matrimonial obligations. Besides which, your devoted Papa threatened to call me out if I endeavored to slip the noose."

Emmalina, who neither played the pianoforte nor painted in watercolors, was known to swoon divinely. The moment was not entirely propitious—she preferred a larger audience—but telling herself that when needs must . . . she slipped into delicious oblivion, punctuated only by a distant rattle, which might have been the rain beating on the stained-glass windows or the murmur of voices.

When she awoke, after what seemed a sennight, Emmalina still felt decidedly unsteady, as if the ground were moving beneath her person. A ground, she discovered on pressing down with her hand, which was uncommonly soft and well sprung. Never plagued by quickness of mind, it was some moments after she raised her beleaguered lids and perceived the earl seated beside her before she came to an awareness that she was in a coach traveling across a landscape fast fading into dusk.

Leaning back against the squabs Emmalina fixed her fine magenta eyes on the wedding ring encircling her finger and opined that she was, willy-nilly, a married woman. She did recollect having murmured the word *yes* in response to that distant rattle of voices, but she had thought she was being offered a reviving whiff of smelting salts.

"Feeling more the thing, m'dear?" The earl pursed his lips until they appeared ready to pop.

Emmalina, heedless of the proprieties, bared her pearly teeth at him.

His lordship looked ready to leap out the door, but mindful of his manners, if not his manhood, said with some energy, "If your ladyship and I are to deal comfortably together you should be aware that mine is a sadly delicate constitution."

"Indeed?" Emmalina brightened.

"A war injury." The earl coughed behind a pudgy hand and stared hard out the window.

"Your leg?" His wife looked almost fondly at the gouty member propped upon a footstool.

"No, no! That comes from a fondness for port wine. Deuce take m'doctor! The old sawbones has made me swear off the stuff. As if a man ain't entitled to enjoy what pleasures are left him." The earl hacked out another of his coughs leaving Emmalina to conclude that his ailment was in all probability that angel of death, consumption, incurred from sleeping in tents with the doors and windows not properly closed to keep out drafts from horrid old battlefields. Unaccountably cheered, she realized the horses had slowed to a clop and between one breath and the next the carriage swayed to a halt. Rubbing a peephole in the fogged window she made out a house with many battlements jutting ominously against the sky.

"Here we are, m'dear!" the earl said as a groom leaped out of the night to open the door. "Welcome to Withering Heights."

Shivering in her bridal muslins, Emmalina followed her husband across the courtyard and up a flight of steps to a heavily carved door, whose forbidding aspect was reflected in the countenance of the black-garbed woman who admitted them.

"So this be the new mistress." A smile, thin as a scythe, sliced the face in two. "Do step in out of night, Your Ladyship, before the house takes the ague." Sound advice, for the hall in which Emmalina found herself already appeared to be suffering from a malaise. The walls were dark and dank, the ceilings low and moldering, and every time someone breathed, something creaked.

"And you must be . . . ?" Emmalina's heart quaked at the thought she might be addressing her mamma-in-law, for the widow's cap was as sallow as the face beneath it, and the ebony eyes as glassy as those of the fox heads on the wall.

"I'm the housekeeper," the woman ducked a belated curtsy, "Mrs. McMurky."

"Her ladyship is wishful to retire." The Earl of Witherington spoke from behind them in a voice plump with pride.

"I'm none surprised, on this night of nights." Mrs. McMurky raised a threadbare eyebrow. "I have the bridal chamber all ready, if you do be so good as to follow me." Her ghoulish chuckle caused the flame of the candle she held aloft to tremble as she trailed her black skirts up the stairs to a gallery haunted by the painted faces of long-dead Witheringtons in gilded frames.

Emmalina's gaze met that of a bewigged gentleman possessed of one blue eye and one green, putting her forcibly in mind of Jim Coachman. Taking the coincidence as a good omen, she experienced an elevation of the spirits.

"Here we be!" Mrs. McMurky flung back a door opening into a wainscoted apartment dominated by a bed, whose tapestry curtains depicted scenes from every battle fought during the Hundred Years War.

"How sweetly pretty!" Emmalina exclaimed. She was in truth not beyond being pleased. The night was young and so was she, and not even the realization that the earl had followed her into the chamber could quite subdue her vivacity. Thanks to the novels of Mrs. Radcliffe, the gothic was all the rage, and Emmalina desired above all things to be in the mode.

"I went and set out a decanter of your favorite port, my lord." The housekeeper gave a murky smile from the doorway.

The earl inclined his head.

"Shall I be off, then?"

"You are a gem beyond price, Mrs. McMurky."

At the closing of the door, a silence, thick as the fog, which blanketed the windows, descended upon the room. Emmelina could not but experience a certain sympathy for the earl, for while it was inconceivable that she return the ardent affection which must have assailed his breast upon first beholding her golden ringlets and alabaster curves, she was not insensible to the good breeding which caused him to refrain from prostrating himself at her feet.

"M'lady," he puffed around the room in circles, "there is a matter of a most urgent, not to say delicate nature, which I must in all justice impart without delay."

"Yes, my lord?"

He ceased his perambulations to stand with his hands folded upon his formidable stomach, his coat buttons straining and appearing to watch her with the same shiny bright intensity as that of his protuberant eyes.

"I beseech you to be brave, my dear."

Emmalina did not have to feign incomprehension; it was something at which she had always excelled.

"You are a young and healthy woman and I most earnestly feel for the bitterness of your disappointment. Indeed, I attempted to give you a hint in the carriage as to the nature of my infirmity."

"But I guessed, truly I did!" Emmalina clapped her hands. "You have the silly old consumption."

Blushing painfully, the earl strove for speech. "South, m'lady. What ails me is south of the lungs."

Never had Emmalina regretted more acutely her failure to master the rudiments of geography, especially where they applied to human anatomy. She was not entirely certain if the heart was east or west, or perhaps it was a matter of whether one was left or right handed. As for the other internal organs, she pictured them now as a number of unnamed continents, adrift in an uncharted black sea. Her magenta eyes blurred and a tear trickled gracefully down her ivory cheek.

Much moved, the earl constrained his own embarrassment, cleared his throat, and said, "M'dear, tax your pretty little head no further. When I fought for Mother England against old Boney I sustained an injury to my male person which prevents . . . ahem . . . my rising to the occasion as your husband."

"Oh!" A memory came, clear and pure as a blue sky above a woodland glade, and Emmalina was back amid the buttercups with Jim the coachman and she grasped the full import of her situation. That mysterious member with which gentlemen were beset would seem, in the earl's case, not to be in proper working order. At first she was elated at the prospect of being spared the necessity of fulfilling her wifely obligations, but, swift as a bird of prey, came a darker realization. Having permitted Jim to avail himself of certain felicities, she must assuredly be with child. And, were she not to be afforded the opportunity of passing it off as the earl's own, she was ruined. Never again would she be permitted to wear white, which was far and away her favorite color.

Desperation, which is the grandmother of invention, made Emmalina do something contrary to her nature. She came up with an idea. Hidden in her reticule was her mother's bottle of laudanum. Rather than doing away with herself, which now seemed excessive, she would add a few drops to his lordship's glass of port, and when he awakened from his drugged state she would be entangled with him amid the sheets, eager to impart the glad tidings that he had miraculously mastered his infirmity to make her the happiest woman alive. For certain he would moan that he could not remember, but she would assure him that she had liked it of all things.

The difficulty was in persuading the earl to overcome his fear of the gout and indulge his taste for port wine, but Emmalina pouted prettily and entwined a golden ringlet about one finger.

"Surely, my lord, we would not wish to disappoint Mrs. McMurky. She did most particularly fetch up the decanter."

"You are right, m'dear. But I suspect she did so for your benefit for she supports the doctor's dictum that I not partake of anything stronger than beef tea."

"La, sir! This is surely a night for uncommon revelry."

When the earl, appearing ready to succumb to a fit of the vapors, buried his face in his silk handkerchief, Emmalina whipped out the laudanum and poured several drops surreptitiously into a glass, before topping it up with gentlemen's ruin.

"Will you take your refreshment upon retirement, sir?" Emmalina dipped a wifely curtsy. It was a most happy thought. The earl disappeared into his dressing chamber and returned after a short interval, cozily attired in his nightshirt and cap. Ascending the mounting block he drew back the bed's tapestry curtains and plunged, as nimbly as a man of his considerable corpulence could do, beneath the bedclothes.

"Here you are, my lord," Emmalina proffered the glass with much trembling of her eyelashes.

"Are you not to join me, m'dear?" The earl looked sadly out of countenance.

"Pray accept my excuses, sir, but spiritous liquor does most seriously disagree with me."

"Fiddledeedee!" His lordship took a mighty swig to show how palatable was the stuff.

"It gives me the convulsions." Emmalina watched his majestic cheeks pale, before begging permission to retreat and disrobe. Within the sanctuary of the dressing chamber, she took a moment, while removing her petticoats and stays, to congratulate herself. All would come about with the utmost harmony. Her child would be born heir to Withering Heights. And with a measure of good fortune and a great many beefsteaks and suet puddings the earl would not live to a ripe old age. Meanwhile, as befitting her youthful charms, her life might yet be solaced if she fetched Jim Coachman into service at Withering Heights. Surely even the most prattle-tongued persons would have little to say if she were to occasionally enter the stables and be found with him amid the hay.

Garbed in a tucked and pleated bedgown, Emmalina returned to the nuptial chamber and upon climbing into bed was much struck by the earl's appearing to be deeply asleep with his eyes wide open. Happily, Mrs. Woodcroft having instructed her that gentlemen were in all ways so very different from females in their habits, she concluded this to be but one more trial of the married state and not to be blamed particularly on the laudanum, any more than was his leaving the wineglass sprawled in slovenly fashion upon the coverlet. She was cheerfully engaged in unbuttoning his lordship's nightshirt, so as to create the necessary state of dishabille to which he would awaken, when the door was peremptorily thrust open to reveal the beaky nosed Mrs. McMurky in her nightmare black.

"You rang, Madam?"

"No!" Emmalina cowered against the capacious pillows as

the housekeeper advanced with the unrelenting tread of an army of foot soldiers to stand by the bed.

"What ails his lordship?"

"Nothing!" Emmalina rallied to smile demurely and avow with a peachy blush. "He is but somewhat fatigued, which is surely not a wonderment after asserting his husbandly rights."

"Fatigued!" Mrs. McMurky's eyes burned like coals in her sallow visage. "My master is dead!"

"You must be funning!" For the moment Emmalina was sadly discommoded, then her mood lifted. She would so enjoy being a widow and there could be no doubt her child's future was ensured. For would it not readily be decided that the earl had succumbed to the apoplexy due to certain exertions? The only puzzlement must be that whole kingdoms of gentlemen did not routinely meet the same fate. Emmalina would have liked above all things to dance upon the bed sheets, but she knew she must be at pains to repine.

"Oh, woe is me!" She assumed a doleful mien. "I killed him!"

Mrs. McMurky's eyes shone with a strange, gloating light, as without a word she moved to the window, drawing back the curtain so that the moon stared balefully into the chamber, probing and pointing its silver fingers at the young woman who stepped from the bed to stand shivering in her bridal night attire.

"Providence be praised!" the housekeeper exclaimed, "I do be seeing Dr. Leech riding his piebald mare Polly up to the door."

"What a happy chance."

"That it is." A smile strayed across Mrs. McMurky's stark features, but before more could be said, the doorbell pealed and she departed with a rustle of black skirts to admit the doctor. Voices in the hall, followed by footsteps mounting the stairs. Their sound echoed the beating of Emmalina's heart. She told herself it was not unreasonable to be anxious; she had never before been widowed and was thus uncertain as to the social niceties. Would she be expected to wear black bedgowns?

She was occupied in reaching for a shawl when Dr. Leech entered the chamber, with Mrs. McMurky hovering like a shadow behind him. He was tall and spare as a long-case clock. Indeed, his head almost scraped the ceiling as he advanced upon the bed, and his countenance was too long and bony to be immediately pleasing. But Emmalina, having determined not to remarry upon encountering the first man to cross her path, did not hold his looming presence or unpruned eyebrows against him. Thinking he might need something to steady his nerves, she offered him a glass of port.

"No, I thank you." He exchanged a look with the housekeeper before bending over the earl. "My lady, I have been your husband's physician these many years and know him to have enjoyed the most robust health."

"Doctor, I was telling you as how she confessed to . . ." At the lift of his knobby hand, Mrs. McMurky fell silent.

"My husband died with honor, in the performance of his manly duty." Emmalina squeezed out a tear. "Indeed, it would seem to me he should be posthumously awarded a medal, as are other gallant men who fall upon the field of battle."

"Balderdash!" The doctor whipped off the bedclothes to leave the late earl exposed to the chill that had descended upon the room. "His lordship was incapable of such action. The last time he saw battle he lost the family jewels."

"I hardly see what that has to say to anything!" Emmalina responded roundly. But when she turned her magnificent orbs to where his lordship's nightshirt was lifted to reveal those most private parts of his person, she perceived with much lowering of spirits that he was missing certain baubles which, if all men are created equal, might not be of any great rarity, but which must needs have been present for her story to have possessed the ring of truth.

"But I thought him to have meant . . ." Delicacy forbade Emmalina's endeavoring to explain further, that she had understood his lordship to mean that the necessary equipment was present if not operational. What a wet goose she was! So this was what was meant by missing in action!

"Murderess!" The housekeeper was hugging the bedpost and dancing a jig in venomous ecstasy. "Couldn't content yourself with being a hussy, could you."

"I do declare, Mrs. McMurky, I have not a notion what you are talking about!"

"Don't make me laugh!" The unearthly cackle blew out a couple of candles. "You poisoned the old goa . . . dear's port!"

"No!" Emmalina had never mastered the art of talking and swooning at the same time. Was it possible that she had been too unstinting with the laudanum?

"And if I b'ain't missing the mark, you did away with Hugh."

"Who?"

"The fifth earl. Very peculiar it was him having that riding accident, and him jumping before he was out of leading strings."

"Hanging's too good for her!" The doctor's lips flapped with fury.

Vastly cheered by this reasonable approach, Emmalina would have embraced a lifetime diet of bread and water, but before she could bat her eyelashes, Mrs. McMurky had drawn a coil of rope from the bowels of her skirt pocket and was tying her to the bedpost in the manner of one who would have enjoyed watching her burn at the stake like Joan of Arc. There was, alas, no appealing to Dr. Leech, for he was off into the night gloom to seek the assistance of the Justice of the Peace, a crusty gentleman of the old school who had never been known to get out of bed on the right side in forty years.

It was with a melancholy hope of any continuance, that Emmelina awakened the next morning in one of the dungeons of Foulwell Castle, which served the county as a makeshift prison until such time as a habitation even more incommodious could be built. After waiting in vain for the arrival of her morning chocolate, she determined to bear her misfortunes bravely. But the prospect from her barred window, being a wall that even the ivy seemed loath to climb, was not conducive to merriment. And the wretchedness of the room she shared with at least forty of the great unwashed soon made itself felt. There were no portraits upon the walls nor any carpets upon the floor. When she went in search of the bell rope in order to summon the butler that he might have a word with the upstairs maid about the chamber pots that appeared not to have been emptied in a sennight, she discovered there was no bell rope.

"What do you think this is, Hampton Court?" A toothless crone, swatched in rags, broke into gales of mirth.

"You leave 'er be." A younger woman with frowzy red hair sidled up to Emmalina and stroked her ringlets. "The good fing about being 'anged is that they don't chop of your 'air, like what they do when they use the ax."

Emmalina stopped squealing only when she felt someone picking through the folds of her gown. "Don't let me bother you, love," an urchin faced girl of about her own age said.

"I'm just lookin' for fleas. We have races with them, don't you know. Helps pass the time."

" 'Ush up, everyone," bellowed another voice. " 'Ere comes Mr. 'Orrible with our grub."

The fellow who brought in the bowls of slop did not resemble any butler Emmalina had ever encountered. There was a fiendish look to his eye and she was forced to speak sharply to him about his failure to shave the pirate's stubble from his chin. Time, alas, did not compose her. The uncertainty of her situation weighed heavily upon her spirits and she found herself looking forward with utmost eagerness to the day of her trial. Her youth and beauty must surely touch the heart of judge and jury and she could not fail to believe her father, however heretofore indifferent, would be in the court, eager to attest to her having been well tutored in the minuet.

How melancholy it was for Emmalina to discover, when guided into that chamber of justice by her wardens, that the spectators' gallery was unoccupied save for an elderly woman in dark bonnet and cloak and a man in rough country tweeds seated, with head bent, beside her. Mrs. McMurky and Dr. Leech were installed where their presence could not be missed, and indeed, Judge Blackstone Smyte, when he finally deigned to put in his velvet and ermine appearance, seemed to be very much taken with the pair.

"Tell me, Madam," he sat with ponderous chin resting on his palm, his wig sliding over one ear, as he addressed the housekeeper, "did Her Ladyship confess to the murder of her sainted husband?"

"Yes, M'Lud!" The denouncement bubbled from Mrs. McMurky's lips. "As true as I'm standing here, and strike me down if I tell a lie, the prisoner's very words was 'I killed him.' "

"But I meant only . . ." Emmelina cried out.

Frowning, the judge rebuked her. "My lady, did you, or did you not secret a drug in his lordship's port wine?"

"I . . ." The golden head hung low.

"A bottle of laudanum was found in her reticule." Slick as an eel, Dr. Leech rose to his monstrous height in proffering this contribution to justice.

"Tut, tut!" the judge said, more in sorrow than anger.

Most bitterly did Emmalina regret her imprudence in being caught out in a crime she had not committed. "But, Sir! I have witnessed my mamma partake of the entire bottle to no ill effect, save for the occasional fall from her boudoir balcony."

"Silence!" The judge had bethought himself of his dinner, which today was to be his favorite braised kidneys and buttered cabbage. "In the name of mad King George, I find you Emmalina, Countess of Witherington, guilty of murder most foul. It is my sorry duty to sentence you to be hanged by your comely neck until you are quite dead. And may God have no mercy upon your soul." Rising in a flurry of velvet he made to quit the room, but was forestalled by a voice floating down from the spectators' gallery.

"Not so fast, my love!"

The judge's face turned first the color of his crimson robe, then white as its ermine trim. The speaker had removed her black bonnet to reveal a powdered wig above a painted face. At the instant Emmalina recognized her spinster aunt, his lordship cried aloud in thrilling accents, "Jane! My lovely lost Jane! In the days when I worshipped at the shrine of your loveliness I was a lowly law clerk. But on the day your father forbade me pay you my addresses, I determined to rise in my profession so as to be worthy at last of making you mine. Then came the day when I knew I was no longer young, and could not trust that you would even remember me."

"I would not have done so." Aunt Jane drummed her fingers upon the gallery rail as if it were a pianoforte keyboard. "I have been afflicted in my mind these many years. The physicians spoke of shock treatment as the only hope of cure, but the thought of being dipped in scalding water did not vastly appeal. However, all is well that ends well. For the news of my niece's tribulations brought me back to full possession of my powers. So sit yourself back down on that throne of yours, Blackstone, while I tell you a thing or two."

"Yes, my dove! At once, my dove!"

"Forget all this twaddle about my niece murdering her husband. I was engaged in reading my teacup this early morn and beheld the face of the real villain floating in the murky . . ." she drew out the word, ". . . murky depths. And I can tell you, Blackstone, you need not resort to your eye glass in searching out the true villain." Aunt Jane stopped drumming to point her finger. "The earl's death lies at your door, Mrs. McMurky."

"You are mad, quite mad!" Hollow laughter.

"No, it is you, Minerva McMurky, who don't have both oars in the water. I ascertained there was something not quite nice about you when I was staying at Withering Heights, many years since, and discovered you had made fate your accomplice when you and the countess both gave birth to boys on the very same day. At dead of night you switched the infants so that your son would be heir to an earldom, leaving the rightful scion to grow up a hireling."

As was Emmalina's wont, she could make neither head nor tail of what she was hearing.

"It was your son," Aunt Jane pressed on inexorably, "your son, Hugh—"

"Who?" the judge inquired with a seraphic smile.

"Hugh, who was killed yesterday on his return from

Hartshorn Hall. In one terrible stroke all your plans had come to naught, Minerva. It was then, I believe, that your evil took a nasty turn. You blamed my poor Emmalina for your son's demise. And it was she, not the sixth earl, you determined to kill. He was known to abstain from port wine on account of his gout. But you shrewdly suspected that a young woman married off to a man with whom she had established but a day's acquaintance might be anxious to steady her wedding-night nerves with a glass of something stronger than ratafia."

"Lies! All lies!" Mrs. McMurky's screams tore through the court with the force of a hurricane. Dr. Leech could not quiet her, even as she babbled that he was the father of her child and that he had been all for the murder plot when he thought it would leave her mistress of Withering Heights. The judge cried "Guilty," but instead of pounding out the verdict with his gavel, he tossed it aside, knocking out one of the wardens in the process, so as to be free to hold out his arms to Aunt Jane, who ran into them with mature squeals of joy and promises of giving up the pianoforte.

As for Emmalina, she did feel that somewhat more fuss might have been made of her who had so narrowly escaped the hangman's noose. Mrs. McMurky did not have the grace to offer one word of congratulation as she was dragged screaming from the court. And Dr. Leech was no better. Sighing, Emmalina doubted that even swooning could alleviate the tedium of this day, and her magenta eyes blurred with tears so that the man in rough country clothes, who had been with Aunt Jane in the spectators' gallery, came toward her out of a fog. And it was not until he was within a hand's breadth that she recognized him.

"Why, Jim Coachman!" Emmalina cried.

"The Earl of Witherington to you, my lass. I was the true heir, switched at birth." The lofty tone was belied by his kneeling at her feet, and Emmalina most ardently hoped that after they were wed he would continue to touch his forelock before taking those liberties which gentlemen would seem to hold so dear.

"Beloved," he rose to clasp her to his breast, "there is a dark and morbid revelation I must make before you pledge your love and life to me."

Emmalina shook her golden head, unable to hazard a guess as to what could make him look so melancholy. Pray heaven he was not about to confess a dislike of turnips, for they were of all things her passion.

"I tried to tell you at our last meeting, but mayhap did not make myself clear, that I put a burr under the saddle of the earl."

"Who?"

"Hugh. The one what was me when I was him. I was determined that he should not marry you. So you see, my angel, his death was no mishap. I . . ."

"Hush!" Emmalina pressed a finger to Jim's lips, lest the judge have ears in the back of his wig. She was by no means unmindful of the compliment her love had paid her in removing a rival suitor from the bridal path. But she could not but think wistfully back to her former husband; for surely a tendency to gout might more readily be accepted in one's lord and master than an inclination to murder should the breakfast ham and eggs perhaps not be to his liking.

Another young lady might have quaked at the prospect before her, but Emmalina, perceiving many opportunities in the coming years to indulge her natural inclination to melancholy, gave him her most droll smile and said, "I will marry you, my lord Jim, and I do most dutifully suggest that given the perilous state of the world you arrange with Mr. Lloyd of London for the insuring of the family jewels."